# Vengeance

## A novel

### WILLIAM CROW JOHNSON

# DEDICATION

To the citizens of Howarth County, Indiana, not far north of the Ohio River.  You know who you are.

**Also by William Crow Johnson:**

Earth 2.0:  Prison Planet

Earth 2.1:  Regenesis

Earth 2.2:  Rite of Passage

Sedalia, Indiana

Sedalia, seat of Howarth County, Indiana, lies near I-65 not far north of the Ohio River, but you will not find it on any map. It lives in the hearts of Midwesterners everywhere—especially Hoosiers.

# ACKNOWLEDGMENTS

My long-suffering wife and chief enabler, and the BC Story Spinners, who offered advice.

WILLIAM CROW JOHNSON

CHAPTER ONE

Sheriff Earl "Tip" Tungate surveyed the farmhouse yard. For once
Chief Deputy Chet Biggle was silent.

The crocuses had passed. A few hyacinths and daffodils persisted, and the air smelled of freshly tilled soil in the nearby field.
Humidity was low. Clover pushed above brown grass in the yard.
The clapboard house baked in the warm sun. A spring drought
was building.

Most of the grass didn't need it, but Mr. Sampson would have
mowed today, it being Saturday. Just the kind of man he was. He
kept a neat farm even though he was up there and didn't work his
own land any more. But raggedy, deep-green poop clumps surrounded the bare-dirt area by the barn where the chained dog
watched. He wouldn't have let that go long.

Tip brought his attention back to the body at his feet. He took
off his Raybans and squatted for a better look. *"You'll always look
cool when you wear these, Dad,"* Katy had said at fifteen on his

birthday. He did not consider himself cool but had worn them every day since she left.

Mr. Sampson lay face down, head turned to one side. A dandelion pressed up under his nose, too close for the staring eyes to focus on. Crows cawed over the cornfield, chisel-plowed but not yet replanted. Rented land always came last.

It was a fine Saturday morning. Or had been. This was going to kill the fishing trip. But that was probably OK. He liked Eileen well enough, but they were really going because people at the café had teased them into it. She talked a good game, but he was pretty sure she was only going along with the joke. Plus, once burned, twice learned.

Back on his feet, he hooked his thumbs in his squeaky pistol belt and chewed on his toothpick. In his third term as Howarth County Sheriff after a required term out of office, even he had seen only four killings in Sedalia. Before this one. And frankly, the others had not bothered him that much. The last two, just last year, were righteous shootings. The "victims" had been out-of-town thugs who, best he could determine, had been killed in self-defense. Plus, their bodies had been found outside his jurisdiction. So even though he knew who did it, who had her own reasons for not talking, he didn't pursue it. And the other two had been drug-related. It was hard to get worked up over scumbags killing each other.

But this was different. He knew the victim well. And there was absolutely no reason for anybody to kill this fine old man. Dick Turley from down the road had been distraught when he called it in. "I've known him for forty years!" Turley had protested. "Nicest person you ever want to meet!"

Still, Tip was surprised at his detachment. Mr. Sampson looked peaceful. Only the dark crust under his nose and the dark patch on the back of his neatly barbered head suggested violence. His right hand still clutched his electric bill and his *Farm Journal*. It looked as though he might get up from his open-eyed nap and go into the house about his old-man business, reading his periodical and pretending he still had farm business to attend to. He probably looked forward to that magazine all month.

Chet spoke.

"Surprise bullet in the back of the head's probably about the best way to go, you think about it."

Tip resisted looking at him. Crows cawed in the distance. Chet persisted. Trying to seem casual, Tip was sure. In control.

"I mean, you think about it. Never feel a thing, wouldn't see it coming, you could be pounding your pud right till the last minute."

Tip hawked and spat. He didn't like the image. He doubted Mr. Sampson had pounded his pud in years. Maybe never. He was old-school.

"'Makes you think it was a surprise?"

"Back of the head. No sign of a struggle. .22, looking at the hole. Long-rifle, not a .223."

"Rifle from across the road?"

"Way I see it. Probably scoped. You could take a scoped Marlin lever action onto that rise in the woods over there above the cut bank and put it in his ear nine times out of ten if you were any good."

Tip took off his hat and ran a big hand back across his bald head. He scratched his curly fringe and looked at Chet. Runt of an old family, politically connected and unfireable, Chief Deputy Chet Biggle looked more like an accountant than a deputy sheriff. Average height, spectacles, narrow shoulders, and a slight belly made him look harmless, and it was true he was no good in a scrape. But he was smart and mean. Used gossip against people.

Liked to hurt people but was always just kidding. The injured couldn't take a joke. Just the sight of him pissed Tip off. It was some sort of mysterious evolutionary force urging him to purify the species before Chet reproduced.

"And why would you want to do that?"

Chet removed his own campaign hat, smoothed the buzz cut he affected to look tough, replaced the hat, and smiled.

"Not my problem, Tip. You're the sheriff. You're supposed to figure that one out." He broadened his smile and laid a proprietary hand on his belly.

Tip looked away, back over Mr. Sampson's hundred-sixty acres toward the far woods. A redtail launched, sailed, tilted, turned. A buzzard circled higher up.

"Tell you what," he said, watching the buzzard. "Get on the radio and ask the State Police for a lab team. Get Doc Freeman from Elmira, too. We'll need a coroner's report. Then call around, eight or ten calls. Your cell, not the phone inside. See if you can find a home for that dog. Animal Control puts too many to sleep. Go see if the Vet knows anybody; see if the nursing home needs a petting dog. When you're done, come back and pick me up. Say, two hours."

Chet appeared to struggle with this for a moment, then recovered a curl to his lip.

"You're the sheriff." He left.

With Chet safely gone, Tip crossed the gravel road to check the rifle theory. Undisturbed myrtle covered the bank, and uncrushed spring beauties and violets carpeted the edge of the woods in the spots where the sun shined in. No footprints.

He recrossed the road, again startled by the image of Mr. Sampson lying in his front yard in bib overalls. Someone could have shot him from a passing car—adolescents on a random violence spree proving their toughness. Or a stray shot from any-where within a mile radius. People were constantly shooting blind and putting holes in houses and cars on the next mile-square road.

On the other hand, someone could have deliberately walked up from behind and shot him. But there was no good reason to do that. Had to be some kind of accident. There was no exit wound, so either the shell had a light load, really was a .22, or the shot came from a distance, or all three. But the expression on Mr. Sampson's face made it clear he had not been afraid. No one had faced him off.

The kitchen showed no sign of disturbance. All was clean and orderly. Two place settings of plain white china rested on the Formica table, upside down, along with a worn leather Bible and a covered glass jar of cinnamon balls. Tip felt a pang and smiled. Mrs. Sampson had been dead for years, but George still set the ta-ble for two.

On the countertop in front of day-lily canisters of flour, sugar, salt, and corn meal, and jars of quarters and dimes, was a paper bag full of morels with a few ladybugs. Three fourths of a raspberry pie sat on the back of the stove, covered with plastic wrap. Too early for raspberries; they had to have been frozen.

No signs indicated a killer had been there. Nothing appeared disturbed. Mr. Sampson's old-fashioned envelope-sized wallet lay untouched on the desk in the living room. He would have been eighty-two in another week. A locked strongbox still lay in the bottom of a file drawer next to the desk. The ancient TV and radio still rested on the TV cart.

The upstairs likewise gave no evidence of ransacking or theft. Mr. Sampson's bedroom looked untouched, with made-up and turned-back bed, worn knee impressions in the painted floorboards beside it, and a bit of a surprise—a Canon digital camera with telephoto lens on a darkened old writing table by the window. Twelve hundred jpegs, three hundred to go, and a flashing low-battery icon. Not enough juice to browse. The view from the window extended all the way to the pond at the back of the farm. There was no computer and printer anywhere, so Mr. Sampson would have had to make prints at the pharmacy. Tip found none, so he pocketed the chip. Might provide a clue.

The guest room looked unused: bed, oak dresser with mirror, bookshelf with dusty collections of Zane Grey and Edgar Rice Burroughs, closet full of Mrs. Sampson's musty clothes, still with a hint of honeysuckle.

Tip was back downstairs in the living room looking for photo albums when the State Police arrived.

Sergeant Temple came into the living room just as he found a large cloth-bound album in a shelf along with a 1952 set of Encyclopedia Britannica. He had hoped it would be her and not Gates. He pulled out the album and opened it.

"Morning, Sergeant." He knew better than to call her Laura. "'Fraid we got a mystery here."

She pushed back her amber-lensed sunglasses and regarded him levelly, just under the flat brim of her hat.

"Morning, Tip. Screwing up evidence?" She set down a steel-cornered carrying case.

He smiled and leafed through the album. Nothing there. All pictures from forty and more years ago—Mrs. Sampson, their small daughter Ella, who now lived in California. He remembered Ella, an awkward, shy farm girl. He put the album back on the shelf.

"Pursuing a hypothesis." He normally didn't talk like that, but he knew Sergeant Temple liked that kind of talk. She was professional. All business. Really smart. And nearly six feet tall and very pleasant to look at. He was careful to keep his gaze above her shoulder level.

"Care to share it? Might help us focus."

"Just a hunch now. Not enough to share. I'd still say, dust everything downstairs, look for hairs and fibers. I don't think anybody's been in here, but we have to check. Even if someone was, I don't think they went upstairs. But check it all if you want. Any powder traces on his hair? Assume you checked on the way in."

She took a long-legged stride to the aluminum and glass storm door and looked out at the two officers he could also see taking pictures. He allowed his eyes to drift down momentarily from her clipped blond neck hairs to her generous but well-shaped hips. He thought of them as horse-riding hips. She filled her blue-serge State Police pants nicely, but it was death to get a good look.

"No." She spoke onto the door window, fogging the glass, then turned around quickly.

Damn. He realized she had seen him looking in the reflection in the glass.

She met his hastily raised gaze eye-to-eye and stood in a challenging way, hands on hips, but involuntarily drew in her chest. "No foot prints, no powder traces, no skin under his fingernails. Looks like a drive-by. Or a shot from across the road."

He took off his hat and smoothed his fuzz. "Hate to think that. Rather have a serial killer loose. Least that way I could scare up a motive."

"That sounds pretty unprofessional. But then, coming from a man who can't be in the same room with a female officer without looking at her improperly, it's not surprising." She returned to her carrying case and began removing plastic bottles and brushes. "Tell me, Sheriff." Her voice was icy. "Do you ever go through a day without thinking about sex?"

Most people saw him as big and slow-moving and probably lazy and dumb, and he played it. His seedy good looks and good nature generally got him over. People responded positively and forgave his shortcomings. Except Temple and Samantha Parr, the prosecutor. They were a new breed. Acted as if only professionalism forced them to speak to an ogre like him.

"Not yet," he said.

A shot exploded the stillness outside. Both he and Temple dropped to a squat and reached for their weapons, but then a voice from out front by the body yelled, "Damn you, Biggle!" One of the crime-scene team.

Tip realized the dog had quit barking. And the shot had sounded like a .44. Chet. He would have a good story about nobody wanting the dog. And he had probably persuaded someone in Animal Control to let him do the job. Guys like Chet—always wanting to use their guns—gave him a pain in the ass. The County Commissioners were up for re-election in November, so maybe Chet's Uncle Clyde would re-enter the honest work force at that time, and Chet could follow. One could only hope.

Tip and Temple both stood. He replaced his hat and looked at her in his most professional manner, eye to eye. "I'm leaving, Sergeant." It was always important with Temple and Samantha to observe the correct protocols and use the proper titles. "Going to leave the crime scene to the professionals. But I would appreciate receiving a copy of your report as soon as it's available."

She nodded coldly.

He went outside and ordered the smirking Chet, who indeed protested that he had made the ten calls, to find a shovel and bury the dog. Then, listening to the crows, he set off for the pond at the back of the farm to check a hunch.

## CHAPTER TWO

Samantha Parr's voice pushed through the phone and invaded the jail office. "It's been almost twenty-four hours, Sheriff. Who are your suspects?"

Tip held the instrument two inches away from his ear. Even fifteen feet away, Chet could hear enough to know who it was. He smiled an unfriendly smile.

Tip had been admiring Mr. Sampson's photos on the new high-res screen on his desk. Familiar already with the new prosecutor's conviction that she was master of all she surveyed, he took his time. The redtail hawk in the photo looked so close you could touch it. Nothing in the background except blue sky. Not a torn or mussed feather on the entire, magnificent bird. Mr. Sampson had developed serious skill. Kind of unexpected from a man who farmed his whole life, never traveled, and limited extracurricular activity to the Methodist Men's Club.

"Tip?" demanded the new DA. "Are you listening to me?"

Tip paged back to the previous photo. Two boys, Toby McConnell and someone with his back to the camera, tending a planting of marijuana in late summer. There in the background the old thresher still rusted away in the edge of Mr. Sampson's woods. From Sampson's father's day. Mr. Sampson probably never went back there any more, but he had caught the boys in his telephoto lens. And Tip had found a just-sprouted new planting when he went back to the pond to check. He flipped back to the hawk.

"Yes, Madam Prosecutor. I can hear you."

"You haven't answered my question."

"I will when I have a prosecutable case."

Exasperated silence came over the line. "People want to know who killed Mr. Sampson, Sheriff. Do your job."

"Who's asking who killed him?"

Tip doubted anyone had asked. She was a pusher; that was all. Harvard Law and all that. Thirty-two at most, lean with ambition, always dressed in expensive dark clothes. Appointed by the governor after Dave Woods's heart attack.

"It doesn't matter who is asking," she dismissed. "What matters is, you've apparently done nothing in twenty-four hours and have no leads."

"When we have a case, Madam Prosecutor, we'll bring it to you. In the meantime, if someone asked you who killed George Sampson, I want that person's name. Could be material to the investigation. Who was it?"

She gave the exasperated sound again. "It's just an expression, Sheriff. People want you to do your job. I'm holding you accountable."

"The people of Howarth County, Indiana, will hold me accountable, Madam Prosecutor. And I will not fail them. At the next election, they'll hold you accountable too, along with Governor Brandt."

He hung up the phone while she was still talking.

Brandt was a son of a bitch who wanted to be president. As attorney general, he took a run at Tip, who was well known in southern Indiana but of the other party. Indy news helicopters came down to film Brandt "cleaning up Howarth County." This consisted of an interview in front of Big Iva's Truck Stop, where prostitution was rumored, and another in front of the deer-camp meth lab of a cooker Tip had sent to jail, for which Brandt took credit. Then he was gone, leaving investigators to hassle Tip. They finally left after two months of people inviting them in for coffee and pie and schmoozing and telling them nothing.

"She can bring in her own investigators, you know," gloated Chet. "Nothing in Indiana law to stop her. Give you a lot of trouble."

"She would have to pay them somehow. Could be wrong, but doubt the County Council would vote the extra money."

"Governor could get their party to pony it up. Pretty clear, they're grooming her for Congress or the governor's mansion. Some counties already get federal grant money for prosecutors' investigators. With arrest powers. To round up deadbeat dads. But it wouldn't have to stop there."

Tip looked at Chet without expression. Chet was a vile creature, but there was no way to get rid of him, so he had to keep it civil. "You gonna apply for the job?"

"Wrong party. Everybody in Sedalia would disown me. I got a reputation."

"That you do."

The idea was outrageous. An asshole governor appoints a prosecutor, then reaches into the county with outside money to go around the elected sheriff. You did have to pay attention to Chet, because he knew everything about everybody, and kept abreast of political news. But he also loved to get Tip going, so what he said had to be taken with a grain of salt.

Tip had decided some years ago that if he got pissed off about everything worth getting pissed off about, he'd have a coronary every morning before his second cup of coffee. The task for the morning was to find and question Toby McConnell about the marijuana planting. Not get pissed off by Chet.

Toby's dad was pretty cleaned up now after his nickel a few years back for meth cooking. Out in two for good behavior. Worked at the headlight factory in Elmira. And the kid was a cheerful, friendly kid who worked summers at the pallet factory. Probably about to graduate if Tip guessed his age right. So Tip hated to see him involved with drugs. The new patch was small, so maybe Toby and his buddy grew it only for their own use. But it was still illegal, and making a habit of breaking the law was a bad way to start out in life.

The key point was, George Sampson would not have looked kindly on boys growing dope on his farm. He would have called it dope. Had he confronted them when they went back this spring to check their new crop? Had the other kid shot the old man when he threatened to turn them in? Tip couldn't imagine Toby doing it.

But you never knew.

# CHAPTER THREE

Tip sat in the department SUV and watched the McConnell compound through the Zeiss binoculars.

The dirt lane stretched three hundred yards ahead to the house. Willow branches moving in the wind interrupted his view, but he could see well enough. Plus, the tree largely hid his vehicle. He didn't want to just drive in without checking things out. Reformed, yes, but old Luther was still pissed about getting sent up. Tip had to be careful.

Surrounded by cars up on blocks, the double-wide needed paint. The press-board siding bowed out along its seams. The shingles curled. A blue tarp covered the roof peak at one end. Two rusty grills, an electric range, plastic toys, aluminum lawn chairs, and stacks of firewood crowded the raised deck in front. The open windows now had screens, versus last time Tip was here. Three German Shepherds chased each other around the house-and-barn lot, tails wagging. Close to the river behind the house, two old single-wides nosed end to end. Clothes flapped on a wash line in front of one, and two blonde children played in front of the other.

Opposite the house stood a large pole-frame building with open garage door. The interior was well lighted as in body-shop paint booths, and all looked orderly and clean. In front and to one side of the barn, a '68 Chevy pickup truck, minus hood, sat under a chain hoist.

While Tip watched, Toby McConnell tried twice to lower a massive V8 into the engine compartment. In the south wind coming off the river, the engine swung slightly if he removed his hand. Feeding chain to the manual hoist with one hand and guiding the engine with the other was too much. McConnell finally gave up and threw his CAT hat on the ground in disgust.

If the old man had been home, he would surely be helping Toby. So Tip decided to drive on in from his hiding spot. Toby didn't look much like a guilty flight risk.

But he did react when the department SUV drove into the lot between the barn and the house. He looked side to side as if for a means of escape but did not run.

"Toby," nodded Tip as he got out of the car. "Use some help getting that engine onto the mounts?"

Toby looked suspicious, but finally nodded. "Sheriff. Yeah, I could. Never meant to be in there in the first place, but it will fit. I measured."

"348," said Tip. "Last one I saw was in a '58 Chevy. Gas hog. Not that hot off the line. 283 was better. Putting it in for the torque?"

McConnell relaxed and smiled. He shrugged. "What I got. Came out of a '61 Chevy too wrecked up to do anything with. Did a total overhaul. New cam, new three-deuce intake manifold. Figure I can fix up the body and make some money. Rust's not too bad, and I can replace the wood bed. Somebody'll buy it."

Tip nodded and put hands on the engine. "Here. Let's lower this baby in there."

They did so with little effort, and Tip wiped his hands on a shop towel lying on the fender.

"Thanks," said McConnell. "But the law don't come out here to help me drop in an engine." He looked at Tip in a challenging way.

"You're right." Tip watched McConnell's face closely. "You hear about Mr. Sampson?"

"Yeah. Don't know why somebody would do that."

"Why's that?" challenged Tip, still locked on to McConnell's eyes.

McConnell looked a little irritated. Maybe offended. "'Cause he's a nice old man."

"Maybe somebody who was growing marijuana on the back of his farm found out he knew and shut him up."

McConnell blanched.

"I didn't do it, Tip. I like the old guy. He has this one alfalfa field he lets me hunt rabbits in. Gives me a piece of pie if I give him a rabbit."

Tip noticed the present tense but did not remark on it. Guilty murderers probably don't talk in the present tense about their victims. He nodded.

"Yeah. Field west of the woods. Let me hunt there, too, when I was your age. Why'd you grow the dope on his place if you liked him? Didn't you know you could have got him in trouble? Before you answer, let me remind you. The penalty for dealing involves prison time, while the penalty for use can be fairly mild."

"Me and Jason—I mean, me and a friend—grew it for ourselves last year. Used to smoke that shit all the time, but I pretty much gave it up. Makes you paranoid. Beer's better."

"You're still too young to drink."

McConnell smiled. "Well, they *tell* me beer is better."

"Your friend going to back up your story?"

"Sure. Damn it. Didn't mean to mention his name. But there's only so many Jasons so I know you'll figure it out. Jason Willetts. Lives over on the Gilead Road."

"I know where it is. Come on. Get in the car."

McConnell bristled. "But I didn't do nothing! You gonna arrest me 'cause I *said* I grew some dope? You don't even have no proof!"

"Got all I need. But I'm not arresting you at this time. Nope. Gonna take you with me while I go over to question Jason. Not that you'd call him up ahead of time to get your stories straight or anything. But this way, I'll know."

McConnell smiled. "You might be smarter than people say, Tip. Can I call you Tip?"

"Sure." They slid into the SUV seats. "Long as you don't call me dumb again." He smiled. "Then I'd have to arrest you for all manner of crimes." He started the engine, then looked across at McConnell with his toughest expression. "Including growing dope. Which if you don't do it again, I won't say anything about. If I catch you again, I'll fry your ass."

McConnell lost the smile.

"Yes sir."

* * *

Jason Willetts lived two miles from Sedalia in a well-maintained three-bedroom ranch on a one-acre lot with a chemical lawn care service. Dad was a low-level manager, but as a Global Corp employee in Elmira, still pulled down two to three times the income of most Sedalians. Mom was home. Good-looking brunette in mid-forties in form-fitting jeans and an IU sweatshirt.

"What can I do for you, Sheriff?" she asked at the door. "Nothing wrong, I hope." She was nervous.

Tip could already tell she knew why he was there. She didn't look like a user herself. More like a consumer of better chardonnays.

"Like to talk to Jason. He here?"

"He is. But what's this about?" She pulled an errant strand of hair back over one ear.

"Just bring him out, wherever he is," said Tip. He wasn't in the business of easing people's fears.

She swallowed hard. "OK. He's in the basement. Just a minute."

\* \* \*

Jason was bleary-eyed and reeked of marijuana smoke. When he saw both the sheriff and Toby, he started freaking out. His chin trembled. Tip started right in.

"Come outside, Jason. I need to talk with you. Alone. Toby, you stay here and keep Mrs. Willetts company."

All three reacted with nervousness to this. Good. Tip took Jason outside.

"Tell me about your marijuana operation on the back of Mr. Sampson's farm. All about it. And tell me about your marijuana use, and Toby's marijuana use. And then tell me what part you played in Mr. Sampson's murder."

Jason started to cry. Tip let it go on for awhile, then intervened.

"Look, Kid. You ever hear the expression, 'Don't do the crime if you can't do the time.'?

Jason sobbed harder.

"Why'd you kill him?" demanded Tip.

"I didn't kill anybody," blubbered Jason. Then he confirmed everything Toby had said about their marijuana operation and Toby's use. Tip let out a long sigh. This kid didn't deserve it, but he was going to give him a break.

"You got a burn pit?"

Jason looked confused. "A what?"

"Burn pit. Where you burn things outside. Papers. Brush. Stuff like that."

"Yeah."

"Go get all your marijuana and bring it out to the burn pit. All of it. And any other illegal drugs you got. Everything."

Willetts swallowed and stared.

"Your feet grow to the ground? Move!"

\* \* \*

Tip followed him into the house, and down into the reeking basement. There was enough marijuana in large freezer bags to fill two five-gallon buckets. There were no small bags suggesting a dealer operation. Tip looked sternly at Willetts when some pills went into one bucket. The kid swallowed hard.

Then they went upstairs with the buckets, and Tip ordered Mrs. Willetts to bring charcoal lighter fluid. She eagerly complied.

Tip squirted lighter fluid over the pile, and set it all alight. Then he turned to Mrs. Willett, who was chewing her fingernails.

"I was never here," he said. "Tell anybody I was here today and I'll make trouble for you. Keep this kid on the straight and narrow and you won't see me again."

Mrs. Willetts clouded up and looked as if she was going to cry, but she held it together. "Thank you, Sheriff. We haven't been able to control him."

"About seventeen, isn't he? Big enough to take responsibility for himself? Smokes dope again in your house, lock him out."

She crimped her lips, and a tear ran down one cheek. She gave a tentative nod.

He and Toby left.

"You're not as tough as everybody says," Toby said. "You're soft inside."

"So I'm not as dumb or as tough as everybody says?"

"That's right."

Tip looked over at the smiling young man and gave his best poker face. "Recommend you believe the first and not test the second." He held McConnell's eye in a stare-down.

McConnell stared back for a long time, searching Tip's face for a crack. Finding none, he finally looked away, trying to conceal his swallow.

# CHAPTER FOUR

The shy, awkward farm girl Tip remembered had turned into a serious fifty-something looker.

Tall, tawny, fit, and leggy, Ella Sampson Benedetti strode the aisle between Indy airport luggage carousels as if she owned the place. She looked like a million bucks: tasteful gold bracelet, form-fitting light-tan slacks, gold belt, white silky blouse, and gold sandals with ankle straps. All expensive looking. And a shawl. As if to say, as a Californian, she expected lesser climes like Indiana to be cold. Even though it was nearly May. Drab Hoosiers snuck sidewise glances.

But even the mute-colored locals here in the airport were a different breed. Suited men in thin-soled loafers talked intensely on headsets, young women strutted in yoga tights that left nothing whatever to the imagination, and multigenerational Indian families retrieved cartloads of luggage. Indy was only an hour distant from Sedalia, but the culture gulf spanned light years.

Tip watched Ella snag her bag one-handed and straighten to look around for him. She stood half a head taller than those around her. He waved and she saw him and smiled.

"How will I get around if you pick me up and I don't get a rental?" she had asked on the phone. After she quit sobbing.

"Well, there's the old Chevy. Your dad was still driving it."

"The old '76 pickup?" She was incredulous.

"The very one." Tip was incredulous too, but because she didn't know.

"Well, all right." She had called back fifteen minutes later with the flight number.

She gave a big smile as she approached and set her bag down. "Tip, you're handsomer than you used to be." She gave him a big hug and a smack on the cheek.

He was prepared and knew not to take it personally. Hoosiers generally kept their distance, but those California people were huggers and kissers. He hugged her back.

"You've changed, too. California has been good to you."

A stir. Whew. He had to be careful here. After all, she had motive. And a husband.

She beamed. "Well that's a nice compliment. You didn't use to be able to even talk to girls hardly at all. You'd get embarrassed. Remember?"

"Thanks for bringing it up."

"How's Diane?"

"Happy, I think. Her new husband has a lot more money than I do. Indy dentist. Several years ago now." He struggled not to think of the biggest pain in his life. The fact that he had also not seen his daughter for ten years.

"Oh. I'm sorry."

"Some days me too, but most days not. Come on. Let's get you home."

* * *

Even with good make-up, she looked as if she had cried the whole twenty-four hours since he got her cell number from Loma Linda police. The number in George's address book was for a disconnected land line. Driving down I-65, he obliquely mentioned how he had gotten her number. She teared up again and confessed. She hadn't been back in fifteen years. Since her mom died.

"It's just so far," she said. "In more ways than one. There, the sun always shines. Life is bright. Here, everything is stark. People scratch dirt for a living. Kill animals and eat them. Constantly talk about sin, redemption, and death. Carry four generations of history with them. It's easier to breathe in California. Nobody knows anything about anybody, and death and other seriousness have been kicked out of reality. It's Disneyland."

"I think folks here think of all that grim and serious stuff *as* reality."

"Yeah. That's why I left."

"Ever get to be an actress like you wanted?"

"No. But I got a husband in the business. Producer. Makes a good living." She flashed a smile. "Keeps me in the style to which I've become accustomed."

So there was that.

\* \* \*

She broke down when he drove her into the homeplace driveway. The yellow police tape had all been removed, but just the sight of the place dug into her.

"There in the front yard?" she sobbed. "Who would do that? And do you think I'll be safe here?"

"Your dad's shotgun is upstairs in the guest room. Full box of number six shot on the writing desk. I don't imagine a perp would come to the same place twice. But just to reduce chances, I'll have Chet drop by a couple of times every day and evening to check on you. And I'll let everyone know I'm doing that."

She looked sidewise at him. "Chet Biggle?"

"The same."

"Never mind. I don't want that asshole anywhere around. I doubt he's changed since high school. I'll take care of myself."

"Your call."

* * *

Tip spent the next two days digging up Mr. Sampson's financial situation and Ella's whereabouts at the time of death. The mortgage-free farm, which on the trip down from Indy she had said she didn't care about except for its sentimental value, was worth upwards of one point six, according to Lulu Phillips, the local real estate agent. Even gone for thirty years, Ella still would know what black Indiana farmland was worth. Maybe she and hubby didn't need the money, but Tip couldn't imagine anyone not caring about one point six mil.

And it turned out Mr. Sampson had been the old-fashioned kind who bought and paid up whole-life insurance policies. According to Carolyn Spence Biggle at the agency, those were worth a hundred-twenty thousand. And Ella was the beneficiary. And though Jim Brock at Sedalia State Bank wouldn't say exactly—"That's for the lawyers, Tip"—George was a gold-star depositor, meaning more than $50K. So there was that, too.

Tip couldn't help reflecting. Funny how an old guy in Sedalia, who scratched the dirt, never wore new clothes, and drove an old Chevy pick-up, could be worth so much. And tons of Global Corp studs in Elmira lived in half-million dollar houses, drove Beamers, and dressed like a million bucks, mostly on debt. It was all clearly evidence of something, but Tip took a pass on figuring out what.

* * *

It quickly proved clear that Ella didn't do it, at least not personally. According to Loma Linda police, who were very helpful, she had rock-solid alibis: a yoga class attended, credit-card transactions at two clothing stores, a grocery store visit confirmable by security video, and a gas station stop. Her cell phone had never left their area, and TSA confirmed she had not traveled. So unless she conspired with somebody in Sedalia, she didn't do it. But there was a lot of money involved, so he needed to find out her financial situation.

Which turned out to be hard to do. The local prosecutor in San Bernardino County said no judge there would issue a warrant for such records without probable cause, and Tip had nothing at all except motive. No opportunity. But the DA did say he actually knew Leonard Benedetti, and the guy was rolling in it. Ella was not exactly destitute.

So there was that. Looked like a dead end. Which was OK. Tip didn't want it to be her. He thought she'd been shabby to her father by not coming home more often, but he had still always liked her. He understood her explanation about why she didn't come back more. Everybody in Sedalia would understand. They had just made a different choice.

But now he was back at square one. The two likeliest candidates looked innocent. And Samantha Parr would be agitating behind the scenes.

He decided to check the possible shooting locations across the road again. The M.E. said it was a .22 long rifle, as common as dirt in Howarth County, Indiana, not far north of the Ohio River. But maybe he could find some clue.

Any clue.

## CHAPTER FIVE

Tip parked the SUV in a deer hunter's pull-off into the woods around the corner from the Sampson farm. Green catkins hung from leafing hickory trees, and spring beauties carpeted the forest floor. A new theory had occurred to him, and he struck off into the woods humming.

The range of a .22 long rifle was a mile. Drop was about ten inches at a hundred fifty yards, so that was reasonable range for an experienced scope user. Maybe there were clear lines of sight to Mr. Sampson's mailbox from spots well back in the woods. Maybe the shooter had used one.

He chose this way into the forest, a quarter mile through blackberry, multiflora, and hawthorn, so Ella wouldn't see him or his car. She would be crying and reminiscing and puttering around the old house, finding relics of her mother and father, and sitting and thinking about life and death the way the bereaved do. He didn't want to disturb her with grisly reminders of how her father had died.

The leaves were coming fast, though not really on yet, so he quickly found many clear shots through the woods to the mailbox. And in one case, there was a deer stand.

The weathered edges of the two-by-four ladder rungs leading up the ten-foot wooden tower showed fresh scuffs. Somebody had been up there in the last few weeks.

He climbed up, not really expecting to find a shell casing. Most .22's around Sedalia were single-shot bolt-action—all you needed for squirrel or sitting rabbit. The shooter would carefully take out the casing himself and pocket it. Even if he was using a semi-automatic he would probably chase his brass. But it was worth checking.

The view from the top of the deer stand was perfect. A four-foot-diameter tunnel of openness, with no obstructing branches, looked straight into Mr. Sampson's front yard.

This was likely the place. Tip looked around for any scrap of evidence but saw nothing. And of course, the deer stand's wood was so rough there was no sense taking fingerprints.

Just to be safe, he had brought a metal detector, and he swept the ground in a ten-foot radius around the stand. But he found nothing except brass heads of old shotgun shells.

But then, on a hunch, he left the stand and walked a way toward the back road, not the side road where his SUV was parked. Hunters might come in from that direction, depending on the wind. There might be a path.

There was. And beside the head of that trail, thirty yards back in the woods, lay a single nose tissue. It had not been rained on, which meant it had been dropped there in the last four days. Within the time frame of the murder.

He bagged it in hopes of DNA evidence. The only problem was, even if it did belong to the murderer, he wouldn't know whose DNA it was. But deer season was long past, and raspberries wouldn't be in for another month. Blackberries for another two. No one would have had much reason to be here.

Except the murderer.

* * *

Temple was cool on the phone. "Sure you got something?" Not cool. More like icy.

Damn. He had to take more care with his relationship with women. Temple. Parr. They were proximity mines, only requiring his approach to go off, but he needed them to get his job done.

"Yup. Pretty sure it's from the killer. Only question is, is their DNA in the system."

"OK. Bring it up."

So Tip was back in Indy for the second time in a week and not quite back in Sedalia when his phone chirped and he got a shock in his email: the DNA on the tissue was from a woman. Who was not in the system.

He called Temple right away. "What if I asked every woman in Sedalia that I know shoots guns to give a DNA sample? I know who they are, 'cause we all grew up together. It's not more than about twenty. Could you manage that many tests?"

The extended silence made him immediately regret the question. An imperfectly suppressed groan and sigh followed.

"Even if they all waived their *fourth amendment rights*, there's the small matter of *time* and *expense*. It takes between two and twenty hours to do a DNA analysis. We don't have the resources. Besides, what makes you think it's a woman from Sedalia? And besides that, would you ask every *man* in Sedalia to get tested?"

Easy here, Tip reminded himself. Dangerous currents. He chose his words carefully. "Sure. And they would all do it, because they all respected George Sampson. They wouldn't do it for feds or out-of-town cops, but they would do it for me."

There was an exhalation over the phone and a moment of that silent disgust rural dwellers endure from city and coast dwellers— the disdain for flyover country and its values. Temple was indeed a transplant from Massachusetts. She broke the silence.

"There's still the resource problem. Let's limit the DNA testing to women with motive, method, and opportunity, shall we? Remember those?"

Now it was Tip's turn to sigh. He was accustomed to being patronized, taken for dumb, and assumed to be incompetent because of his high-school-only education. Plus military and police training. But it did get old.

"I'll try to bone up, Sergeant. Thanks for the information. Have a good day."

He clicked off without waiting for a response.

*　*　*

He drove up and down River Road, thinking. The driving always helped. The problem was, out of all the women in Sedalia, how could he find out who had been in the woods opposite George's house on the day of the murder? Willy Carson, the mail carrier who had delivered George's mail, had seen nothing. No cars, no walkers, no bike riders.

Then in a fit of disgust with himself, Tip realized he had probably destroyed tire tracks in the pull-off where he had parked when he went into the woods. So just to be safe, he went to George's mile square—the one across from his house—and took plaster casts of the tracks in all the pull-offs. Then he sent them up with Chet to Temple. Let Chet absorb her scorn. Her note back was nasty, as expected. "You'll get these back when you get them," it said. "I put our new guy on them. He can learn on your stuff, since so much of it is pointless anyway."

Then despite Temple's sneering, he decided to collect a few touch-DNA samples from women known to be good shots. But he started with Ella Sampson Benedetti just to clear her from his list. An empty pomegranate-juice bottle from the kitchen trash. What the hell were pomegranates anyway? Some California thing. He told Temple the bottle came from a possible suspect he wanted to eliminate.

"Ella Benedetti," she said. "You're really predictable, Tip. You two had a thing going in high school? Fine. I'll check it."

Then the shock: it was a match with the nose tissue. He hadn't expected that. And given her Loma Linda alibi, it couldn't mean she was the shooter.

Still, he asked if she had been across the road into the woods. He watched her face closely. He considered himself a good identifier of liars.

"Sure. I wanted to see where the bastard stood."

"How far into the woods did you go?"

"Maybe twenty feet. I quit after ten minutes. There were a zillion places over there where a shooter could stand without being seen. Plus, I didn't want to get poison ivy. It's all over that woods."

"You drop any Kleenexes over there?"

She looked insulted. "No. Think I'm some kind of litterer?"

She was not deceiving him.

Tip spied a box of Kleenexes on the sideboard, and a pile of used ones in a small wastebasket near the kitchen door. A chill went down his spine.

"You're 100% sure?"

"Of course. I'm from California, remember? We're all green out there. We don't throw trash."

"Noticed anything out of place in the house since you've been here?"

A chill descended over the room. Ella was no dummy. She immediately saw where he was going with this.

"Now you mention it, I have. That candle stand by the front door was knocked over. Would have fallen but was leaning against the drape. Yesterday morning. I'm ninety-nine percent sure I didn't do it. It's been there fifty years. I wouldn't bump into it even in the dark." She looked wide-eyed for a moment. "You think somebody's been in here?"

"Don't know. Might not be a bad idea to stay in a motel up in Elmira. I think somebody might be spoofing me, and the only person I can think of who would be doing that would be the murderer."

\* \* \*

On the way back into Sedalia, Tip had a sudden thought. He turned around in the Sieferts' driveway and went back to the pull-off where he had parked before.

Starting at the deer stand, he walked ever-wider spirals, intending to go out as far as he had to until he found what he hoped to. It didn't take that long. He found the first where a deer trail crossed the footpath that came in from the back road. The second was strapped to a sapling facing an old scrape, now looking as if it had been rained on since the last time a buck pawed it.

Game cameras.

He wrote notes on sheets from his Rite in the Rain® all-weather pocket notepad and stuffed them between the cameras and the trees: "Will return your camera card in a couple days. If you want it before then, see me at jail. Tip."

Since there was no name-and-address tag on either camera, he doubted if either owner—one camera was bottom-of-the-line and the other was a three-hundred-dollar job—would come and see him.

What he wasn't prepared for when he got back to the jail and looked at the images—deer, coon, a turkey, a distant shot of himself—was the still picture of a man's hands close-up.

One held a Kleenex.

The other was flipping the bird.

# CHAPTER SIX

Tip stared at the middle finger for a long time on his monitor at the jail. Looking at it didn't make the situation better.

This was personal.

The murderer—or at very least, the intruder who had gone into Ella Sampson's farmhouse *while she was there*—was dicking with him. Knew the picture would mean nothing to the owner of the game camera. Knew only the murder investigator would understand what it meant. Knew—*anticipated*—it would be Tip, that he would come back and search the area. Because only a local person would check that far back in the woods, and check game cameras. Which suggested a local murderer. Tip just couldn't imagine who it might be. People in Sedalia were too nice to kill anybody.

Weren't they?

The hands were male. No doubt about that. They were medium to large, with square-cut nails, some of them dirty. But there were no rings, tattoos, or scars, and no shirt sleeves. Nothing to identify the person. The skin tone looked slightly olive, but game cameras were not known for picture quality. The guy could have been albino and his skin might look olive in the photo.

If he asked Temple to analyze it, the case would spiral out of control. She would call Samantha, and Samantha would call the governor. The state boys would barge in. What a political opportunity: a killer with a grudge against a sheriff Brandt wanted gone. Tip no longer wondered why grudges lasted. They just did. He never should have saved Brandt from that kid at Scout camp back in the day. Being saved by a social inferior was apparently worse than an ass whipping.

He riffled through his case files, hoping a name would pop out. What sick bastard would kill George Sampson just to get back at Tip? And for what? Probably somebody he'd put away, and that was a lot of people, but mostly not for very long. Mostly drugs. But then there was the Ortiz case. Turned federal. Danny Ortiz. Fifteen years for meth cooking. Indy operator cooking meth in Howarth County. Did Ortiz have a brother? He sent a note to the warden at Terre Haute to find out.

On the other hand, it might have nothing to do with him at all. It was some kind of performance art. Some asshole who wanted to demonstrate how clever he was, and tap dance all over Sedalia's forehead. The sneak job into Ella's house was the act of an asshole seriously into *control*. Or gamesmanship.

The question was, why George Sampson? Inheriting big money was out as a motive. Unless he didn't really have the skinny on Ella and her husband, and they had a local operator. Or there was a scumbag grandson who would inherit.

He needed to know what was in George's will.

Jason Quibble was the only lawyer in town, therefore the will's likely author. So he would need to convince him to show the document. Or get Judge Prechter to order it if Quibble balked. Neither felt like a walk.

He should have done it before, but he sent an email direct to Prechter asking for an order to disclose. Ella was almost certainly the executor, and she could reveal the will's contents to him, but he wanted to find out without her knowing. Since there was still the ghost of a chance she was somehow involved.

If the motive wasn't in the will, it looked like plain opportunity. George lived in the country, it was easy to get a shot at him from a hidden location, and nobody would be the wiser or pay any attention. Just another gunshot.

Which was a scary thought, because living situations like George's were common. Sedalia was a farming community.

Dear Lord, were people going to start getting shot off of their tractors in remote fields?

Then, in a sudden fit of paranoia, thinking about the home invasion and the planted nose tissue, he jumped into the SUV and drove out to George's place. Ella was not there, but the door was unlocked, so he went in. With his weapon drawn. People in Sedalia never locked their doors, but after living in California, Ella was probably now a door locker.

He found what he was looking for upstairs in George's bedroom closet. An old Remington Targetmaster model 41 .22 with the old pull-knob cocker. He shook George's pillow out of its case and used the cover to pick up the weapon and carefully open the breech.

An empty shell casing lay in the chamber.

Dread settled on his stomach like cod liver oil. He suddenly knew what he would find out, but he took the rifle out to the SUV and put it and the shell casing into an evidence bag. He was just coming back out of the house after replacing the pillow case when Ella returned.

"What the hell, Tip?" she challenged.

"Might say the same, Ella. Told you to move out of here. Too dangerous. What I just found, if my hunch is right, says it's really,

really too dangerous. By the way, do I have permission to get ballistics on your dad's rifle? It'll speed things up."

Her mouth opened slightly as she processed this. She started to speak twice, but stopped each time.

"No shit?" she said. "You really think so? Who the hell?"

"No kidding. Stay in a motel in Elmira. Or if it gets too expensive, see Mrs. Aubrey, the church secretary. She sometimes takes in boarders."

Ella's creased forehead smoothed, and she smiled. "I remember Mrs. Aubrey. I wouldn't have any secrets for long."

"That's our gal."

* * *

Prechter's response was not long in arriving on his phone: "You must be kidding. Haven't you met the snake in our cucumber patch? The scorpion in our shoe? The spider in our bed? All warrant requests must now go through the prosecutor."

# CHAPTER SEVEN

Jason Quibble, the very picture of well-dressed, revenge-of-the-nerds prosperity, leaned back in his plush leather chair, and looked across his desk at Tip. He straightened a lapel and steepled his fingers.

"Can't do it, Sheriff."

When Slack retired, Quibble became the principal at Quibble and Slack, the only law firm in Sedalia. Now in middle age, he was nevertheless lean, fit, and trim long after his contemporaries had run to pudge. And he was proud of it. He generally found a way to work his fitness regimen into any conversation. Still compensating for always being last pick, people said. Plus that fateful eighth-grade, wrong-basket lay-up. "Wrong-way Quibble" had dogged him for thirty years. But they acknowledged, "Honest lawyer."

"Why not?" Tip asked.

"You've used up your freebies. You wanted to know last year, without a warrant, who inherited Carter Blake's copyrights."

"And you told me before. Without a warrant."

"Reluctantly. Went ahead because I knew Judge Prechter would sign an order to disclose. This is different."

"Why?"

"Number one, it's George Sampson's will. He was better liked than Carter Blake. People will want all the i's dotted and t's crossed. "

"And number two?"

"Come on, Tip. New prosecutor. Ball buster. Even Prechter is afraid of her. Scuttlebutt is, he already refused your request."

"He's an elected judge. She's just a prosecutor. Appointed."

"By the governor. Who is of the other party. Who also by stroke of luck was able to appoint three of the five justices on the Indiana Supreme Court. Which can remove a county judge."

"Ah. Delightful guy, our governor. So I have to get Samantha to ask Prechter?"

"Afraid so."

"There are things I'd rather do."

"I imagine it's a long list."

\* \* \*

Samantha Parr's office in the Howarth County court house had the spacious dimensions common to nineteenth-century public buildings: at least twenty-five by twenty-five, with a twelve-foot ceiling and an eight-foot-tall oak door topped by a frosted-glass transom. Samantha sat behind an ancient walnut desk that must have weighed half a ton. A two-foot-long sign on her desk said "District Attorney Samantha Parr."

Tip hated himself for it, but he took off his flat-brimmed campaign hat as he approached her desk. His Smokey hat, as people called it. If you wore it just right, with the brim pulled down low in the front, you could look like a serious badass. Intimidate the hell out of people. He usually wore it tilted back on his head so as not to obscure vision. And not intimidate people.

She made him wait twenty seconds or so, then looked up imperiously.

"Crawling to me for help, Tip? Need a warrant or something? Why didn't you go straight to Prechter the way you used to do?"

It was true that previous DA Dave Woods, though himself an asshole of the first rank, had had a practical view of such things. "You need a warrant, Tip, go straight to Prechter. I've told him I trust you and know you only ask for one when it's legit. All I ask is that you make sure I get a copy right away, and that I know right away when you serve it."

"Just dotting i's and crossing t's, Madame Prosecutor. Following the process. Need to know who inherits in George Sampson's will. I don't think there's an issue there, but I want to know for sure. Ella Sampson checks out clean, but I want to rule out anything complicated, like surprise heirs."

"Cut the 'Madame Prosecutor' crap, Tip. Call me 'Sam.'"

There it was again. When Tip first met her, she had come around her desk in a semi-aggressive way, stuck out her hand like a man, and said, "Call me 'Sam.'" It was her signature line. He would rather eat a dog turd than call her Sam.

She cocked her head in such a way as to suggest suspicion. "I'm told that Michelin off-road tires, the kind used on Jeeps, were recently in a pull-off near the Sampson place. Also that a nose tissue you sent for test was used by Ella Sampson. One does wonder why you sent that in. But the real kicker is that the rifle you sent in is the murder weapon. Care to comment on that?"

"Nope. Just want an order to disclose what's in the will."

"Come on, Tip. How do you know she's clean? I'm betting the rifle is George's, am I right? You don't have some sort of old high-school flame going with her, do you? Ugh." She shuddered and took a second to recover from her disgust. "You just believe what she says? You tell me the rifle is George's, I'm going to charge her. The rifle's enough."

He handed her a folded slip of paper. "It's all in the affidavit. The Kleenex and the gun are enough probable cause, but the Loma Linda police have proof she was there when the shooting occurred."

"Got physical evidence of their proof?"

This pissed Tip off, but he didn't let it show. As if this was his first rodeo, and she was going to tell him how it was done.

"On the way."

"All right. I'll get your warrant. But I expect daily reports from you on your progress on this case."

Lots of people expected lots of things, but they didn't necessarily get them.

"Looking forward to getting that warrant."

# CHAPTER EIGHT

Tip stared like a statue at the girl lying face-up on the school playground gravel.

How could it be?

Prechter's order to disclose still stuck from his shirt pocket. The judge had responded to Samantha's request right away, and Tip had been in Quibble's office when the lawyer rolled in at nine o'clock. But there was nothing complicated about George's will. A straightforward will from a straightforward man. Ella inherited everything.

Now, that early-morning business seemed a distant comfort. The urgent call from Chet—with no hint of his usual insolence—had abruptly ended the meeting in the plush comforts of Quibble's office. Somebody was killing Sedalians, and it wasn't Ella Sampson.

The last-day-of April sun illuminated the tragedy like an over-exposed photo. The girl lay open-eyed on the gravel beneath the swing set. A .22-sized hole marred the center of her perfect fore-head. Blood had dripped back into her blond hair. She was an adorable little girl. Had been. For some reason, the Velcro straps on her pink sneakers nearly brought Tip to tears. Janice Hauck, the principal, sobbed behind him. His chest heaved as he struggled to control his own emotions.

"Who would *do* a thing like this?" she choked.

Indeed. He was barely able to contain his rage. The girl looked about eight.

"Her parents know?" he rasped, without turning. He pushed aside the cowardly hope that they did so he wouldn't have to tell them.

"The Clarksons? They're on their way."

"Don't let them see this. Keep them in your office until the medical examiner and crime scene people are finished. They'll put her body in an ambulance when they're done. I'll come and explain to the parents that we have to do an autopsy. To get the bullet."

"I'll try."

Inside the school, children peeked out the windows until teachers loomed up and shooed them away. Surrounding the school yard and the area within two hundred yards, Indiana State Police cruiser lights flashed. All four Sheriff's department vehicles were there as well. All reserve officers were called in. Buses were beginning to arrive to take children home, though it was the middle of the morning.

"Tell me again. How many shots did the children hear?"

"That's just it. They didn't hear any shots."

Gravel crunched behind with someone's approach. Tip didn't turn. His eyes were locked on the girl. Corporal Jarvis of the State Police spoke. Tip knew him from way back.

"Bad stuff, Tip. Really bad."

"How's the search going?"

"Nothing yet. We're probably breaking about sixteen civil rights laws, but we're hitting every building within a two-hundred-yard radius. Questioning everybody. Collecting weapons."

"Getting signed permission to search, and giving receipts for the guns, right? "

"Sure. Like you said, that's about max range for a weapon with that bore. And a slug that didn't. . ." He stopped himself and looked at Janice.

"Right," said Tip. Didn't blow out the back of her skull. Meaning a small or weak load. A .22. Not a .223 with a magnum shell.

"So far, though, nothing. You'd think somebody would have seen something."

You'd think.

Jarvis lowered his voice. "You'd think, town like this, somebody would have noticed a stranger."

Tip's knotted stomach twisted even tighter. "You would definitely think that." But if not a stranger, who in this town would do a thing like this?

"No real vantage point," said Jarvis, looking around. "School yard extends out at least sixty yards in all directions, which would make a shooter visible."

The two of them scanned the whole horizon. If it was the same shooter, with a different weapon this time, since the state lab still had George's .22, he might have chosen another hundred-fifty-yard shot. Same MO. Maybe even farther. In any case, the dead-center-of-the-forehead hit spoke of a serious marksman. And probably a close-by vantage point.

"Church tower," said Jarvis.

"Nah. Mrs. Aubrey or Pastor Frank would see him go in and out. Elevator leg. The tower that takes the grain up," he added. "Pretty long shot, though."

Jarvis grinned. "I'm no city boy, Tip. And the elevator leg requires climbing up the ladder cage on the outside of the leg. Somebody would have seen. Look, if nobody heard a shot, maybe a shooter with a silenced .22 just fired from the stop sign over there and drove on."

"Could have. Jesus. What a sick bastard. Shooting a kid is bad enough, but picked at random? Otherwise, people would notice him sitting there waiting for his shot."

"Probably right," conceded Jarvis. "So, one of these houses around the school yard?"

"Gotta be. Sat in there and watched for her for some reason."

"We'll know soon as my men get through these houses."

But Tip's mind had stepped out of the conversation with Jarvis and headed off on its own trail.

A sniper.

There was only one sniper in Sedalia that Tip knew of, and that was Tom Burton. And Old Mrs. Burton's house, his grandmother's, no longer inhabited or habitable, was busy sagging into the earth an easy eighty-yard shot away.

Burton was a mid-to-late thirties Iraq vet who had been trouble as a boy but seemed now to just want to be left alone. He had come back from the service all screwed up, in the technical jargon of Sedalia, and moved onto his parents' old property down on River Road. All close relatives were long dead, father in a bar fight when the boy was about nine, and mother of cirrhosis when he was about twelve. Burton had torn apart one of the two trailers sinking into the soil on the old lot and used the scrap sales to fund his restoration of the other. He lived on disability, since he was apparently too screwed up to hold a job. Mainly, he fished, gardened, drank, and kept to himself.

Still, Alma Fisher, a self-identified excellent judge of character, swore he was no good. She even kept a loaded .38 under the register at Fishers' Groc to deal with him if he got out of hand. But as far as Tip knew, he disturbed no one's peace.

He *was* screwed up, though, as everyone attested. And he had been a military sniper in Iraq. Two tours. But unless he had run totally, murderously amok, motive was the missing piece.

Meanwhile, uncomfortably aware the State boys and his own auxiliaries were probably violating people's civil rights, and a conviction based on illegally seized evidence would be fruit of the poison tree, Tip called Samantha on the cell.

"I've got Chet and the State boys searching every house within two hundred yards of the school. Some people will object. I need a blanket warrant. Right now. Make it happen."

There was a peeved silence.

"Tip, I don't like your tone. Have you gone crazy? Why would you do that? And why would you dare talk to a prosecuting attorney like that?"

"Ah. You haven't heard." He told her.

There was long silence on the line. He could hear the wheels turning in her brain.

"Prechter is in court, but he'll adjourn. He and I will be there in ten minutes."

"You don't have to come. Just send the warrant. But make it five."

\* \* \*

Samantha pushed ahead of Tip and crossed the soaked living room rug in the old Burton house. A small patch of blue shone through the partially collapsed ceiling and roof. It had finally rained a couple of days previous, a brief shower that had barely settled the dust, but water squished up out of the carpet and over the toes of her Italian leather boots. She was careful not to brush her charcoal wool suit pants or jacket against any of the old furniture. The clothes looked incongruous in this place.

"Jesus, this place stinks," she said.

"Hold back," commanded Tip. Samantha turned on him, ready to rebuke him for giving her orders. He nodded at the faint foot-prints leading alongside her own across the wet rug into an adjacent room. "Evidence. Somebody's been in here in the last two hours."

She saw them. "Ah."

The prints barely showed, but he photographed them with his cell phone anyway. A man's size eleven or twelve. Then he brushed past her into the adjoining room. An old bedroom, with a bed still in it. An old woman's room, with a glass, spoon, and Bible still on the bed stand, and a framed needlepoint on the wall: the golden rule. This room was dry.

Someone had knelt in the dirt in front of the window very recently. And disturbed the dust on the windowsill. And poked a hole in the rusty window screen. The line of sight to the school yard was perfect.

Why? Jennifer Clarkson specifically, or just any kid the shooter chose randomly?

No shell casings. No other evidence. And the front door had long ago been broken by kids sneaking in, to use the bed, by the looks of it, so there was no way to conclude that it had been unlocked by somebody with a key. Still, it was Tom Burton's grandma's house. He was familiar with it. And he was a sniper. And anybody could make a silencer. Especially a sniper who used one all the time and knew how they were made.

"This guy has been on my list," said Samantha. "It's time to nail him."

"You have a *list*? Far as we know, the guy has broken no laws. We're *inves*tigating here. We need to establish a connection. And a motive. He might even have an alibi. You do know about those? *Jesus!*"

"Don't patronize me. He's a combat veteran. Sooner or later they screw up. They've all lost the thing that makes us civilized: the unwillingness to resort to violence. To kill people."

This pissed Tip off so badly his vision darkened momentarily. He briefly considered proving her point.

"*I'm* a combat veteran." He managed to sound flat and rational.

"Yeah." She looked him in the eye. "You are." Her self-confidence was unshakable. She was sure she could stare him down. When she realized she could not, she continued. "You now have two dead people on your watch, Tip, and you haven't arrested anybody. The news people will be down from Indy."

"Got their numbers on your cell phone, do you?"

"They'll be screaming for your head, Tip."

"You mean, you and Brandt will. But your problem, Madame Prosecutor, is that if you two get rid of me, you'll never figure this out. And you'll own it. You don't know this town, or the people in it. If you get rid of me, you two'll be next up to bat. You need me to own it."

She gave a thin smile. "I have thought of all that, Tip. That's why you'll pick up Tom Burton. For questioning, at the very least."

"Was going to go see him for that reason. But I won't be arresting him unless I have probable cause. Speaking of which, I could use a warrant to let me search his place for a weapon. Think you got enough probable cause for that?"

She looked thoughtful. Searching a house where no search was warranted was basis for a charge of prosecutorial misconduct. "Hm. Probably not."

"Didn't think so. Not that you'd want your name on." He smiled what he hoped was a patronizing smile. "I'll get back to you."

## CHAPTER NINE

Tom Burton sat in an aluminum lawn chair on the small deck in front of his trailer. It was 11:30 in the morning. He took a swig and raised his beer can in salute as Tip walked up from the SUV.

"Hey, Sheriff. I didn't do it, whatever it is. Beer?"

Burton was a rangy, fully-bearded, camo-clad man with strong bones and little meat on them. Tip stepped up onto the deck and looked around for something to sit on. Burton extended a skinny leg and pushed an unsplit log section toward him with his foot. Tip sat. Sunlight dappled the porch. The smell of fried fish wafted through the screen door. In a patch of sunlight to one side of the trailer, ruler-straight, weedless rows of young potatoes, peas, radishes, and beets belied the book on Tom Burton. Tip hated this visit.

"Beer sounds good, but people would smell it. I'm on duty." He shifted back and forth to find a comfortable position on the log section. There was none. "Not a social call anyway."

"Didn't figure it was. Who's saying what about me this time?"

"Where's your car?"

"Around back. Finally got some gravel back there to park it on. Need more for a driveway."

"Been anywhere this morning?"

"VA. Up in Indy. Just got back. Tell me I got a limited time left to live. If I keep drinking the way I do. But I've cut back. I don't do the whiskey until the afternoon."

"What time was your appointment?"

"Nine. Had to wait. Just got back and had breakfast. Lunch. Whatever you want to call it. Catfish. Want some? Some left."

"How long were you gone? Total?"

"Probably four hours. What's this about?"

"Mind if I search your house?"

Burton's beer paused on the way to his mouth while he looked at Tip, then his face took on a look of disgust.

"I got nothing to hide." He shook his head. "Same shit since I was a kid. 'Burton probably did it.' What is it this time?"

"So I can search your house?"

Burton spat sidewise over the deck rail. "Knock yourself out, Sheriff."

* * *

It took only ten minutes to find the scoped .22 in the bedroom closet with the mouth of a plastic water bottle duct-taped onto the end of the barrel. He sniffed the centered one-inch hole cut neatly out of the bottom. The smell of gunpowder lingered.

"Damn it," swore Tip quietly, and headed back outside.

Burton's face screwed up in shock when Tip showed it to him. "What the hell? I didn't put that on there, Tip. I swear before God, I didn't put that on there! Somebody's been in my house! And the only time they could have done it was when I went to the VA this morning. I ain't even been to town in the last week."

"How long since you used the gun?"

"Probably a couple of days. I shoot squirrels and rabbits with it. Get tired of fish after awhile."

"Mind if I take it with me? Ballistics test. I'm ninety-nine percent sure it was used in a murder this morning."

Burton's face turned white. "Tip, I didn't do no murder! I ain't shot a man since Eye Rack!"

"Wasn't a man. Was a little girl. About eight or nine. School yard. During recess. Girl by the name of Jennifer Clarkson."

Burton's already sallow face turned white.

"*What*? Kenny and Sarah Clarkson's girl?"

"Yes."

"Who would do that? I'll kill the son of a bitch!" Burton stood and threw his beer onto the ground. "I just saw her last week! She's a beautiful kid. The Clarksons are the only people in this town that treat me decent. Invite me over to supper couple of times a month. Their Christian duty, trying to save me from myself, but I don't mind. And the girl is sweet." A tear rolled down his face. He shook his head in disbelief. "Ah, Jesus."

"Did you shoot her?"

Burton took a moment to process the question, then indignantly turned to Tip. "What? You really think I would do that? Jesus, Tip! What kind of sick bastard are you to even ask that question?"

Tip didn't react. "Who knew about your appointment at the VA?" Meaning, who could do this while you were away.

"Hell, could have been a dozen people. Doc Quick. He referred me. Anybody at the VA."

Doc Quick would of course have nothing to do with murder. Unless it was somebody from Medicare. He bitched about government paperwork every chance he got. People laughed about it, but they loved him.

But, somebody from the VA?

Nah. Probably neither Doc nor anybody from the VA. But one of those two connections would lead to the killer.

"You know how this works, Tom. I got no motive for you, and if your alibi checks out with the VA, no opportunity. But a rifle with a silencer in your house looks really bad. Especially since the kill shot was silenced. And sure as I'm sitting here the shot came from your Grandma's old house."

"What?" Burton's voice trailed off. "Who the hell . . .?"

"Wish I knew. I don't think it was you, but the DA is screaming for your neck. So don't leave town. If you do, I'll have to put out a warrant."

Burton kicked a piece of firewood off the deck and for a moment looked as though he might face off. He was forty pounds lighter than Tip but nearly as tall.

"Son of a *bitch*! Somebody is setting me up! Came into my *house*, for Christ's sake. I'm telling you, Tip. I find somebody in my house, I am going to hurt him. Bad."

"You find somebody in your house, tie him up and call me. Don't hurt him more than you have to, or you'll be in more trouble. 'Cause I'll want to talk to him."

"Damn it, Tip, I shouldn't be in any trouble because I didn't *do* anything."

"Tell me what you know about George Sampson."

Burton calmed. "Well, he's a fine old man. Treated me like a son after I had to move in with Grandma. I was kind of wild, and he calmed me down some. Let me hunt. Used to give me moral instruction, as he called it. I love him like a grandfather. I need to go seem him. Take him a mess of fish." He smiled. "He will come right out and tell you he likes catfish, where most people like it but don't admit it."

"So you don't know?"

Burton took on a look of alarm. "Know what?"

"Somebody shot him Saturday."

Burton looked stunned for a long moment. Then he started kicking everything on the deck and yelling.

"Sons of bitches! Low-life bastards! Goddamn scumbags!"

After kicking everything off the deck that would fit under the railing, he picked up a three-quarter axe and looked around, wild-eyed. Tip Tensed, but Burton turned and flung it across his small yard with a whip-like motion. It turned several revolutions in the air and stuck in a young oak, handle at an angle. Then the rage seemed to go out of him, and he sat down, put his head in his hands, and sobbed, a low baritone wail Tip remembered from when his own father died.

Tip decided to leave him alone with his grief. No way was he going to take this fellow veteran in, because he knew in his gut Burton was not the killer. Still, as he left, he said, "Stay in town." And hated himself for having to say it.

* * *

On his way to the Medical Examiner's office in Elmira to pick up the slug, Tip stopped at Eileen's Restaurant and Café across from the court house. He needed a grease infusion, and some of the advice he was sure to get there might be useful. There was some risk since the place was just across the street from Samantha's office. But Eileen's clientele was not her style, so the risk was slight.

Animated conversation penetrated Eileen's plate-glass front window, and he could even recognize voices from the sidewalk. But as soon as he went in, quiet fell. Everybody looked at him. Behind the counter, Eileen yelled "burger and fries" into the kitchen and turned back to him.

"So what's up, Tip?" She tried to make it sound casual, but the silence that followed in the room was electric.

He took his time and bellied up to the lunch counter, resting a ham on a stool. Then he shook his head.

"No firm suspects. Looking day and night. Got some leads."

"Revenge of some kind," offered Dave Schulz, the barber, from two stools down. "I'd start there."

"Nut job," said Al Stefano, the Porters man, unloading boxes of frozen pies, burgers, and fries onto the counter from his two-wheel cart. His freezer truck was parked at the curb. Porters sold frozen foods—burgers, steaks, egg rolls, shrimp, meatballs, ice cream—to businesses and homeowners. Al's route encompassed both Elmira and Sedalia. A beefy man who looked like an Italian wrestler, he was always cheerful, always had a joke.

"You both could be right," said Tip. "But we're talking about an old man and a girl. Nothing in common. And premeditated. Shot from a distance." He knew the sniper theory was already out there, so there was no harm in sharing this information.

"Maybe it's some guy just showing how good he is," said Al. "Doesn't matter to him who they are. Some kid, been watching movies or playing video games."

Schulz frowned at Al. "Hate to think we got one of those loose. But could be. Whole country's going to hell in a handbasket." He sipped his coffee, brushed his perfect mustache with the back of his finger, and looked at Tip.

Tip smiled but didn't engage. The only barber in town, Schulz was a chameleon curmudgeon who would agree with ain't-it-awful rants from all points on the political spectrum. He liked to get people going.

"Smoke screen for some other crime," said Al, piling the last box on the counter. "Keep you from figuring out the motive. You might never figure it out."

"Thanks for the vote of confidence, Al."

Stefano grinned. "Any time, Tip." Then he sat down at a table with his clipboard and began checking off the items on the countertop.

"It's some kind of revenge, Tip," Schulz insisted. "Assuming the same killer did both. Nothing else could connect an eighty year-old man and a nine year-old girl."

"Hm," said Tip. Despite being slippery when it came to politics, Schulz was a keen observer of human nature. "Maybe. But what could those two victims have done to provoke revenge?"

"Maybe they didn't do it. Maybe somebody else who will miss them did it."

"Ah," said Tip. He thought immediately of Burton. "That would mean we were facing a serious psycho."

"It's a woman," said Eileen, both elbows on the counter in front of Tip. "I'm sure of it. You haven't said much, but I heard, whoever it is plants evidence to make it look like somebody else did it. A trickster. That's a woman. Men aren't that smart."

Tip suppressed a smile. Eileen liked to poke him. He laid his Smokey hat on the counter and scratched the back of his fringe. "Where'd you get that from? About planting evidence?"

"Come on, Tip. You been here all your life. You expect to keep secrets in this town? Mr. Sampson's own rifle?"

Damn Chet's mouth. Or Samantha's, looking to undercut him. And neither even knew yet about Burton's gun, waiting in the car to go to Indy with the slug from little Jennifer Clarkson's head.

"I believe she's right," offered Eldora Quick from the corner booth. She and an elderly lady friend sat with coffee and the halves of a cinnamon roll they'd divided. "*Cherchez la femme.*" She nodded and smiled sweetly.

Eldora was the eighty-something grande dame of the local writers' group, and author of several self-published crime novels.

Surely considered herself a crime expert by now. She was also Doc Quick's mother.

"You may be right, Mrs. Quick. But which femme?"

Mama Alma Fisher banged through the front door carrying a plastic grocery basket full of canned goods, onions, potatoes, eggs, and bags of buns. She grunted as she reached up and set it on the countertop in front of Eileen. Five-two on a good day, in her seventies, and skinny as a grasshopper, she was still going strong. Everybody stopped talking and looked at her expectantly. She always had something to say.

"*What*? she demanded, looking around in confusion. "You all been talking about me? Sherry? My new son-in-law? He's doing very well, thank you. Even helps us with the grocery store."

This referred to daughter Sherry's scandalous marriage to Andy McCall, the salvage yard owner. Scandalous if you'd lived around Sedalia for forty years, but otherwise unremarkable.

"We were offering the Sheriff our valuable advice," explained Pastor Frank from the window table with a slight smile. He looked at Tip. "But as we were discussing before you came in, we can't offer much in the physical realm. Still, I'm sure I speak for every-one when I say we stand ready to offer what we can." He folded his paper, set his coffee cup down on it, and shook his head. "This is a horrible situation."

There were several nods. Tip caught the hint and nodded soberly as well. "Thanks, Pastor Frank. I would appreciate what-ever help you can arrange from the man upstairs." Tip was not a religious man, but it was important to give due respect. And to engage Pastor Frank's bully pulpit.

Pastor Frank acknowledged with a nod. The Sedalia Methodist Church congregation would pray energetically for the Lord to guide Tip.

"Never spends much,' Eileen said of Pastor Frank once. "Buys coffee and reads his paper, but kind of sets the tone."

"Well," sniffed Mama Alma, turning on Tip, "you ask me, Tip, I think you're not doing your job. You're in here wasting time when you should be out arresting somebody, instead of playing footsie with Eileen."

Eileen and Tip both smiled and shook their heads. People had been teasing them for years. Mama Alma continued.

"You got the perfect suspect living out on River Road, a crazy man that killed people for a living over in Eye Rack. It's him for sure, and the wonder is, why haven't you arrested him?"

Eileen slid Tip a cup of coffee, and he stalled for a moment while he took a sip. Then he set the cup down and smiled at Mama Alma. "You have to have probable cause to arrest people, Mrs. Fisher. Evidence they did it, whatever it is. You can't just arrest people because you don't like them."

"It's him, I'm telling you," she snapped. She looked around the restaurant for support. A couple of people nodded. "Do your job, Tip. Get out there and arrest him. You won't be sorry. You heard it here first."

Next to Tip, Al nodded silently as he handed Eileen his clipboard for her to sign. "Seems logical to me," he said. "Sometimes, things aren't complicated. If it quacks like a duck, it's a duck." He tipped his hat and rolled his two-wheel cart out the door.

With that, Mama Alma handed Eileen the bill for her delivery and left, which pretty much ended the speculation.

But seeing Mama Alma and Pastor Frank in the same place gave Tip an idea.

Mama Alma was probably number three on the gossip hit parade after Chet and Mrs. Aubrey, Pastor Frank's church secretary. Chet's info always came with a load of agenda, and had been useless in this case. But Mrs. Aubrey was more of an unbiased collector and dispenser of information, with extremely delicate sensors. If anything touched the gossip web, anything at all, no matter how lightly, even the most insignificant crumb or morsel, Mrs. Aubrey rushed to gobble it up. And instantly to re-gurgitate it. To all the right people. To be helpful.

* * *

Tip looked at Mrs. Aubrey across her desk in the church office, plump, well-dressed and well-groomed, and asked the one question he knew would pique her interest.

"Can you keep a secret?"

This touched the right button. She smiled modestly, smoothed her hair, and looked both ways to make sure nobody was listening. Then she leaned across her desk to speak in confidence.

"I'm pleased you came to me for help," she said. "Of course I can keep a secret. What is it?" He could almost hear her salivat-ing.

"Before I tell you, you must agree. Don't tell anybody I was here. Or anything I say. Or anything you tell me."

She actually wriggled in excitement. "Oh, of course, that's easy."

Her expression told Tip it would be a short time before she broadcast all three. Good. Might flush a snake or two out of the grass.

"Who all would know Tom Burton had an appointment at the VA during the playground shooting?"

Her mouth opened and closed. Twice. Good. She also thought it was Tom Burton. For a moment she took on a covert expression and her forehead wrinkled and her eyes shifted sidewise like a guilty person. Then she looked back at Tip.

"Well. Doctor Quick. Melinda McConnell. And Carmen Turner, his paperwork gal. You know. He gripes about paying her to do nothing but government paperwork. Poor woman. But she probably made the appointment. Knows all the government connections. For all the good it did if Tom didn't go." She looked at him expecting a reaction.

He left her dangling. Why didn't he think of Linda McConnell? Doc Quick's nurse. Married to Frank McConnell. Separated. Lived in one of the two trailers. Frank in the other. Wouldn't let him move back in until he quit drinking. She would have heard about the appointment from Carmen. Maybe mentioned it to one of the McConnells. Maybe Frank. Maybe Old Luther. Word was, Luther really liked her and had kicked Frank's ass over the drinking. So she might have an easy relationship with him.

Luther. Could it be him? Revenge would be a dumb motive for an ex-con. Way too obvious. And besides that, revenge for what? On an old farmer and a little girl? Or her parents?

"Thanks, Mrs. Aubrey. Not sure it helps much. But thanks anyway."

\* \* \*

On his way up to Indy, he called the VA and confirmed what he already knew: Tom Burton had indeed been at the VA at the time of Jennifer Clarkson's murder.

# CHAPTER TEN

WSTV from Indy and WMKY from Louisville were parked in front of the jail when he got back from the crime lab, their satellite dishes already trained on the southern sky.

Tip recognized Trudi Wingate who did WSTV's signature ambush interviews. The sports-jacketed guy from Louisville normally reported horse racing from Churchill Downs, so he might not be so bad.

Both wore jeans but were neatly groomed and formally dressed waist up. The make-up on their faces made them look like they were wearing masks.

The instant they saw him coming they moved to block the door, clutching logo-festooned microphones and giving instructions to their cameramen. Tip could imagine their urgency: get a killer sound bite in the next ten minutes for the six o'clock news.

"Sheriff Tungate," shouted Trudi, though there was no need to shout. "Why haven't you arrested Thomas Burton for the murder of little Jennifer Clarkson?"

Tip imagined the adorable picture of Jennifer that would play while this question was being broadcast. Just as viewers reached for the tissues, up would come an old pre-army, trouble-making-days mug shot of Tom Burton.

"Sheriff Tungate," shouted the guy from WMKY. "Are you aware people are calling for you to resign for what appears to be incompetence? Two murders in one week, no suspects, and no announced leads? How do you explain that?"

They blocked his path to the door and stuck their microphones in his face. The cameras and their lights focused in. He summoned his best public-servant expression. While thinking, so much for an easier time from the horse reporter. Plus, it's this guy and his producer who sat in a room alone and called for me to resign so he could say, "people" were calling for his resignation.

"Good evening, and thanks for this opportunity to update concerned Sedalians and Hoosiers on this investigation. To your question, Tom Burton is not a suspect. He was provably elsewhere when the shooting occurred. However, we are making good evidentiary progress and have uncovered key facts we are not at liberty to share at this time. We don't always announce our leads." Then he turned toward the Indy camera. "Suffice it to say, we are closing in on enough evidence to charge the culprit, and that person should be worried. Very worried. Thank you. That will be all."

It was thin, but not falsifiable. And he had used words that made him sound professional. He saved words like "suffice" and "evidentiary" for just such occasions. He just wished he felt as confident as he had sounded. And that he knew who gave them Burton's name. Could have been anybody in town, but he knew. He shrugged between the cameramen and opened the door.

"Sheriff! What about Burton?" insisted Trudi.

"Sheriff! Why aren't you resigning?" demanded WMKY. "I mean, seriously. Two in a week in a town the size of Sedalia?

Something's seriously wrong here. How many more must die before you figure it out?"

Tip asked himself this question about twice an hour, but he did not respond. He nudged a cameraman aside and slipped through the door, hoping their microphones didn't pick up his exasperated sigh.

At least he now had three solid pieces of information. Multiple witnesses plus security-camera footage confirmed Burton's VA alibi. The slug that killed Jennifer Clarkson was fired from Burton's rifle. And it was metallurgically identical to the Remington Super X .22 Long Rifle slug that killed George Sampson: same mix of lead, antimony, tin, copper, and other trace elements. Same box, by FBI rules. At least the same batch.

\* \* \*

Inside, there was no peace and quiet. Luther McConnell glowered up from the chair by Tip's desk.

"Finally," he carped. The hatred Tip remembered from their last encounter was mostly suppressed. McConnell looked determined.

"Evening, Luther," Tip said cheerfully. "What brings you in this evening?" Though he knew.

He sat down heavily in his desk chair and looked at Luther. The elder McConnell wore a beat-up leather jacket with the collar turned up and an oily iron-gray ducktail. He smelled strongly of cigarettes. His thick hair pissed Tip off. In general, most guys with thick hair didn't deserve it and pissed Tip off.

Luther put a big hand on each knee and leaned forward as far as he could to get into Tip's face. His fingernails were dirty with auto grease. "I didn't do it, Tip. Got nothing to do with it. Neither one. The girl or Mr. Sampson. I'm clean, and I been clean. But I didn't get clean for you. I did it for Prechter." His tone was arrogant. Dismissive. Contemptuous.

Tip was familiar with the attitude. Most chronic repeat offenders had it. He looked closely at Luther. He didn't look like he was using, but then he mostly hadn't used when he cooked.

"Linda told you about Burton's VA appointment." Tip stated it as a fact. As planned, Mrs. Aubrey had blabbed and the whole town knew about his visit and his question, and that was why Luther was here. "You're the only ex-con in Sedalia who's done hard time. Your son and his buddy were growing dope on George Sampson's place. Maybe you found out he was going to report them and shot him. I don't know why you would shoot a little girl. Maybe to muddy the waters. Maybe just to make me look bad. Where were you this morning at nine thirty?"

"Jesus, Tip," snapped McConnell. "What kind of asshole are you to even *think* shit like that? I don't give a shit about you or making you look bad. Linda did tell me, but I *told* you. I didn't *do* it. But I know how people like you think." Luther's voice was rising. "I got no alibi for the girl, 'cause I was home helping Toby work on his truck. I don't even know exactly when Mr. Sampson was killed, so I don't know when I need an alibi *for*, for that. You bastard."

"Anybody but Toby to verify you were helping him with his truck?"

"No. Well, maybe. I was on the phone maybe with Hoosier Auto Parts ordering a clutch plate. With my cell phone. You could check the GPS. Toby don't have no credit, so he pays me back."

"Anybody else? Make any other calls?"

Luther looked at Tip with the expression of a mean dog biding its time. Rumor was, his cell mates had fared badly. "Nope. But I

didn't do it. I been clean, just like Prechter made me promise."
Prechter being the judge who had handed down his sentence, then
reduced it after two years to time served. "You ain't my favorite
person, Tip. You know it, and I ain't hiding it. In fact, you're a
son of a bitch. But I wouldn't lie on something like this. Don't
know what kind of man would shoot a little girl. I know what I
would do to him."

"So who'd you tell about Burton's VA appointment?"

"What? Nobody. I don't give a damn about nobody else's
doctor appointments. Linda might have told somebody, she knows
everything that goes on at Doc Quick's office, and I did hear her
say Burton went there, but you'll have to talk to her. But you
better treat her right." His tone was threatening. "She's a good
little gal. Maybe she talks too much, but she don't mean nobody
no harm."

"All right. Go. But don't talk to those reporters outside. And
don't leave town. Tell Linda I'll be right out."

* * *

Tip followed Luther out of town and up his long lane. He could
see him on his cell, for sure warning Linda. Damn it. He should
have made Luther ride with him. Oh well.

Linda was a sweet gal about ten or fifteen years younger than
Tip who nobody could ever figure out why she had married into
the McConnells. Rumor was, to defy her controlling mother.

Short, blond, and trim, still dressed in her nurse's uniform, she
swung open the screen door to her trailer.

"Come in, Tip. Luther said you'd be coming. Pretty quickly,
too, I see." She flashed a smile. "Afraid I'd run?"

"Something like that. More like, I need to find out pretty quick
who's doing these murders and arrest him."

"Or her."

"Or her. So who'd you tell?" Tip was sure Luther would have told her what he wanted.

"Dave Schulz."

Linda wore her hair in a short, no-nonsense page-boy and had Schulz cut it because he was half the price of the beauty parlors in Elmira.

"Anybody else?"

"Mrs. Aubrey."

"Ah, Jeez."

Mrs. Aubrey already knew about Burton's appointment when he visited her. Even when it was. And she knew he was innocent. And that she had maybe helped the murderer by blabbing. That was why she raised the possibility that he skipped it. She felt guilty.

"Yeah. Sorry. She was in his shop selling her cinnamon rolls."

Mrs. Aubrey's cinnamon rolls were good, even memorable. But everybody bought them because they knew she didn't have a lot of income.

"How'd it come up?"

"She was doing an ain't-it-awful about Tom killing himself with alcohol, 'why Jimmy Ray Cheatham refused to sell him any more whiskey,' and so on." Her imitation of Mrs. Aubrey was pretty good. "Dave like he does agreed with her, but I had to open my big mouth and defend Tom by saying he had an appointment at the VA to get help with his drinking."

"Ah. And you just had to mention exactly when it was."

She shook her head in disgust. "Dumb. Unprofessional, I know. But Mrs. Aubrey gives me a pain in the—"

"Yep," said Tip. "You're not alone. Tell anybody else?"

"Nope. Really sorry. Really, really sorry. That little girl and her parents had enough problems."

"Oh? Like what?"

"Lymphoma. Couldn't control it."

A small tingle in the back of Tip's brain stopped him for a moment. A connection tried, then faded, like an elusive word that won't come.

"OK. Well, don't let out any more secrets to Mrs. Aubrey. Might as well call up Bud Tatum and put an ad in the *Democrat*."

"I know, I know," she said ruefully. "You don't think it helped the murderer, do you?" Her anguish told the story. She was pretty sure it did.

"Don't think about it. And don't talk to anybody else about it."

\* \* \*

Tip tried to catch Eileen still open so he could get a hamburger and fries. She was still inside, he could see her in the kitchen, but when he rattled her locked door and knocked on it, she waggled a finger at him.

"You do this at least once a week," she yelled. It was dull through the glass. "The dishes are all clean. I'm closed, damn it! Can't remember when I close, Tip?"

"I got nothing at home," he yelled back. "Can I at least have a ham sandwich? I'll make it myself. And clean up and lock up."

Just as she shook her head in disgust and came to unlock the front door, Tip heard a low voice behind him. He turned and saw two men on the other side of the street carrying weapons in holsters, right in front of the courthouse. The light was dim, but one thing about Marine combat experience and three terms as sheriff, you became very attuned to when people were carrying.

He drew his service weapon, pointed it at the sky, and yelled, "You! With the weapons! In front of the courthouse. Hands up! Now!"

Both men raised their hands.

"It's just us, Tip," called one reasonably. "Don't shoot. We're on your side."

Tip stepped into the street and headed toward them, still holding his weapon at the ready. It was too dusky to see who they were, but he had no trouble seeing their weapons.

"Who's 'us'?" he called out.

He was in the middle of the street now and saw. Orville Freeman and Tim Schneck. Decent enough men. Gun fanciers of a type you usually only saw among non-veterans, but honest folk. Tip had hunted quail with them in years past. He re-holstered his weapon and approached.

"What you boys doing?" He nodded at their weapons. He had to be respectful, because with Indiana's Open Carry law, they had every right to be carrying pistols. Both had concealed-carry permits. He had that list virtually memorized.

"Citizens' Watch," said Tim. "On the look-out for the murderer. We figure the same guy did both, and he's looking for another victim. We know you and Chet and your auxiliaries can't cover the whole county by yourselves, so we're helping."

"Ah," said Tip. Just what he needed.

Just at that moment, Ralph Burke's camo-painted Hummer drove up and three paunchy camo-dressed men in combat boots climbed down clutching AR15's. With thirty-round banana clips. Ralph himself leaned out the driver's window.

"Hey, Tip. Hope you don't mind I organized a citizens' committee to help catch the murderer. Got thirty people posted all over town. Make people feel safer. That son of a bitch won't try nothing now."

Over his shoulder, Tip saw the light go out at Eileen's. Damn it. Great way to end the day: hungry and surrounded by gun-happy minutemen. About whom he couldn't do a damn thing. Well, maybe a couple of things.

"Tell you what, Ralph." Ralph ran Ralph's Sporting and ran as a write-in candidate for President every four years. "Conservative" was a euphemism for his views. "I could use some of your boys out around Ella Sampson's place to protect her. Can't talk about why, but she needs the protection. I'll call her and let her know you're coming. Also, Tom Burton. He won't like having your guys out there, but there's a risk somebody could try something on him. He's not a suspect, but some people want him to be. Also, Luther McConnell's place. Can't talk about that either, but need to keep Linda and Luther safe. S'pose you could help me out on that?"

Ralph looked closely at Tip for a moment. Tip put on his best worried face. It wasn't hard, surrounded by six armed men looking for excitement.

"If you say so, Tip. Won't be able to cover the town nearly as well."

"Can't share everything, Ralph, but trust me, this'll help reduce overall risk, even with fewer of your men in town."

## CHAPTER ELEVEN

Tip woke to bright sunshine, ravenous hunger, and the tantalizing feeling that some revealing dream had just slipped back into darkness.

He lumbered out of bed, cursed his knees, and took a look outside. The daffodils were all hanging over, spring juices spent. The yard around his 3BR 2BA on a slab just west of the tracks was badly clumped up. He hadn't started the mower yet this year, and he suspected that would be a job in itself. But of course, he had no time. He would have to pay the Chambers boy to mow. He was just lucky the damned reporters weren't clamoring in his front yard. They would be in a few days if he didn't move his ass.

He had got a deal on the house a decade ago when Diane left. Next to the tracks and all, and he had to reroof it, but he didn't care. Only two trains a day. She freely admitted cheating with the Indy dentist, but Indiana was a no-fault state, so the settlement required "fair and equitable division of assets." Which left her well off and him nearly broke. He didn't feel like paying her for his share of the old house, so he found a cheap one for the same money. He didn't want to stay in the old place anyway. All its memories seemed false. And since Katy never came to visit, being an important New York news figure and all, and convinced her Mom was the wronged party, there was no nostalgic reason to stay.

But the new place had never been home. More a crash pad, really. He finally took Pastor Frank's advice and employed Lucy Smith to clean once a week, same day she did the parsonage. Which meant he had to be careful what he left lying around. Still, the risk of gossip was better than living in filth.

But he never seemed to get around to buying groceries, and now he was pretty sure all he had in the kitchen was an ancient box of pancake mix. No cereal, no milk, no eggs, no sausage, no bacon, not even any cooking oil.

Ah, well. Pancake-batter dumplings, boiled in water, ended up being better than nothing. He would just never tell anybody. At least he wasn't eating more grease, which Doc Quick had made him promise to lighten up on.

Which got him to thinking about health matters. Which yanked up the lost thought like a bluegill out of deep water. George Sampson. The rumor had been that he had some kind of health condition. Men of his kind didn't talk about that stuff. They just soldiered on until they dropped. Just the way life was. So nobody knew for sure. Maybe Doc Quick.

But if he did have a health condition, maybe even a fatal one— like Jennifer Clarkson's lymphoma—then that would be a huge flashing light.

He looked at the last three off-white balls of boiled dough on his plate. He pooched out his cheeks in disgust, and said, "Jesus."

He dropped them in the trash, showered, dressed, and went to work. Meaning in this case, Doc Quick's office.

Doc wouldn't tell, told Tip he ought to be ashamed of himself, but Carmen gave him Linda's cell number. She was busy in the back, so he went back outside Doc's office and called her from the department SUV.

"Why didn't you just come and talk to me?" she said. "I saw you in here talking to Doc."

"Didn't want him to hear what I asked you."

"Asked me what?"

"Did George Sampson have some kind of fatal condition?"

There was a long quiet moment.

"You asked Doc and he wouldn't tell you."

"Right."

"So why do you think I'll tell you?"

"Because you feel guilty about blabbing about Tom Burton's VA appointment. And because you know it's the right thing to do. George is dead. And the answer might help me find out who killed him."

"Colon cancer," she whispered.

"Colon cancer?"

"Yes." Then her voice dropped to a whisper again. "Metastasized. He didn't have more than six to nine months."

And there it was. Mercy killing. Maybe. Just like Jo Ann Meyers from back in Ed Spurling's sheriff days. Jo Ann was dead and gone, so it couldn't be her. But it put a whole new light on things. Particularly on who might have that motive. Up until now he had been thinking evil, evil, bad, bad people. Now all sorts of people came into the picture.

"Thanks, Linda. You just racked up some karma points."

"You know about karma?"

"I'm not as dumb as people think."

* * *

Chet quickly X'd out of whatever screen he was on when Tip came in and sat down at his desk in the jail office.

"You got a list of calls to return, Tip. There by your phone."

"You'll grow hair on the palm of your right hand, Chet. Plus make it look bad for the office if anybody ever checks your browsing history."

"Got it set up to automatically delete. Keeps the matrons from seeing what I've been investigating, then blabbing it all over town."

"What *are* you investigating?"

Tip knew better than to ask Chet for help on the murders. He spent his time gossiping, undercutting, and facilitating any scandal that might force Tip to resign. Work and initiative were out of the question as long as Spences and Biggles were in county politics. He could only be expected to follow direct, tightly defined orders—and to work behind the scenes to tarnish Tip's image and burnish his own.

"You probably ought to look at that list of calls," persisted Chet.

"Did you call the Indy and Louisville news people?"

"They're always interested in local murders, Tip. You know that."

"So it was you that called them."

"Didn't say that."

"And gave them Tom Burton's name?"

"Didn't say that either. But I hear you been busy. Been out to Luther McConnell's. Found out it was Burton's gun. And the same box of bullets that killed the Clarkson girl and George Sampson. So what now, Tip?" Chet grinned. "Looks to me like you got squat. Still no suspect, unless Burton wasn't really at the VA."

So Temple was feeding information to Samantha, and she was feeding it to Chet. But Chet would not know of his nugget from this morning: they could be mercy killings.

"Working on it, Chet. What's your angle?" Meaning, what could he possibly be investigating besides some internet gal's physiology.

"Better look at that list of calls, Tip."

Tip sighed and looked at Chet's obsessively neat handwriting. Samantha, Samantha, Mrs. Aubrey, Samantha, Governor Brandt, Doc Quick, Linda McConnell, and Godiva Randall. Big Iva. Hmm. Governor Brandt was underlined. In his peripheral vision, he could see Chet leering, waiting for his response.

He suppressed all reaction and punched in Brandt's number.

An officious female voice answered on the first ring. "Governor Brandt's office."

"Sheriff Tungate, Howarth County. Returning the governor's call."

"Please hold. It could be several minutes. The governor is quite busy."

"He called me. I'm not holding. You have my cell number on your screen. When he's ready to talk to me, he can call me back."

"Well!" sniffed the voice. "In fact, I see through the door that he's just finished what he was doing. I'll put him on."

There was a click, followed by rustling paper sounds.

"Hey, Tip. Thanks for calling back."

"You're the governor, Jim. I do have some class."

"But not much luck finding murderers, it appears."

"I'm looking."

"This is looking bad for Indiana, Tip. There's actually a national news story coming this evening. You need help."

"What kind?"

"A prosecutor's special investigator."

"Nope. Not participating in your protégé's elevation."

"You won't have a choice if I appoint one."

"Sure I will. I have many skills. Law enforcement is only one."

"You'd quit?"

"In a heartbeat. And your investigator wouldn't stand a chance. Wouldn't know a soul."

"Your deputy would."

"Wrong party."

"Turns out he's willing to ignore that. Ambition is a funny thing."

"Problem for you is, it's not always paired with competence. The other problem for you is, I'd let everybody here in Sedalia know what you'd done. And the news people from Indy and Louisville. You would own the whole thing. Just like I told your fair-haired girl."

"Her hair is black."

"Yeah. She's into that color. Look, Jim. May I call you Jim instead of Governor? You got five seconds to decide. Then I either go back to work or make good on my threats."

Four seconds passed.

"All right, Tip. But you'll pay for this."

"You been trying for forty years to make me pay for saving your ass at Boy Scout camp. You could just say, 'Thank you.'"

Tip punched the "end" button without looking directly at Chet. But he sensed him swelling behind his desk, like an overinflated balloon. The conversation had obviously not gone as he had hoped. And just at that moment, it occurred to Tip, like another tickle at the back of his brain, that Chet had motive. Strong motive. And he might in fact have known about the fatal health conditions both victims had had. If there was something to know in Sedalia, Chet generally knew it. And used it. And he of course knew about the Jo Ann Meyers story from many years ago. And he would possibly feel OK about killing people who were going to die anyway in order to satisfy his ambition: become sheriff.

Could it be?

Surely not. The man was a career law enforcement officer, and a Sedalia boy born and bred. He wouldn't do something like that.

Would he?

Tip quietly resolved to find out where Chet was at the time of both shootings. Just to rule him out.

He punched up Big Iva on his cell phone. She actually answered herself instead of letting it go to the truck stop phone and Missy answering.

"Come see me, Tip. Pronto. Stuff you need to know."

When Big Iva said come see her, you went to see her. And when she said pronto, it had to be serious.

"Be right there."

# CHAPTER TWELVE

Two miles out Road 50 South, Big Iva's I-65 Truck Stop had been a favorite for forty years with independent truckers. It offered cheap fuel, good food, clean showers, and the cleanest girls between Chicago and Mobile.

And all was good as long as the men—and occasional women—paid cash and treated Iva's people with respect. Such men ran their own businesses, so they mostly respected Iva's rules. Not tipping a waitress would get you a comment. Fouling showers or restrooms would get you a warning. And abusing a parking-lot girl—Big Iva called them "cleaning ladies"—would get you a beating. Often from Big Iva herself. Or a close look at the muzzle of her Beretta Pico, and a warning never to come back.

Everyone in Sedalia knew what went on at Big Iva's. Young men claimed adventures there; older ones denied it. But the respectable stayed away and the powerful left her alone because she had something on nearly everybody. She played a hard game. But she had her own code, and as long as she kept things under control and stayed out of the drug trade, Tip left her alone. It was a mean, nasty world out there along I-65, she had told him once, and he and the mild folk in Sedalia weren't equipped to deal with it. Maybe so, he had thought at the time, but the main reason Sedalia's leading lights didn't mess with her was her Album full of candid photos, and her memory full of inconvenient history. Only Samantha Parr was immune. Which would turn into a problem at some point.

The last time a call came in from Big Iva's, last year, there had been a gunfight. Two stolen Escalades from Chicago were destroyed in a hail of gunfire, and the men who drove them disappeared without a trace. Except for a wound in Big Iva's side, and a mob corpse that floated up in the Cumberland River near Corbin, Kentucky, weeks later, there was no connection. Nothing provable. Tip's take at the time was, it served them right. They were probably trying to shake her down. But he feared another shoe would eventually drop. He was guessing this call was about that other shoe.

Big Iva greeted him as soon as he walked in the front door of the shabby main building, which housed the dining room, kitchen, and upstairs in the back, Big Iva's apartment.

"Hey, Tip. Come in. Sit down. Take a load off. Have some breakfast. I happen to know you didn't get any supper last night unless you fixed it yourself or went to Elmira." She called toward the kitchen. "Cindy! Full breakfast!"

Tip was immediately suspicious. She was way too friendly. Usually she just stared at him and waited for him to state his business, which always gave him the uncomfortable feeling she was thinking sexual thoughts about him.

She sat in her usual place at the left end of the dining room, on her custom-made oak love seat, twice as thick in the bottom, with her back to the knotty-pine paneling. Light-colored plastic wood filled several holes in the wood, almost certainly bullet holes, to her upper left. Well over four hundred pounds, her bulk filled her denim pants and Prince T-shirt like a half-barrel of yoghurt in a garbage bag, pooched out at the bottom and thinner at the top. Wisps of brassy hair hung in their usual forlorn ringlets. She smiled a gat-toothed smile, and he marveled again at how close together her eyes were in that massive moon face.

But he was not fooled by the smile. The pig eyes—intelligent eyes—never left his face. And they did not smile.

"You're being way too nice, Iva. What's wrong? Can I have some coffee, too?"

"Cindy! Coffee too!"

"I don't know how you know, but you're right. No supper last night, and damned little breakfast this morning. But I'm paying for the breakfast. You've already got the album. I'm not being more beholden."

She waved away the comment about the album. "Ralph's vigilantes told me. Wanted to post a guard here last night. I ran them off. Bunch of nimrods. But your money's no good this morning, Tip. 'Cause you're right. Something nasty may be coming down the pike. And it may be because of me. Sort of. Kind of. Maybe a little bit."

She fidgeted with her hands. OK. Must be something serious. She never showed weakness.

"The Chicago boys," Tip said, watching her eyes. "Armando Dalek's colleagues. The ones who didn't get killed in that shootout here last year."

Her eyes took on a hard look. "Don't be insinuating things you can't prove, Tip. I don't know any Armando Dalek. And I don't know where those Escalade drivers went. I'm just saying the Russian mob might show up and do something because I won't pay protection. I'm getting scuttlebutt."

So there it was. The corpse in the river down in Kentucky. Dalek was a Polish name. Tip had looked it up. Family might have been from Polish Russia. Or the guy just learned Russian growing up. So Dalek had almost certainly been one of the Escalade drivers. But Tip didn't get it. She feared reprisal? A year later? What was she afraid of now?

"You expecting a full scale attack, or just a repeat? You're well armed. Everybody here has a carry permit. And I'm guessing you got heavier stuff, you need it. You got rid of them before. And the evidence. What are you saying?" It still pissed Tip off that she had probably had their bodies in the kitchen when he answered Missy's call, and he had been too stupid to check.

"You have a fine imagination, Tip. All that stuff. But nobody wants a war. Or something worse. That's what I'm saying." Her eyes bored into his.

A chill went down Tip's back. She looked worried. He had never seen her worried. Then a thought flashed. Could the Sedalia murders have something to do with the Russian mob? Surely not. What would be the motive? Test Big Iva's love for her neighbors?

Nah. Especially not with the new connection he had ferreted out: the fact that both victims had had fatal illnesses. It suggested mercy killing, and implicated people who knew about both illnesses: Linda McConnell, Doc Quick, probably Chet and Mrs. Aubrey, and maybe Luther McConnell. Cross-reference those with good shots and you came up with Chet and Luther. Cross-reference those with people who he didn't know where they were when the murders occurred—somebody who would climb up in a deer stand and knew how to make a silencer—and you came up with Chet. Not a Russian mobster.

But still, there were those Michelin off-road tire tracks. Which were maybe connected to the murderer. An out-of-town murderer. Nobody in Sedalia bought tires that expensive. Certainly not Chet.

"Look, I appreciate the heads-up, Big Iva. But what do you want me to do about it? All I got's Chet and a couple part-time deputies. And my hands are full. Not sure how much I can protect you."

Cindy approached his table and slid a gigantic platter of scrambled eggs, bacon, hash browns and toast in front of him. Damn it, Big Iva really had it down—how to get to a man. He immediately dug in with a will. The food was glorious. He nevertheless shook his head in self-disgust while he chewed. He was weak, weak, weak.

She watched in quiet approval for a minute while he shoveled in food. No one ever saw her eat, but she obviously enjoyed her food, and she famously liked to watch her customers eat. She made sure her food and cooks were first rate. Finally, when he was hogging down his seventh bacon strip and third slice of honey toast, she spoke.

"You're not the brightest bulb in the pack, Tip, but you're not as dumb as you like to act. You like people to underestimate you. I know you instantly had an idea when I mentioned the Chicago Russian mob. That's where you should start."

"I did have an idea, but I don't want to do it. If I call the FBI and ask what their mob intelligence unit has picked up about this, it could raise questions you don't want to answer about the shootout last year. Questions I don't want to answer, either. About why I was never able to find the drivers of those cars. Makes me look pretty bad."

"It's a mystery, Tip. Was then, and is now. But both those Escalades are pig iron by now. Legally. And there's just no evidence for the FBI to dig up. I wish I could figure out what happened, too."

Tip snorted. "The slugs in those patched holes in the wall behind you might just match slugs from crimes in Chicago. Why don't I just dig them out and find out?"

"No slugs there, Tip. Those are woodpecker holes. Big pileated woodpecker got in here and caused a lot of damage. Besides which, if anybody fired a weapon in the commission of what later might be maliciously interpreted as a crime, that person would be a fool not to melt that weapon down. The FBI's got nothing. They can't figure out what you and I haven't been able to figure out. But they might have info on the Russian mob. What it's planning. If they have somebody inside. Least that way, you might get tipped off who to watch for. Probably show up in Elmira, though. No outsider would be fool enough to try to snoop around Sedalia without getting noticed."

Damn it. He had not got around to checking *Elmira* for those tires. Maybe he *was* the dimmest bulb in the pack. Trouble was, with the money there was in Elmira, with all those studs working at Global Corp, dozens of people could have those tires. Still, he understood she wanted him to fish for information to protect her ass, even if they both caught heat. So she was worried. And he needed to keep her sweet, even if it distracted from solving the murders.

"All right. I'll check it out. How's Missy doing? Still your legal intern?"

It always pleased Big Iva if you asked about Missy. She smiled.

"Starts law school this fall. Thanks for asking."

Missy was Big Iva's knock-out right-hand gal, twenty-eight or so, graduated from service in the furnished shipping containers out back to helping run the business. She was Iva's favorite among the runaway girls she had taken off the rest-stop circuit, de-toxed, given a place to sleep and work, and educated. Sedalia's young men bought gas there just to get a look at her, but the buzz was, she preferred girls. Iva also had an accounting intern she had sent to Ivy Tech. The poor gal had to get a hell of a workout doing books for a business rumored to have millions in cash in hidden safes.

Tip polished off the rest of the food and laid a twenty on the table.

"Thanks for the food and advice, Iva. This here's a tip for Cindy, if you won't take money for the food."

Big Iva's face crinkled into a smile.

"Thanks, Tip. You're a gentleman."

\* \* \*

Agent Rudolpho Sanchez at the FBI Eurasian Organized Crime Unit said they had heard nothing. A little too fast, Tip thought. But of course he wanted to know why Tip was asking.

"Just a tip." Tip savored the pun. He assumed Sanchez was recording the conversation.

"Have anything to do with Armando Dalek?"

Tip's neck hairs prickled. "Don't know. Who's he?"

There was a five-second silence pregnant with suspicion.

"He was suspected of stealing a Cadillac Escalade whose VIN number we found on a report from US Recycling in Indianapolis. Sent there by McCall Salvaging in your town. Signed over to McCall Salvaging by Chester Biggle, your deputy. Picked up at a truck stop owned by one Godiva Randall, all shot up. Then Dalek turns up rolled up in plastic in the Cumberland River in Kentucky, with several 9 millimeter slugs in him. On which we have ballistics. All very mysterious. You know anything about that? Any reason we shouldn't test all the weapons at Godiva Randall's

Truck Stop? Based on their carry permits, looks like everybody there packs heat all the time."

"No reason at all. Test them out if you want. But on my end, being an elected official and all, I gotta have probable cause to do stuff like that. Motive. All that fourth amendment stuff. You got any? Other than location? And suspicion of stealing that Cadillac?"

Another silence. Finally, "No. Just looks suspicious. What do you know about that incident?"

Sweating, Tip relayed the facts of the case: got called out to Big Iva's, truckers playing target practice with two Escalades, later found to be stolen, no drivers or passengers to be found, and no one knew anything. It was all in his report. State Police had been present. He left out the apparent bullet wound in Big Iva's side, which she claimed was a dog bite, and the puddle of blood on the floor she claimed was dog's blood, but which the counter gal accidentally spilled bleach on before Tip could get a sample.

Sanchez was unimpressed.

"Look, Sheriff, how can you not see this Godiva Randall's dirty? The IRS says her books are squeaky clean, but they're suspicious as hell. She handles a lot of cash. Prefers being paid in cash, even pays her vendors in cash. Sends bags of cash to her fuel supplier. Something going on there. And you just about have to know what it is."

"Cash illegal?"

"No. Just suspicious."

"Look, she's never given me reason to look into her affairs. Couple complaints about drivers being roughed up, but that's it. And I called you for help, not an interrogation. She thinks the Russian mob may be after her because she won't pay protection. And now I'm wondering if they might be behind two murders we've had here in the last week." Tip didn't really think this, but it was a good lever. "In our little town where nothing ever happens. And for the life of me, I can't figure out who from Sedalia would have motive. Which means somebody from out of town. And the only thing unusual going on is Iva's concern the Russians might do something violent. Now, do you have anything for me about the Russian mob or not?"

Another silence, this one full of exasperation.

"All right. We did hear something. They're really pissed at her. They're sure she killed four of their guys. Including Dalek. *And* she won't pay protection. But they're afraid of attacking directly for fear she'll shoot *their* ass, so they may try something different. Can't see them murdering small-town strangers though. More their style to park a trailer full of explosives at her place and leave."

"Any names? Descriptions?"

"If I get any, I'll let you know."

"Thanks a million. You been a big help. Any time you need anything, let me know. I'll respond in kind."

"One last thing, Sheriff. Probably has no impact on what you're looking into. And it's confidential. No repeating."

"Got it. What's that?"

"Why I'm involved at all with the Chicago mob and the Armando Dalek death. We're picking up that the Russian mob is laundering money for an Iraqi terror group. Possible Chechen connection."

"Can't see how that plays in."

"Neither can I."

* * *

Big Iva was grateful for the warning, but shocked.

"Damn, Tip, a bomb? Never thought of that. But thanks for the warning. We'll be on the look-out. Guess we'll start checking trailers with no seals, and make sure no drivers just walk away."

# CHAPTER THIRTEEN

Samantha rested a hip on Tip's desk and leaned across into his face. It was very distracting. Not the leaning across. The hip. A well-shaped hip expensively clad in slightly snug black slacks. He was used to her space-invader tactics. What he wasn't used to was the unbidden thoughts he was suddenly having in her presence. Damn.

"Ask for some help, Tip! You're out of your depth."

"Been saying that for a long time," added Chet from across the office. He appeared also to be appreciating Samantha's posture.

Tip leaned back in his chair and did his best to look relaxed. He knew laid-back people pissed her off. "It's unusual for you to come onto my turf, Samantha. What prompts this visit?"

"You have to be kidding! There you sit, leaning back, doing nothing while we have a crisis on our hands! I can't do anything about your indifference and incompetence, but it's making me look bad. The governor!" She flipped a hand in the air. "News people!" Another hand flip. "Citizens!" Another hand flip. "They're all calling me to complain that you haven't arrested anybody. I'm here to offer you some help."

Her breath smelled like chocolate. Aha.

"Your special Prosecutor's investigator."

"No. You made clear to the governor where you stand on that. It's political. I can understand that. No. Somebody different. Effective. No politics involved. She's top-rate. You know her. I'll get her on TDY from the State Police."

He suppressed a groan. "Temple." The one person he least wanted to see walk into his office and offer help. She would be like a bad rash.

"Exactly."

He forced himself to think constructively. It would in fact reduce the heat on him. And he saw an opportunity. And no real way out. "Fine. One condition."

"Which is?"

"She reports to Chet."

"Why? She won't like that, and I don't either."

Chet looked pained.

"Because Chet's familiar with the community, he's a seasoned deputy, and the two of them will work well together. Temple thinks I'm some kind of chauvinist pig, and she and I would clash."

Plus of course, Chet was already the info conduit to Samantha. And Chet and Temple wouldn't find out anything he didn't want them to find out. And the kicker: Chet would piss her off even more than he himself would. She would leave within a week.

"Ah. Well, you do radiate a lot of unrepentant maleness, but it's big of you to admit it. Fine. I'll arrange it. You want to tell the news people, or shall I?"

"I'll leave that to Chet. He's being doing a good job so far of passing along information."

* * *

There was one last task to perform at the VA, which he couldn't really do over the phone: interview everybody there who had contact with Tom Burton. The scheduling people there had confirmed he had been there for his appointment, even that he had sat for an hour in the waiting room. But there were other patients who sat beside him, the doctor who saw him, the pharmacist who dispensed his pills, the counseling psychiatrist who was helping him deal with his PTSD, even a couple of buddies from his unit who worked there as orderlies.

Nothing came of it. The VA cooperated and made people available. But no one had any connection to Sedalia. And Burton's shrink, Dr. Hammadi, was shocked that anybody could think it of the troubled veteran.

"He is gentle soul," said Hammadi. "A man of low station who joined service to escape situation and, how you say, straighten himself. We know, he made much trouble as young man. Hooligan. But I am sure, it was anger. He was poor and not respected. Abusive and absent father. Now he wants only be peaceful. Irony is, he was good shot as boy, so army made him sniper. He killed many, many people. He suffers guilt. Maybe not enough, but he suffers."

Tip thought this last comment odd, but said nothing. It was probably just some shrink thing where if only Burton suffered more he would get it all out of his system. Or maybe it was just Hammadi's unfamiliarity with the language. Or he thought sniping was not honorable. Certainly, soldiers felt that way about the other side's snipers.

Anyway, it was a wasted trip. No Sedalia connections popped up. Nobody at the VA knew anybody in Sedalia except Burton. And they were all horrified that anyone might think Burton had shot a little girl.

* * *

Back at the office, Temple was already there. She and Tip exchanged a long look of mutual wariness. Tip was careful to keep his eyes above her collar.

Chet broke into this with news that he and she had unearthed something odd. "Probably just weird and unconnected," said Chet, but Tip immediately made a connection. Though he didn't let on.

Evelyn Spence, Chet's aunt and County Clerk had called him a couple of weeks prior and complained that somebody had been messing with the Clerk's Office computers. How did she know, he had asked, and she had explained that for a couple hours one day, one computer went off on its own. Wasn't usable by anybody else. Acted like somebody was using it, but nobody was sitting there.

Chet did nothing about this at the time, for the very good reason that he had no idea how to do anything about it. But with Temple in the office, he had this race-car-engine of a brain at his disposal, an engine housed in a sleek race-car body. Being unaccustomed to supervising people, as Tip surmised, and clearly liking to work closely with her, he put her on it because he had no idea what else to have her do. In half an hour, with help from the forensic IT staff in Indy, she determined that somebody with a Chicago IP address had routed a hack through Amsterdam, Hong Kong, and Dubai to try to cover their tracks. Whoever it was had looked at local records in some detail.

"What records?" Tip asked.

"Plat records. GIS. Land ownership," she said.

"Any specific area?"

"Sedalia Township."

That left out Elmira, but still covered a lot of ground, including Sedalia itself. Hmm. Chicago. Russian Mob. Murder. Property records. Tom Burton's grandma's house. Burton's trailer. George Sampson's farm.

Nah. Surely not. What could the connection be? The motive? Surely the Russians would blow something up at Big Iva's, like Sanchez said. And what did they care about an old farmer or a little girl?

"Tell you what, Sergeant. And Chet. That's good work. Really good work. How about asking Doc Quick if he minds if you look to see if *he's* been hacked."

"Why?" demanded Temple.

"A hunch."

"If we're going to work together, we have to trust each other," challenged Temple. "What do you know you're not telling us? Based on your skimpy case notes, you don't know anything."

Chet nodded for emphasis. She had him twisted around her little finger already.

Tip looked at Chet, the odious worm, with his falsely cheerful, postal-clerk face, round glasses, and phony buzz cut. He looked back at Tip in a calculating way, clearly scheming as always how he could make this all work for him personally. But he was also smart, and with Temple on board for him to perform for, maybe he would help.

"George Sampson had inoperable colon cancer. Jennifer Clarkson had incurable lymphoma. Neither had long. Probably only Doc Quick and Linda McConnell, his nurse, knew both things. You already know the slugs came from the same box."

Temple looked at Tip in a whole new way. The disdain was dialed way back. For once, she looked uncertain. "Oh," she said quietly. "A mercy killer?" She semi-frowned at Chet. "Why didn't you know about the health angle?" Chet looked embarrassed. She turned back to Tip. "How does Chicago fit in?"

"Good question. But first, we'd have to connect the hacker to both. If Doc even has his records computerized."

"Got it." She looked at Tip in an evaluating way. "Don't shut me out, Sheriff. I can help here."

"I can see that. Just don't talk to the TV people. We don't want the killer or killers to know anything we know."

\* \* \*

The answer was not long in coming. Doc Quick's office systems, such as they were—a server and three laptops—had indeed been hacked. All patient records had been downloaded by another Chicago IP address, this hack routed through Chechnya. Doc was furious.

"By God, this is the Federal Government's fault!" he shouted over the phone to Tip. "I wouldn't even have the damned computers if it wasn't for the feds' damned record-keeping requirements! Now some asshole somewhere knows everything about all of my patients, back to five years ago when we started that crap! Including your hemorrhoids, by God! It's outrageous! Do you know, bless her heart, nothing against her, I employ Carmen *full time* to do *nothing but* that crap? I'm telling you, Tip, the day is coming—"

"—Seems like you may have mentioned that before, Doc. And I'm with you on Big Brother. But I'd say in this case, best thing to do would be follow Temple's advice and get some security support from that Indy outfit she told you about. She said you don't even have anti-virus software."

"I help people get rid of REAL viruses, by God! And the federal government is the only reason I have to spend MORE MONEY to deal with these damn ELECTRONIC viruses. At least you sent a good-looking young gal over to deliver this bad news, and I will follow her advice. But I'm TELLING you Tip—"

"Scuse me, Doc. Gotta go. Other phone's ringing off the hook."

Which in fact, it was. Tip picked up. "Sheriff Tungate."

There was only the sound of breathing, then a click.

"Hmm."

When he got home for the evening, there were the usual bills, flyers, etc., in his mailbox. All of which normally came at ten in the morning. On top of the mail was a computer-printed note, in bolded font:

> **Now I have your attention. The first two were merciful. Arrest Tom Burton and get him convicted. Then resign your office and confess all your crimes. If you do not, you will lose everything. And everyone. You will be powerless to stop me.**

He immediately called Sandy Hoechst, the postmistress, on her cell. He had virtually the entire community on his cell-phone directory.

"Who delivered my mail this morning?" he demanded.

"Why are you yelling at me, Tip? I didn't do anything."

"Who?"

"Well, Willy, like always. There's nobody else. You know that."

"Thanks."

He called Willy Carson.

"What did you put in my mailbox this morning?"

"Well howdy to you, too, Tip. At the jail or your house?"

"The house."

"Well, the usual. Your credit-card bill, your electric bill, couple of collection-agency letters. Bunch of advertising crap. Your copy of Field and Stream. You really ought to get help paying your bills on time, Tip. I know you make enough money. My sister's an accountant, and she—"

"Thanks for the advice, Willy. Anything else? No typed note?"

"No. That would be illegal, Tip. You know that. Everything that goes into a post box has to be postage-paid. What's this about?"

"Never mind. Thanks."

Damn. Who had done what to this guy? He was sure it was a guy.

And of course, none of his neighbors had seen a thing, with his house backed up to the railroad tracks, and screened on both sides by overgrown lilac and forsythia bushes. The purple lilac blooms were turning brown, and the forsythia had long since shed its glorious yellow blooms and gone to full leaf.

The bloom was coming off of spring.

# CHAPTER FOURTEEN

**I**t was afternoon in Jimmy Ray Cheatham's drinking establishment, the only one in town, and the lunch crowd, such as it was, had left. Bud Tatum was always in as soon as he put the *Democrat* to bed, but today he was late.

"Probably trying to come up with an angle on the killings," Jimmy Ray smiled when asked. "Always trying to make his advertiser into the *New York Times*." Then he wiped the walnut bar and looked at Tip with an evaluating expression. "What'll you have? Not like you to come in during the work day."

"Sasparilla with a dash of cherry."

Jimmy Ray smiled. "Still watching those old western reruns, huh?"

"Best thing about that satellite TV. Can't sleep, sit there on the couch at three in the morning and watch *Sugarfoot*."

Jimmy Ray dug deep in one of the coolers behind the bar and came up with a root beer. He popped the top and set it in front of Tip. "You're going to have to do without the cherry."

Tip gratefully took a long pull. "That's all right. I've just always wanted to walk into a bar and say that." He leaned an elbow heavily onto the bar and took a swig with the other hand.

"You look like shit, Tip, like you *have* been watching TV all night."

"*Osculare meum tergum*, Jimmy Ray." A relic from their days in Latin class decades ago: 'Kiss my rear.'

"Well, in your situation I'd probably lose sleep too. And thanks for getting the deponent verb right." Jimmy Ray liked to show off his memory.

"You're welcome. And thanks for holding back on the advice. I'm full up."

"Bet you are. But I'm in the bar business. I listen."

Tip shook his head. "It's bad, Jimmy Ray. I think we might have something like a terrorist on our hands." He told him about the note and the mercy angle and swore him to secrecy.

"Damn. What's the motive?"

"Trying to figure that out. Revenge on Big Iva I can understand. Her enemies list would stretch to Louisville. But I don't see any connection to her yet. Looks like they'd go after her directly. Personally. No. There's something else."

"Maybe something Tom Burton did."

"Well, yeah, he shot a lot of Iraqis, but that was war. And they're over there, and we're here."

"Maybe it's something you did."

Well, there it was. The abyss that drew Tip toward it in his darkest hours. The source of his recurrent dreams since Gulf One. The young Iraqi soldier hiding in a house with his rifle. He could still see his scared face. Still see him starting to raise the AK. Still see him stuttering backward as his own M16 rounds tore into him. Still see the empty chamber in the AK47, and its empty banana clip when he checked. Still hear the screaming Iraqi woman shouting in Arabic, translated for him later: "You murdered him! He was giving up!" Still see the accusing look on the face of the small boy cowering on the couch. A close relative to the soldier, by the look of him. He saw it over and over and over. It always ended the same way. It had tapered off in the last few years to once every couple of weeks. But since the murders had started, it was pretty much every night. Only Jimmy Ray and Butch Bauer, friends from boyhood, knew about these dreams, and neither would ever talk. Principal of the high school now, Butch had his own Gulf One memories to deal with. And Jimmy Ray absorbed information; he didn't dispense it.

Tip took a long pull on his root beer. "Hate to think that, Jimmy Ray. Hate to think that. But I know it's somebody who is really smart, with a lot of resources at his disposal."

"Well, right there you go," said Jimmy Ray. "Smart and rich? Lets out everybody from Sedalia. Question is, who's next? And why? And who in Sedalia might be giving the bad guy infor- mation?"

Tip confirmed this thinking with a slow nod, then shook his head in despair.

"Damn, Jimmy Ray. Come in to get cheered up and you make me feel worse. Thanks a lot." He put his hat on and made to go.

"Any time, Tip. What friends are for."

* * *

Tip had thought about the Sedalia angle. A lot. Was there any- thing the murderer needed to know that he or she could only find out from a local? Chronically ill? Doc's records. Addresses? Courthouse records. Burton's grandmother's house? A stretch, since it was his maternal grandmother, with a different surname, but still, maybe courthouse records. His own address for what his ex-wife had sneeringly called the railroad house? The phone book. When Burton was going to be gone? Doc's records. Maybe. Elementary school recess time? The school website. What seemed clear, though, was that a stranger would have to stay out of sight while either reconnoitering or on his way to doing the murders. And that it would be a hell of a lot easier for the murderer if somebody was feeding him information.

Or the murderer was somebody from Sedalia.

# CHAPTER FIFTEEN

Morning came with a break and more sunshine: a tip from Elmira police in response to his Be-On-the-Look-Out. A rental jeep with Michelin off-roads was parked outside a motel on the I-65 motel-and-fast-food strip. Rented to an Andrei Dalek. Sure as hell had to be the brother of Armando Dalek, the Chicago-based corpse who floated up in the Cumberland River. Tip didn't want Dalek to know he'd been spotted, so he put on civilian clothes, drove his F-150, and watched the guy's room until he went next door to IHOP for breakfast. A casual check of the tires showed a missing chunk that matched the casts.

Revenge. But still. George Sampson? Jennifer Clarkson?

The hotel clerk confirmed the man had been there for two weeks. Tip showed his badge and warned the clerk of legal problems if he told Dalek he had been inquired about. The clerk gulped and said he would say nothing.

Tip would have liked to put an RF tracker on the Jeep, but that only happened in TV shows and big-city or federal outfits with money. Howarth County had little money, and Elmira sucked up most of that. But he had Dalek's phone number from the hotel clerk. He drove back to Sedalia a modestly happy man. Or as happy as he let himself be these days.

But of course, he had nothing except the tires, and a loose conception of opportunity. And motive. Which didn't fit with Dalek.

Casual questions to the jail matrons and people in Sedalia confirmed that Chet was nowhere near either murder. So there was that. There was still the possibility he was somehow feeding information to the killer, but Tip didn't believe it. He hadn't known about the chronic illnesses. So it seemed safe to ask him and Temple to run a geographical track on Dalek's phone.

Within half an hour of putting the two on getting phone company records, he got a call from Samantha. "Why didn't you ask permission to search phone records? You're going to poison any case you're building. And why haven't you updated me on latest developments? Clearly you know something you haven't told me or Temple."

Tip didn't react to this blatant concession that Temple was a spy. He had decided on a different tack.

"Why don't I come over and update you?" he asked reasonably.

There was a surprised silence on the phone.

"Of course."

He walked the three blocks to the courthouse listening to the mockingbirds on the maple branches. Under his arm was the box of expensive milk chocolate slabs he had bought in Elmira's Chocolateria for this purpose. It was a good day.

In her office, he slid an upholstered chair over to face her desk, made himself welcome and comfortable and set the chocolate in front of her. She looked down at it, at the spare, elegant logo on the cream-colored box, then up at him, unsure how to react.

"Bribery, Tip? Is nothing beneath you?" She leaned involuntarily over the box, from which he had removed the cellophane wrapper, and sniffed ever so slightly. Her nostrils flared. She could smell the chocolate.

"Just had them around. Don't eat much sweet stuff. More into salty crunch stuff. Thought you might appreciate them more than me," he said easily.

Her cheeks flushed, and she brusquely pushed the box to one side of her desk, handy, Tip noticed, for a snack after he left. She made no move to return the box.

"Why I didn't ask you for a warrant," he continued. "According to a recent 4$^{th}$ US Circuit Court of Appeals ruling, I don't need a warrant to look into cell phone records. As long as I'm just asking the phone company for them. The agreement users sign says the company owns the data, not the users. So technically I'm not violating the fourth amendment."

Her eyebrows rose. He smiled inwardly. He loved surprising her with the fact that he wasn't an idiot.

"You're right, but that's never been tested in the Supreme Court. You always need to ask me. We don't want to prejudice any case with civil rights violations. Why do you want to look? Who is this guy?"

This was delicate. He did not, repeat, not want under any circumstances to tell her about his suppositions about the connection between the deceased Armando Dalek and Big Iva. Or that Andrei was his brother. Way too much explaining to do.

"He has a Jeep with the right type of tires. The right front tire even has a chunk out that matches the casts we made. Which proves his Jeep was there in the pull-off around the corner from George Sampson's place. I want to see where else he's been. In fact, I want to see where he is all the time going forward."

"So you have opportunity. Maybe. Method, you can assume. Could be anybody broke in, took George's gun, and shot him with it. But what have you got for motive?"

This was where it got tricky.

"Rather not talk about that yet. Just working a hunch. Don't have enough to arrest him, but I'm going to watch him. The tire's enough for me to do that. That plus the phone records, if they show the Jeep was there. And they will."

"All right. I'll get you the warrant."

* * *

A check of the National Criminal Information Center database produced the skinny on Andrei Dalek: failed car thief, two-time loser as a second-story man, reputed bag man for the Russian mob, and implicated in extortion schemes run by his now deceased brother, Armando Dalek, though never charged.

So. Second-story man. Sneak thief. Experienced at sneaking into people's houses. That fit with accessing the murder weapon in both cases.

However, it turned out that Dalek was smarter than Tip had assumed. Temple and Chet triumphantly reported that the phone's GPS location remained resolutely at the motel during both murders. Hm, Tip wondered. Were Chet and Temple drawing together into an anti-Tip cabal? They took way too much shared pleasure in supposedly destroying his theory.

But the Jeep's rental company was happy to help, especially when he hinted that the vehicle had been involved in a homicide.

"Sure," said the voice on the phone at the rental agency's St. Louis headquarters. "Send us a fax with your bona fides proving you are who you say you are, and we'll give you daily updates."

"How about a warrant? Would that suffice for proof of good faith?"

"That would definitely do the job."

The warrant for telephone records sufficed because it specified "any and all electronic records." He fired it off immediately by email and next-day air, and the results came back within hours: a user ID and VIN giving him access to location data for the Jeep.

And bingo. He sat at his high-res monitor looking at the interactive map. Put in a date and time, see the Jeep signified on a map by a blinking asterisk, accompanied by coordinates. There it was in the pull-off around the corner from George's. On two different days. Problem was, the first time was the day *before* George was murdered, and the second was the day *after* he was murdered. Consistent with stealing the murder weapon and putting it back, but not with the murder itself. And there he was at Burton's place the morning of the Jennifer Clarkson murder, twice, two hours apart: once for stealing the murder weapon, and once for putting it back.

Damn it. Was the guy just an accessory, or was he the killer?

At least there was enough to bring him in for questioning for the Jennifer Clarkson murder. But what could his motive be? Or for George Sampson's murder, for that matter? They made no sense. Revenge on Big Iva made sense. But not them.

Still, Samantha would be delighted. Until she found out he didn't have enough to charge the guy. Opportunity, yeah. But the clincher? Nah. Anybody smart enough to leave his cell phone in his hotel while he committed a crime was not going to leave fingerprints on the weapons. Even if he was dumb enough to rent a vehicle with GPS tracking.

And the really odd thing about the tracking data? It showed the jeep going out to Catfish Bend several times, and staying there for fifteen minutes each time. Catfish Bend being a place three miles out on River Road where the county kept dumpsters as a way to keep people from trashing River Road. But during the week, it was a lonely, unfrequented place, since most people who produced a lot of trash were working. Retired people produce little.

But the unnerving part was that data from a few hours ago showed the Jeep parked at the end of County Road 50 North, where it ended at I-65, having been cut off decades earlier by the interstate's passage.

Tip knew the place. The nearest house was half a mile east, on a north-south road. No one would have noticed the Jeep driver turning west on this long-unused, unmaintained country road, now gone over to weed-filled cracks. And at the end of the road, where it abutted interstate right of way, there was a cluster of Russian olives which could hide a vehicle.

Sweat formed in Tip's fringe. What could the guy have been doing there?

The answer occurred immediately. Jesus. The killer was looking for a spot to shoot at Big Iva's. The place was only a mile north of County Road 50 South, whose intersection with I-65 was the location of Big Iva's Truck Stop.

In both cases so far, a very good shot or a trained sniper was clearly at work. Tip pictured in his mind where a shooter might locate.

The fence row separating the two bean fields that lay between the roads offered only small cedars for cover and no vantage point. Larger brush lined the highway right-of-way, but traffic was in the way of a shot across the interstate at the truck stop. But where the fence row between the fields T'd onto interstate right of way, a too-steep-to-farm wooded rise offered both cover and a clear shot. The freeway had cut through the rise, leaving a cut bank on the east side of the road and an unobstructed three-hundred-yard shot. A shooter could park at the end of 50 North, walk south under the Russian Olives to the cut bank, hide on the rise and shoot without being seen. Straight out of Big Iva's nightmares.

Tip never got around to checking where the jeep was right then. He knew what he had to do.

"Chet!" he bawled, reaching for his Kevlar vest. "Temple! Come with me! Pretty sure we got a sniper's nest out along I-65. Let's catch the bastard before he shoots somebody else."

"We're looking at Dalek's phone records," griped Chet. "Like you asked. It's a burner phone, which he turns on only when he makes a call. And all his calls have been to other burner phones. But one of those burner phones stays on, and moves around Howarth County."

"Do that later. We move now, we can stop something terrible from happening."

He showed them the data and outlined his plan. One of them would advance south along the brushy interstate right-of-way, pre-pared to take down a shooter hiding on the rise. Another would converge west along the cedar-lined fence row between two fields.

"I'll do the fence row," volunteered Temple. She gave Tip a steely look. "The work you've been having me do here is so bor-ing it's an insult."

"OK. So Chet goes to Big Iva's in case there's a direct-attack component to this. Assuming this is not a wild goose chase. If it is, we get the owner of that rise to cut down the trees and brush that would hide a sniper."

"Direct attack?" whined Chet. "Just me? Why do *I* always end up in the line of fire? You *al*ways do this. I don't get paid to get *my* ass shot off. I'm just a deputy. You're the sheriff, Tip. The people elected *you* to take the risks." He noticed Temple staring sidewise at him in disgust. "Not that I'm afraid. Of course I'll do it."

Tip continued. "I'll go down the highway from the parking spot to see if I can flush anybody out. He'll come toward you, Temple, 'cause there's no other direction he could run. He'd have to go through the drainage ditch if he went south. Dry now, but pretty steep. Could be I'm imagining things. But at the very least, I think I'm going to find a sniper's nest."

\* \* \*

But it was all too late. Tip had just started down the line of Russian olives, having noted the mashed-down chicory and pig-weed in the old road on his way in. A deep boom reverberated along the highway from the direction of the cut bank, rising above even the sounds of the sixteen wheelers singing along the asphalt.

Jesus. Serious rifle. He accelerated his pace, cursing the black-berry and multiflora thorns tearing at his clothes. Thirty seconds later, his phone vibrated.

"Jesus, Tip," said Chet. He sounded in a panic. "They got Missy. Sniper. She was outside talking to the fuel truck driver. You must have heard the shot, too. I think you're right. He's on that rise. I've got everybody inside. Big Iva is on a rampage. Wants to do a sweep with her people."

"How bad? Missy dead?"

"No, but bleeding bad. Left shoulder is pulp. Had to be a big round."

"OK. Get an ambulance. Keep Big Iva and her people from going nuts. I'm going to call in the state boys."

He called Corporal Jarvis and explained. A sniper was shooting at Big Iva's.

"Need you bad, Jarvis. Like, five minutes ago. Many guys as you can rustle up. Help me surround the guy. Watch out for Temple." He explained where she would likely be.

"Twenty minutes is best we can do," said Jarvis. "Three guys."

"I'll take it."

A sudden buzzing sound close to his head followed by another deep boom drove Tip to the ground.  He rolled deeper into the brush. Holy shit. His heart pounded. The guy must have a spotter, because the Russian Olives obscured the line of sight.

He called Temple.

"Stay down and zig-zag," he said, out of breath. "Son of a bitch just took a shot at me. Got Missy at the truck stop."

"Copy," she said, her voice ragged. "Running along the fence row toward the bluff," she panted. "I'm running at a crouch, cedar to cedar. I'll get to the top of the bluff in about two minutes."

Another deep boom and a grunt from Temple.

"Temple! Talk to me!"

Hard panting came over the phone. "Holy crap!  I felt the shock wave on my left shoulder!  I'm pinned down. In the honeysuckle behind a cedar.  Don't think I'm hit, but I can't even move to check. It's a skinny tree."

"All right," said Tip. "Don't move. I got this.  I got more cover than you do. I'm gonna move deeper into the brush and come at him from the north, like I planned.  Be ready for him to flush your way."

"Copy that."

It all sounded braver than Tip felt. Holy shit. The feeling was back. The feeling from his two firefights in the Gulf. Like you couldn't get enough air in your lungs. Like your heart might explode. The only positive was, it was like the guy was sending messages this time instead of killing. A good sniper could easily have hit Missy in the head.

He got up and moved south as fast as possible, staying close in under the Russian Olives, between them and the blackberry canes. Before long, he was panting hard. Damn all those cheeseburgers and fries, all those chips and beer on lonely nights in the railroad house. When this was all over he would get back in shape. But no Quibble gym-rat stuff, in stupid-looking skin-tight clothes. Nah. The old Marine Corps workout. Plus jog a couple miles out River Road, while carrying. Get a twofer: the running, plus a few people seeing him "patrolling" the notorious road.

If he didn't get his ass shot off in the next few minutes.

He fought his way to the bottom of the rise. To his left, stretching east, was the fence row concealing Temple. He called her.

"I'm seventy yards north of your fence row, in the brush along the edge of the highway right-of-way," he said quietly into his phone. The traffic noise was terrific, and he hoped it would cover up whatever noise he made. "Where are you?"

"I sneaked into the woods at the bottom of the slope leading up to the cut. I'm behind a log, waiting for him to come down. Somebody's been through this way. Cut through the blackberries with a machete."

So much for Temple following orders and not taking risks.

"OK, good. Means he'll likely run that way if I can flush him. I'm going in."

"Careful, Sheriff."

"You bet." He was tempted to say, "I didn't know you cared," but he understood. In combat, things changed. Petty rivalries fell away.

He quietly low-crawled forward through the brush, tearing hands and shirt on the rose and blackberry thorns, but taking care to keep a substantial tree or log between him and where he thought the shooter was. He struggled to quiet his breathing.

But it was a bust. The closer he got to the top of the rise, the more he was convinced no one was there. Indeed, when he got within thirty feet of the crown, clutching his Glock tightly, ready for the worst, he saw a dull shine on the ground.

"Hands up!" he shouted. "We've got you surrounded!"

No response.

"Come out!" he shouted.

No response.

Taking no chances, he low-crawled forward until he could see what produced the dull shine: a reflection off the lens of a scope. On a rifle leaning against a fallen branch. Carefully, he stood, walked over, and examined the rifle without touching it. Russian. An old Mosin-Nagant 91-30 sniper rifle. .30 caliber with the bottleneck shell. Plenty enough to blow the shit out of you.

Nowhere was there evidence of a person. But Tip could smell him. Some kind of essential-oil cologne. Like a cedar, but not as sharp. He called Temple.

"Found his rifle, but he's gone. See anything?"

"Nada."

"OK. Let's figure out where he went."

Which didn't take long. There was indeed a perfect view of Big Iva's from the shooter's spot.

And down below in the cleared right-of-way yawned the open end of a large drain pipe that ran under the interstate to the woods on the other side.

## CHAPTER SIXTEEN

The inside of the culvert pipe smelled of mud. And sure enough, splash marks on its crusted walls showed that someone had gone through very recently. In a hurry out of fear, Tip wondered, or just caution? The guy knew he was being pursued. The shots at him and Temple said that much. And he had left his rifle behind, maybe for speed, but likely, just not to be connected with it. Doubtless, there were no prints on it. Still, was the shooter waiting at the other end with another weapon? A pistol?

Tip gulped the funky air and his heart pounded as if he had been running. He had to move at a crouch through the five-foot drain, nervously aware he was vulnerable to a shooter at either end. Still, weapon at the ready, bent uncomfortably, he pushed ahead the eighty yards to the end of the second culvert. Second culvert, because in the median yawned an open space. He paid no attention to the clumps of Russian Olives and willows on either side of the rip-rapped ditch bed there, but pressed on into the second pipe.

But at the other end of the second drain, nothing. The grass around the stone inflow apron looked undisturbed, and farther into the woods, the lush, easily-broken mayapples showed no signs of passage. It was impossible to tell where the shooter had gone. Maybe straight up the ravine into the woods. Maybe he did a U-turn and climbed up to the interstate for pick-up. Or maybe he just called Scotty and had himself beamed up.

Jesus, this guy was slick.

Tip called Jarvis.

"He got Missy in the shoulder. Should be on her way to the hospital now."

"Ah, Jeez. Any sign of the guy?"

"Must have been in a hurry. Found his weapon. Nagant sniper rifle. How about sending your boys to the west side of I-65, on roads 50 South and 50 North? Converge between the roads. Look for somebody on foot."

"Just the guilty ones, right?"

"Go ahead. Joke. But catch this bastard."

"50 North dead-ends at the highway, right?"

"Right. I'm pretty sure he was brought in on 50 North on the east side of the highway. There are tracks through the weeds on the old road. I think there are two of them. I'm betting the pick-up guy might be on the west side."

"Got it. Wait one."

Tip heard him giving orders over the radio. Then he was back.

"You do know that professional shooters often have their weapon delivered and picked up? That way they minimize their exposure."

"See, that's the kind of thing you professional state boys learn at the academy. Us dumbos out here in the sticks, we just try to catch bad guys."

* * *

The stake-out of the two road ends produced nothing. A trooper each from the north and south swept the woods toward Tip in the middle, where he had searched a fan-shaped area in front of the drainage pipe inlet. They all met in the middle and reported nothing.

Then in a flash, Tip realized there had only been splash marks in the *first pipe*. Without a word, he left the troopers standing gape-mouthed and ran back into the second culvert. At the open space between the northbound and southbound lanes, nerve sweat running down his brow and the middle of his back, he crouched in the end of the culvert for cover and scanned the thick clumps of brush. No movement. Nothing. The foliage was too thick already, even though it was still pretty early in the season.

"Come out with your hands up!" he barked. "If I have to chase you, I'll shoot your ass."

Nothing.

Carefully, still crouching to minimize his target profile, he crept into first one, then the other clump of brush, gun ready, safety off. There was nothing in the first clump except trash, but deep inside the second, a fresh footprint showed in the soft earth, and a willow root displayed a fresh white scrape where the bark was skinned off, as by a boot. And in the wind-protected space, he caught a whiff of that same cologne. His neck hairs stood up. The asshole had watched from the bushes *while he came through*, then gone back the way he had come.

Then Tip remembered the broken-down '88 Dodge Caravan. Maroon. Visible from the sniper's nest, it had been sitting on the berm, facing north. A piece of blaze-orange tape was stuck on the back window, as if State Police had marked and logged it. Desperate not to have been so easily snookered, he ran up the embankment to the inside edge of the northbound lanes and looked across.

The van was gone.

Tip threw his hat on the ground and yelled, "I'll be dipped in SHIT!"

People honked and waved as they blew by.

\* \* \*

By the time he got to Big Iva's, Missy had been taken to Indy by chopper. Blood still puddled outside on the concrete. Big Iva was furious. Her face looked like the oncoming black cloud wall of the simoom he once saw in Kuwait, a storm so dark and threatening all you wanted to do was dig a hole and hide.

"You let it happen, Tip." She didn't yell. Her voice instead was a low and deadly contralto. "I oughta shoot your ass."

"Easy, Iva. You can't talk to me like that. I'm a law enforcement officer."

"You're a broken-down, over-aged high-school football hero elected because you used to be good looking, to do a job that's way over your head." Her voice thickened. "Wait until somebody shoots somebody close to *you*."

Of course that had happened more than once, but he said nothing. He watched as her body began to shake in an odd way. At first he thought she was laughing, but then he saw the tears on her massive face.

"She's my favorite, Tip," she sobbed. "And she could have died. Might still. As it is, she'll probably be crippled on that side for the rest of her life."

"Trauma surgeons can do amazing things, Iva," Tip said quietly. He knew Missy was more than her favorite. "And the ones in Indy have a lot of experience with gunshot wounds."

"You gotta get these bastards, Tip. I'm telling you. Otherwise, I'm going to war. I'll go up there and clean those cockroaches out. Every last one. I know who they are. I know where they live."

"Now's a fine time to tell me. Who *are* they? How about some names? And where *do* they live?

She gave him a list of names and Chicago businesses, mostly bars and restaurants, where her sources had it that they hung out. No addresses. He didn't see how it could help, but he said nothing. Now was not the time to talk about probable cause, his inability to engage the FBI without raising questions neither she nor he wanted to face, or his inability as sheriff of a mostly poor county in southern Indiana to put his own watch on these guys.

* * *

Temple took the rifle straight up to the Indy lab for ballistics and fingerprint testing. She called back with bad news within two hours.

"No record of the serial number in the NICS, which means nothing. Only that it hasn't been used in a crime before. That anyone knew of."

"It's Russian," Tip growled. "How did it get here? There must be an import record."

"Usually, yes. When weapons are imported, their serial numbers are captured on the State Department's form DS1504. But this Nagant's number is not there."

"Smuggled in? Still, wouldn't there be a record if it was sold?"

"Maybe, maybe not. It's a pretty old weapon, before record-keeping was very good. Even so, if a licensed firearm dealer filled out the required Form 4473 Firearms Transaction Record, that record stays with the dealer. There's no way, given the serial number, of knowing which dealer might have sold it. It's a needle-in-the haystack scenario. And there's no matching record on ballistics."

"And, let me guess: no fingerprints."

"Correct. We're working with a professional here. The stock had been thoroughly rubbed with linseed oil, and the only thing sticking to it was talcum powder from latex gloves."

"Terrific. Well, at least two positive things came out of this one."

"I'm waiting."

"Missy is still alive, and we know we're dealing with a professional."

"You're easily pleased. What's next?"

"These days, I'll take what I can get. But I think I gotta go after my guy with the Michelin off-roads. He's dirty in this." He told her about the vehicle tracking data. Then, "Be pleased if you would keep that to yourself."

"Ah," she said. Then a second, brighter, "Ah! You think the perp has a local information source. Who might hear what I might say."

"Could be." He noticed a change in tone from her normal snarkiness toward him. They were now partners in a tough investigation, colleagues, and together, they had come close to the perp. And been shot at. Maybe he was halfway forgiven for looking at her ass that day out at George's.

* * *

He knew you could buy Nagant 91 30's all day long in well-stocked gun shops across America. But the fact that it was Russian—and apparently never legally imported—had to be significant. So it looked like Big Iva might be right. He was dealing with the Russian mob. On Missy's shooting, at least. And the motive was revenge. But how would they have known to target Missy? And what possible connection could there be between this shooting and the other two? Could the note have been right? The first two were mercy killings just to get his attention? It gave him a headache just thinking about it.

All he had was a boot print, the smell of someone's aftershave, and some suspicious vehicle tracking data. Plus the suspicion that the perp had a local information source. A check with the State Police confirmed that they had not marked a 1988 Dodge Caravan near the Sedalia exit as abandoned. Going to Chicago and rattling cages was a non-starter. Dangerous to boot. No, he had nothing except Mr. Andrei Dalek. Otherwise, he was pretty much swimming in the ocean out of sight of land.

It was time to rattle Dalek's cage and see what he knew.

* * *

Tip sat in the IHOP parking lot and waited until Dalek got into his Jeep and headed out of Elmira. He wanted to get him in a remote place.

Dalek crossed the Wapamoni in Elmira, then turned south toward Sedalia on River Road. Any car that drove down it raised a dust cloud visible from a distance, so Tip hung back behind a couple of curves and called Chet. He was to watch the south end of the stretch, where the Sedalia bridge crossed the Wapamoni. If Dalek tried to pass, Chet was to stop him.

"On what charge?" Chet demanded. "We don't have enough from Andrei Dalek's phone records to charge him with anything."

"Accessory to murder."

"Got proof?"

"Nope. Just a bunch of strong circumstantial evidence. Gonna interrogate him."

"Ah."

Chet regularly undercut Tip on other stuff, but kept quiet about his sometimes unorthodox interrogation techniques. Playing good cop before and after made him feel powerful. He would give prisoners to understand that as Chief Deputy, he could add charges—resisting arrest, battery on a law officer, visiting a common nuisance, being a habitual criminal—that lengthened jail time and were impossible to disprove. And he could turn hard cases over to the sheriff—again—for questioning.

At Catfish Bend, a place where the river took a loop away from the road, and where generations of parkers had changed their lives in one way or another, Tip came upon the yellow Jeep sitting beside one of the dumpsters. He switched on his light bar, gave the siren a single whoop, and turned on the speaker.

"Do not exit your vehicle. Place both hands on your steering wheel and wait for further instructions."

Tip got out with his weapon drawn and approached the driver's side of the vehicle. The driver's window was down. Neither hand was on the wheel.

"Both hands on the wheel or I shoot!"

The hands moved slowly to the wheel. Tip approached and ripped the door open. Inside sat a city-looking dude with oily hair perfectly combed back in a pompadour, expensively dressed in clothes a city person might imagine he would need in the boonies: brand-new hiking boots, Khaki cargo pants, long-sleeve shooting shirt with notepad pockets on the sleeves, and a multi-pocket fisherman's vest.

"Easy, officer. I'm just here enjoying nature." "Officer" came out "awwfisuh," and "nature" came out "naychuh." "Brought my bird-watching log."

"Uh huh. Get out of the car, slowly, keeping both hands in sight. Then turn and place both hands on the roof of the car, and your feet wide apart."

Slowly, reluctantly, with an insolent expression no birdwatcher ever used, the man did as ordered. Tip then kicked his feet farther apart and farther away from the Jeep so he was off-balance. Then he frisked him and started going through the many pockets.

Just as he realized there was a small automatic in the man's right bottom vest pocket, there came the sound of a vehicle far up the gravel road toward Elmira. He had maybe three minutes. Just to be safe, he cuffed the man and told him to get on his knees. He did, gingerly. "Ow," said the man. "This is police brutality. The gravel hurts."

Tip fished the automatic out of the man's pocket. It came with a small leather wallet containing the man's carry license. "What the hell?"

"Hah," said the man.

"How'd you get it?"

"Petitioned the state after four years of clean record. I know you know who I am or you wouldn't have stopped me, so you know my record. It's minor stuff, so they let me have my carry license back."

"But you're from Illinois."

"Actually East Chicago."

"So what are you doing in southern Indiana? In my county?"

"Birdwatching."

"Uh huh. What's a mockingbird look like?"

"Wings. Feathers. The usual."

"Uh huh."

Tip kneed the man in the back, hard, driving his face into the door of the jeep. His nose spurted blood.

"Damn it!" shouted Dalek. "You can't do that!"

"Why was this vehicle parked near George Sampson's farm the day before and the day after he was murdered?"

"Who is George Sampson? If I was parked near his place, I was bird watching, not killing anybody. I don't kill people."

Tip kneed him in the back again, driving his face into the Jeep door again, this time leaving blood smears.

"Why was this Jeep parked this morning at the end of 50 North near the interstate, less than half a mile from where somebody just fired a rifle shot that nearly killed a woman at Big Iva's truck stop?"

"I don't know!" wailed the man.

"Where were you two hours ago?"

"Bird watching."

"Uh huh. Where?"

"Between here and Elmira."

"What roads? Whose woods?"

"I don't know. Maybe sometimes I trespass, but I don't cause any damage."

"Mind if I search your vehicle? The correct answer is no."

"Knock yourself out, Sheriff. Just don't hit me again."

The search produced little. A pair of binoculars, which Tip assumed were part of his cover. Also, a walkie talkie, which was strange but not unusual. And the car being a rental, all the storage spaces were empty and clean. The carpet showed no signs of mud, as it would if this guy had run through a drain. And the worst of it was, this guy's complexion didn't match what he had seen in the game-camera pictures. Nor were this guy's hands as thick as the one in the picture.

This was not his guy, but this guy was dirty. He was sure of it. Still, he planned to take him in and hold him for a couple of days, the law be damned, just to take him off the street. And to further interrogate him. How did he make a living? Who did he work for? Etc.

Just as he was loading Dalek into the back of the Sheriff's Dept. SUV and chaining his cuffs to the eyebolt in the floor, the Porters truck came around the bend from the direction of Elmira and stopped beside Tip. Stefano lowered the right-side window and greeted him.

"Hey, Sheriff! Looks like you caught a criminal. Maybe the shooter? Need any help?"

"Nah, that's all right, Al. Just doing a little proactive police work."

Tip liked to use words like "proactive" with the public. He thought it made him sound professional.

"You sure?" He nodded at Dalek. "Looks like a rough customer you got there."

"Yeah. He fell during the arrest. But look, Chet should be waiting at the Sedalia turnoff. With a State officer. Tell him to come this way, if you would. Need to clear this vehicle from the road." He nodded at the Jeep. Stefano and Chet were fellow horse-racing fans who traded gibes about the other's losses when Stefano brought Chet, who did not cook, his weekly stack of frozen dinners.

"You bet, Sheriff. Hope you got the right man."

He smiled, tipped his Porters hat, and drove off.

Tip got into the front seat of the SUV and turned. "Now, let's go over your answers once more. But start with where you work, how you pay your bills, where your bank is, where you have a safety deposit box, and where you sleep. I think you're dirty, Dalek, and I'm going to prove it."

Just then, Tip's phone rang. Area code 212. Manhattan. No caller identified. "Hello," he said, probably sounding too gruff. Who the hell would be calling from New York City?

"Daddy," said a woman's voice. "I'm really scared. Can I come home?"

## CHAPTER SEVENTEEN

**K**aty. His gut instantly twisted into a knot. For a moment, he couldn't breathe. Then he spoke, for fear of losing the connection.

"Baby, you know you can come home. Any time. And stay as long as you like." He hesitated, suddenly aware again of Dalek handcuffed in the back seat. He checked the mirror and saw a smirk on the man's face. "Just a sec."

He rolled up the SUV windows, got out, and walked over to one of the dumpsters, where he could keep an eye on Dalek but feel private. She sounded really scared. "Tell me what's wrong."

"People are after me, Daddy. Following me. Leaving threats in my mailbox. Breathing on the phone. The last one said twenty-four hours, and I'd be dead. Then I found a dead cat. Inside the door to my apartment."

"What about the police?"

"Worthless. No serious crime committed, they said. Come back when I'm dead. Not quite that bad, but close."

"Gotcha." He couldn't help smiling. She had her mother's sharp tongue.

He had not heard her voice in ten years. His only child. Not since she left for New York, blaming him for her mother's departure. "You're an emotional bankrupt!" she had accused. "Drove her away!" And she had gone off to the big apple and become a TV producer. He regularly googled to see how she was doing, but she never answered his emails or phone calls.

"What about your job? Looks like you're doing great, TV news producer and all. Can you get off work?"

There was a long pause during which he suddenly feared he had screwed up again, the call would end, and that would be the last time he heard her voice. Finally, in a soft voice she said, "I'm touched that you check, Dad. But the job won't do me any good if I'm dead. I don't know who's after me, or why, could be terrorists pissed off about some news story, extortionists who haven't delivered their demand yet, or just some nut job. But I need to get out of town and go someplace where people don't do that kind of thing. At least until Detective Margolis figures out who's doing it."

"Tell me your flight and I'll pick you up. I live in a different house now, but it has empty bedrooms."

"The railroad house. I heard." Meaning, she kept in touch with her mother.

"That's the one. Only two trains a day, so it's not so bad."

There was a brief silence. Then, "There's, uh, nobody else living there?"

"Just me. Pastor Frank's cleaning lady cleans it once a week, but we'll have to get some groceries. Haven't done too well on the cooking front."

Another silence. Then, "Ah."

* * *

Back at the jail, after Temple was back from the lab in Indy, she and Chet couldn't understand why he was suddenly in a good mood. He admitted he'd been grumpy since the murders started. Temple raised her eyebrows at the blood all over Dalek's face and shirt but said nothing. Chet simply nodded and said, "What'd you get out of the interrogation?"

"Nothing good yet, but the guy's dirty. You and Temple, do the full detailed rundown on his finances, including safety deposit boxes, even safes in his house. You'll have to drive up to East Chicago. Also his movements for the past two weeks. Interview him separately, then compare. We'll get something. He may not be the perp, but I think he's working with him. Oh, and search that motel room in Elmira, all his luggage."

This was too much for Temple. "You do know you don't have enough for search warrants, or for an arrest? Not even enough to hold him. Or do you intend to just violate his civil rights?"

"That was pretty much what I was planning, then not telling anybody about it. I'd search the motel room myself and not tell anybody, but I have to make a run to Indy."

She shook her head in disgust and crossed her arms over her chest. "I won't do it."

There went the new collegiality he had imagined between them. Behind her, Chet nodded yes and winked. "Me either."

You could just never tell where help was going to come from.

"By the way," said Tip on his way out the door. "I found a pack of latex gloves in the glove compartment of that rental Jeep. On my desk. Kind of an odd thing to find in a rental car." He looked at Temple. "Any way you can test the talcum on those gloves to see if it matches the talcum on that Nagant?"

"Did you have permission to search his car?"

"I did."

"Then that I can do."

*　*　*

Tip could hardly believe his eyes. His snot-nosed teenage daughter had turned into a head-turning bombshell. She was dressed like a million bucks in a blue suit, white blouse, and dove-gray shoes worth a week of his salary. And she herself looked like a million bucks, fit, trim, with her mother's blond hair styled in a short, no-nonsense, but feminine wave.

She gave him a hug. He hugged her back, hard, but careful not to hang on too long. She pulled back.

"You're looking . . . prosperous, Dad. And very official."

"You mean I've got a belly and I'm bald."

"Actually, I'd say, you look distinguished."

"Nice save. Come on." He grabbed her bag. "You can tell me in the car everything you can think of about what's been happening. Then give me this Detective Margolis's phone number."

On the way down to Sedalia he told her nothing about the murder spree. Or about the threatening note in his own mailbox. She would find out about the first soon enough. He was just so pleased to have her back, if only briefly, that it felt as if his happiness had swollen his being outside his body. He wanted only to enjoy her presence, to protect her, and keep her from harm. No goddamn New York scumbag was going to hurt his daughter. He would feed the bastard through a wood chipper. After running a weedeater on his dick.

They stopped in Elmira for groceries, then he deposited her in the house, gave her a key to his old F-150, the password to the Wi-Fi, and showed her where the loaded .38 was, up in the kitchen cabinets.

"Same gun you taught me on," she said, hefting it in her hand.

"Yup. Hasn't been fired since."

Then he headed back to the jail to see what had developed with Mr. Andrei Dalek. But not before stopping at Eileen's for a ham sandwich, and learning once again that there were no secrets in

Sedalia. A couple of retiree widowers and Dave Schulz were the only patrons. All looked at him with shit-eating grins.

"Hey, Tip," said Eileen and winked. "Thanks for coming in before closing time this time." She looked at her watch. "Barely. Need to fuel up before the evening's activities?" Wink, wink.

"Well, yeah. It's probably going to be a long evening. We've picked up a suspect."

"Tell us something we don't know," said Eileen. "Mrs. Aubrey came in to sell some of her cinnamon rolls."

"Buy any?"

"Yeah, they're pretty good. And if I didn't buy any, I'd hear about it from everybody. She needs the support. But it's just how she maintains her gossip network."

"She told you we'd arrested a suspect?"

Eileen raised an eyebrow. "Wasn't all she told us."

"What the *hell* are you hinting at?"

"Your, uh, houseguest. Young knock-out. Sherry Fisher saw the two of you in the grocery store in Elmira, and Mrs. Chambliss saw you drive down your street to your house, with her in your car." She waggled her eyebrows. "And I thought you and I might get something going."

"Ah. Well, we still might. Long as you're not jealous."

The ham was only a quarter of an inch thick this time, compared with its usual half to three quarters of an inch.

* * *

Morning brought two surprises and one break.

One was, Katy could cook. "Self defense, Dad," she said as she took over mid-omelette. He always thought all those New York sophisticates ate out all the time.

Two was, everybody in town still thought he had shacked up. "You dog," leered Chet. Temple folded her arms over her chest and sniffed.

The break was, the talcum powder was a match. "Still circumstantial," warned Temple.

"You mean because tons of people have latex gloves. Deer hunters, for example. For field dressing. People cleaning toilets. Some people even wear them while washing dishes."

"You, Tip?" smiled Chet. Normal snarkiness aside, they were apparently buddies now, sharing a male moment at the triumph of Tip's move-in. Wink wink, nudge nudge.

"Have to protect my sensitive skin. So what about our friend, Andrei Dalek?"

Chet took a sidewise glance at Temple, then back at Tip. "Well, he had a brother, name of Armando. Former KGB, according to the NICS. Found dead floating in the Cumberland River. Definitely a member of the Chicago Russian mob."

He and Chet exchanged a private glance. So Chet had not told Temple of the probable connection to the shootout last year at Big Iva's. Good. He didn't want to explain to Samantha.

"OK. What else?"

Temple took over. "It wasn't necessary to go to Chicago to find his bank and phone records. He used a burner phone here, but Mr. Dalek has been very indiscreet. His regular phone in his name shows a lot of interaction with suspected Chicago crime figures. He has two bank accounts, one for his money, and the other, at a different bank, with only a few thousand in it, is what he uses for his debit and credit cards, and his internet purchases. The first account, at Polish American Bank of Merrillville, has sixty-two thousand in it. Fifty thousand of that was deposited one month ago."

"Ah. Where'd it come from?"

"Krepinsky Gold Bullion, Inc. In payment for forty-five one-ounce Krugerrands."

"Which of course, there's no record of Dalek ever buying. Meaning this Krepinski outfit is dirty, and a money laundry."

"Correct. On the FBI watch list, but they are very slick. No smoking gun yet. I called them, and they are willing to show me forty-five Krugerrands and a record of purchase."

"And what's Dalek's explanation about where he got the gold coins?"

"Inherited them from his brother, of course."

"Of course. And where's the guy work?"

"Very murky. Has a P.I. license. And a license to carry in both Illinois and Indiana."

"Yeah, saw that."

"Does consulting."

"I can just imagine. Who's hired him to consult in the last year?"

"Says we can talk to his lawyer about that. Who will be here within the hour. Had to let him make his call. And here's the kicker. Fifty thousand left the account two weeks ago. In cash. Withdrawn to pay a personal debt, he told the bank manager."

"Or some contractor who demands spendable, untraceable cash. So Dalek is cutout number one. Wonder if there's another one. Damn it. Where's the lawyer from?"

"Chicago, of course."

"So when did Dalek make the call?"

"About an hour ago."

"Hmmh. Fast driver."

* * *

Robert Miklaczewski was the picture of a mob lawyer: dapper, mannerly, affable. And tough. His suit looked like it had cost at least a thousand bucks, but it could not hide the bull shoulders that came from daily workouts on the weight machines. Though it did hide his shoulder holster, until he intentionally let his jacket fall open so Tip could see it.

"Let's see your license to carry that," said Tip with a smile. He refused to get up from his desk chair.

"Of course, Sheriff." The man pulled the weapon, a Browning 1911 .45, and laid it on the desk in front of Tip. Then he pulled an expensive, check-book-size leather wallet out of his inside coat pocket and laid it open in front of Tip. "Now hand over my client."

Tip looked the license over, then flipped through the other cards in the wallet without looking up and said, "And your attorney identification card." Then he smiled up at Miklaczewski. "If you don't mind."

"Of course not." He reached down and flipped to the back of the plastic envelopes. "Note that I'm licensed in both Illinois and Indiana. To carry and to practice."

"Hmmh." Tip pulled out the attorney ID and the man's business card, which listed his cell number. "Hey, Temple, how about making a copy of these? You don't mind, do you, Mr. Miklaczewski?"

"Of course not."

Tip handed the cards to Temple, who copied them, handed them back to the lawyer, then sat down with the copy at her laptop. Tip turned his attention back to the lawyer. "Tell me, Mr. Miklaczewski. How did you manage to get here so fast? From Chicago. Which is at least four hours away?"

"I, uh, was doing some business in Indianapolis, though that's none of your business. Now fetch my client, or I'll need to take it up with your prosecutor. With whom, I strongly suspect, you have not made application for charges?"

"It's only a matter of time, Mr. Miklaczewski. He is not to leave the country, or the state of Indiana. But if I see him or you around here again, there's going to be trouble. "

"I can't believe you just made a threat to an officer of the court, Sheriff. I may need to report it to your D.A."

"Mind showing me your phone log, Mr. Miklaczewski? Showing all your incoming calls for the last six to eight hours? And mind telling me whom I can talk to in Indianapolis to confirm your presence there?" Tip liked to use "whom" when dealing with officious assholes.

The lawyer was cool. "I don't have to show you anything, Sheriff."

"What I thought. Get yourself and your client out of my town, Miklaczewski. You're dirty, both of you, and I'm coming after you."

Chet brought Dalek out. He was still wearing his bloody shirt, though the matron had taped a patch of gauze over his nose.

"What the hell, Sheriff? What kind of town are you running here?"

"One where Chicago assholes don't come in and murder my neighbors. Now get out."

* * *

"So what'd you get, Temple?"

She looked up from her laptop.

"Two interesting things. First, the number Dalek called was a Chicago cell number, ID blocked. But the interesting thing is, a cell using a local tower, ID blocked, also called that number yesterday afternoon about an hour after you, uh, arrested Mr. Dalek. That Chicago number then called Miklaczewski last night around eleven. So, yes, Miklaczewski's phone was indeed in Indy an hour ago, but on the move. But how he got here so fast? He started five hours ago."

"And no way to find out who made the local call."

"Correct."

# CHAPTER EIGHTEEN

Tip had four threads to follow: Dalek's binoculars, Hammadi, and Detective Margolis. And of course, the Chicago connection.

Those binoculars bothered him. He was pretty sure what Dalek had used them for, and it wasn't bird watching. In the history of Sedalia, no one had ever been caught bird watching. As well, something about Dr. Hammadi didn't seem quite right. It nagged at him. He remembered how the folk in Iraq would smile and deal with you on the straight-up. You thought. Right up until they tried to kill you. While still smiling. Yeah, such thinking was un-PC. Screw PC. Its high priests should serve their own tours in the military.

But Margolis had to do with his daughter, so he started there.

After using his cell phone to leave three messages on Margolis's phone with no call-back, Tip finally called on the Sheriff's Department land line. The detective's phone screen would identify the caller as the Howarth County Sheriff's Department, not some anonymous number from a flyover-country area code. The man picked up on the third ring.

"Yeah?"

"Sheriff Tungate, Howarth County, Indiana, following up on a case of yours."

"Yeah? How are things out in Mayberry?"

"Probably better than things in that festering shithole you New Yorkers are so proud of," said Tip cheerfully. Tell me about the Katy Tungate case. She's my daughter."

"No shit? Babe like that came from Indiana?"

"She did. We corn feed them out here. Now, the case. What have you found out?"

"The B&E? Dead cat in her apartment? Frankly, haven't spent any time on it. Questioned the neighbors up and down her hall. Nothing."

"What about the threats? The people following her? Calling her and breathing?"

"Got nothing there except calls from blocked numbers and her word. Nothing to follow up on."

"You don't believe her?"

"Look, Andy—"

"Sheriff Tungate."

"Sheriff. We get calls like this all the time. Women who think men are after them. Women who hope men are after them. Eventually, they go away."

"The cases, or the women?"

"Hah hah. The cases."

"Look, if you're not going to do anything about it, how about emailing me what you've got. This is my daughter we're talking about. She's so scared she left her job and came back to Indiana."

"That's pretty scared. And I got a daughter, too. I understand. I'll send the stuff."

\* \* \*

He had a theory about the binoculars. He didn't actually think Dalek was the shooter. This went with the fact that his jeep was parked around the corner from George's before and after the murder, but not during.

Dalek was the scout and the look-out man.

The question was, if you were going to shoot somebody at Big Iva's from the sniper's nest where he found the Nagant, where would you want your lookout?

He drove back out to County Road 50 North, and took a look. The weeds growing through the cracks in the oil-mat pavement showed no new mashed-down tracks besides the ones his SUV made when he was after the shooter. And he was pretty sure any lookout would have avoided the busier road one mile south, which intersected with I-65. So maybe the guy parked somewhere in the woods up the north-south road east of I-65 and walked in to his lookout post.

And bingo. A quarter mile up the north-south road a pull-off led east into the woods and curved out of sight behind a brush pile. And it showed the same Michelin off-road tire tracks. From there, he looked across the road to the west. A woods there offered a south-facing tree line that looked across 50 North, the bean field, and all the way down to the wooded rise the sniper shot from.

He walked along the edge of the woods and within ten minutes found what he was looking for: a deer stand in that south-facing tree line. And fresh chips off of its two-by-four ladder rungs.

So Dalek parks his car in the woods across the north-south road, takes up look-out in this deer stand, and warns the shooter by walkie-talkie when he sees Tip park on the abandoned road and sneak south along the band of Russian olives. The visibility was perfect.

Great story; no proof. These guys were professionals. That much was clear. The question was, who hired them? Sure, the Russian mob. That explained Missy. But not George Sampson or

Jennifer Clarkson. The only thing that looked sensible there was mercy killing. But then the mailbox note made it clear the same killer planned to strike again. And somebody was after Katy. And there was that unexplained local call to the Chicago number, almost certainly a mob number, from which somebody had called Miklaczewski, almost certainly a mob lawyer.

Just to check, he took out his phone and googled Miklaczewski. Sure enough, high-profile cases defending alleged mobsters. And he won nearly all of them. Dangerous guy.

So. Maybe same killer, two different motives. The first two looked like mercy killings, the note even sort of said so, which implied local knowledge plus sympathy. So, maybe the killer was a local with some sort of nasty Chicago connection.

It didn't wash. Everybody in Sedalia had been born and raised there, or moved in years ago. And they stayed put. They didn't go to Chicago. Usually not even Indy. And very few people actually moved in. He could think of only two: Paige Colfax and Ann Christopher, aka Anna Christoph.

The Colfaxes had moved in several years ago when Sander completed his Chile assignment for Global Corp. He was on the short list for CEO at the Elmira headquarters, so they had built a house on a hill above the Wapamoni and settled in. She had been unpopular at first, striving to improve the locals with one unpopular initiative after another. But then the corporate jet crashed in Texas, killing Sander, and she changed. Despite being wealthy, by local standards at least, she became an accepted member of the community, giving her time and money to help with initiatives locals cared about.

Anna Christoph was a former Bloomington art gallery owner and jilted girlfriend of Carter Blake, the unloved English teacher who made it big as a writer and moved to New York. On a trip home to sell the house, he was poisoned by Anna's aunt, his next-door neighbor. In his will, not updated to recognize his new wealth and new girlfriend, Anna got everything—copyrights, money, and house. And though her aunt confessed to the poisoning, then poisoned herself, the out-of-control diabetes and congestive heart failure found in her autopsy made Tip suspicious. Did the aunt take the fall with a well-timed exit? It was all too neat. But he had nothing to go on, so he had let sleeping dogs lie.

So, Paige Colfax had no motive to kill anybody, and no experience doing so. Anna Christoph had no apparent motive, but might have experience. But he couldn't see either of them shooting anybody. In fact, the one thing Paige still did that pissed off locals was loudly support gun control.

Still, he decided to talk to both of them. He could not afford to leave any stone unturned.

* * *

Paige liked to hit Jimmy Ray's about one in the afternoon for a gin and tonic up on the patio. Just one, never two. The draw of catching her at Jimmy Ray's was, Jimmy Ray had the best breaded tenderloin sandwich in town—the competition being Eileen, who for some reason bought these dinky little stamped-out and breaded pork patties, while Jimmy Ray got these gigantic hammered tenderloins from Al, the Porters man. So Tip went for a twofer. He didn't need the calories, God knew, and he would go on a diet just as soon as he had this case figured out, but for now he deserved some comfort food.

She was indeed up on the patio, taking in the sun out from under the porch-style roof, with a drink and an *Economist* open on the table in front of her. She was actually reading, not the *Economist*, but a trashy paperback murder mystery. Tip took his hat off and approached.

"Mind if I join you for a couple of minutes? Can't take long, 'cause Jimmy Ray's gonna put a breaded tenderloin on the bar for me in a couple of minutes."

She smiled a big smile. He loved that smile, and the fact that she always looked great, even if she just went out for gas, always dressed in clothes nobody in Sedalia could afford. Her hair and make-up were always perfect. But she was out of his league.

"Well hey, Tip. No, I don't mind. Have a seat. And you can share my table for your lunch, if you want to. Have your sandwich sent up here." Her smile brightened. "You do know, by the way, that deep-fried food will kill you. As well as, umm," and here her gaze dropped to his stomach, "have other effects."

"Yes Ma'am," he said and sat. "And I can see clearly that you don't eat any." He laid his hat on the table. "But something's going to get me sooner or later, and I need my comforts now and then. And you'll probably want to hear what I have to say before you invite me to your table."

Her smile disappeared. "Has something bad happened again? Something even worse than what's been going on?"

"It's what's been going on that I need to talk to you about. And I need you to promise not to reveal what we talk about."

Now she looked really concerned. "OK."

"What did you know about the health status of George Sampson and Jennifer Clarkson?"

"What?" Her voice trailed off to express her total confusion. "Nothing. I barely knew George, a nice old gentleman, by the way, sometimes we would talk in the bank, and I didn't know the girl at all. What's this about?"

"Do you know Tom Burton, and are you familiar with his habits?"

"*What*? Tip, this is getting strange. I know who he is. Now, after all the ruckus."

"Didn't you once enter a complaint about Big Iva running a prostitution operation out at her place?"

Now she got hot. "You know damned well I did, and neither you nor Dave Woods at the time did a blessed thing about it. I let it go because nobody seemed to care. Maybe Samantha finally will."

"Did you talk to anybody outside Sedalia about it?"

"No. Tip, what the hell is this conversation? It's sounding a lot like an interrogation."

"Do you have experience firing rifles?"

"Of course. I learned how as a girl scout. But you know my views on weapons."

"Where were you the morning Jennifer Clarkson was killed?"

Her mouth dropped open, then broadened into a big smile. She put the book down on the table. "I get it! I'm a suspect! Cool! Just like in the mysteries!" She leaned across the table playfully and asked in a low voice, "Is this where I say I'm not going to say another word until I talk to my attorney?"

"If that's what you want. Where were you?"

"This is not going to be any fun. I'm afraid I have an alibi. I was with the Women's Book Club at Eldora Quick's house. I do wish she wouldn't try to get us always to read her books, as it's rather uncomfortable discussing them in front of her."

"OK. One last question. What contact have you had with people from Chicago in the last month?"

"None. I don't know anybody from Chicago."

"OK. You're off the hook. I never believed you were on it, but the exigencies of the investigation required that I talk to you, as the closest thing we have to an out-of-towner."

She smiled. "'Exigencies'?"

"My word of the day. People think I'm uneducated, so I've become an autodidact to prove them wrong."

The tenderloin plate's arrival stopped their conversation. Jimmy set it in front of Tip with a flourish, then asked Paige if she needed anything. She put her hand over the top of her drink. He turned to Tip. "I see Katy's back in town. Damn, Tip. It's clear she takes after Diane."

"Good thing, too. Or she'd never stand a chance. She go out to Fishers' Groc or something?"

"Yeah. Whole town is buzzing. First they didn't know who she was and thought you'd shacked up. Now they can't believe what she looks like, and that she's a famous New York TV person and all. She back for good or just visiting?"

Paige was looking quizzical.

"My daughter," he said by way of explanation. Then he turned to Jimmy Ray. "Just visiting. Got some business to straighten out."

Jimmy Ray looked back and forth between Paige and Tip, neither of whom made effort to keep the conversation going with Jimmy Ray. "OK, then," he said. "I'll just be down at the bar if you need me."

"You mentioned your daughter once," said Paige quietly when Jimmy Ray was gone. "That you hadn't seen her in a long time."

Tip flashed her a sharp look, then nodded. She looked sympathetic, and he knew she did not gossip. He, Jimmy Ray, Butch Bauer, the high school principal, and Bud Tatum, who owned the *Democrat*, had all befriended and supported her when she lost her husband. She was only trying to reciprocate.

"Yeah. Happy she's back. Just don't like the circumstances."

She looked thoughtful. "My maid in Santiago was a wise old Mapuche Indian woman named Sayen. She used to say, when bad things happen in strings, it is the same devil doing it. Is something bad happening, Tip? To your daughter?"

Now he squinted hard at her. "What makes you say that?"

"Coincidence. Strings of bad things don't happen by coincidence. You don't like the circumstances that brought her back, and she comes back after a long absence, when all these bad things are happening in Sedalia. Is someone trying to get at you through your daughter?"

He had wondered this about once an hour since Katy called. Who had he put in jail? Who was out of jail? Who had he hurt or killed? Iraqis. But that was a long time ago, and he had been a soldier. In a war. And they were there and he was here.

But then came the dream again. Only this time he was awake. Once again he was in the house, and the woman was looking at him, screaming, shaking, holding up her hands, and the little boy was looking at him in terror. There was the soldier hiding in the corner, now raising his weapon. There was no choice. He had to shoot. But the woman was his mother or sister, and the boy was his son or brother, by the looks of them. Still, he shot. Right in front of them. He had to. It was war, and it was him or the Iraqi with the AK. Except that the guy's weapon was empty and he was trying to give up.

Sweat beaded on his forehead. He had been over this a thousand times, and it was always the same. Him or me, him or me, him or me. And then it wasn't.

"Tip? Tip." Paige looked concerned. "You with me?"

"Yeah, sure. Was just thinking of something."

"You kind of zoned out there for a minute."

"Yeah." He abruptly stood and made to leave.

"Aren't you going to eat your sandwich?"

"Nah. Tell Jimmy Ray to put it in the fridge. I'll get it later."

And he left, a new idea racing around his head. Forget Anna Christoph. Chances there were one in a million.

Hammadi.

# CHAPTER NINETEEN

His idea was to get Temple to go through Hammadi's bank accounts, his personal history, every bit of information in public and private databases. Of course with her being such a straight arrow that would be a challenge, since no probable cause legitimized such a search. Who would believe a too-ready smile was reason for suspicion? But he remembered those smiles from the war: all lips, no eyes. Then a shot in the back.

But when he got back to the Jail, he found that Temple's scruples were no longer his immediate problem.

TV trucks were there again, and Rebecca Schulman, the Lieutenant Governor. Even a small crowd of onlookers. A squad of four state troopers surrounded her. Each looked as if he had been selected for size and poker face. Two of them normally stood outside the governor's office as part of his personal protection detail.

The lieutenant governor was a pleasant-looking woman in her early fifties, a popular school superintendent Brandt had plucked from East Chicago where he needed the black vote. She met Tip at the door in front of the TV cameras. An official-looking document trembled slightly in her right hand. The cameramen closed in.

"Sheriff Earl J. Tungate?" she said. Her voice was loud and firm. She crimped her lips. She was nervous, and he could see she was steeling herself to do whatever dirty work Brandt had sent her to do. He felt sorry for her.

"It's OK," he said quietly, so the microphones couldn't pick it up. "Do what you gotta do."

She gave a slight nod and smile and continued, forcing her voice to be louder than normal. "As Temporary Sheriff of the Indiana Supreme Court, I have the duty to inform you that the Court has removed you from office as Sheriff of Howarth County Indiana for failure to perform duty. Please forfeit your badge and your gun."

Tip spoke loudly enough for the microphones. "Jim Brandt is too busy to come and do this himself?"

The troopers closed in.

"Your badge and gun, Mr. Tungate," demanded the Lieutenant Governor.

Tip removed his badge and handed it to her. Then, using only his thumb and forefinger to keep the State boys from getting jumpy, he pulled his weapon from its holster and handed it to her. She recoiled in disgust, and one of the troopers took it. Tip turned to face the cameras.

"Since the governor's allies on the Supreme Court have now given him control of the investigation into our string of shootings, he's going to need all the help he can get from you, the public. So I ask you—"

"That's enough, Tungate," snapped one of the troopers, step-ping between him and the camera and pushing him back roughly. "No statements."

"You just assaulted me," said Tip calmly. "And violated my first amendment rights. Touch me again and I'll hurt you."

One cameraman moved a few feet to his right and squatted down, in anticipation of the action. The trooper bristled and said, "That's a threat to an officer of the law." He reached for his cuffs. "Turn around."

"Go to hell," said Tip.

The trooper, one of the two on Brandt's personal protection detail, signaled to his squad members to surround Tip, but Schulman shook her head. "Let him be," she said quietly. She, at least, understood political messaging: Tip was incompetent, so he was out, per an efficient-manager governor; but the governor was no sponsor of jack-boot policing.

Tip turned back to the cameras and continued what he had started. "This string of shootings is the biggest threat Sedalia has ever faced. We all need to hang together, because it's not clear who might be next. Looks like I'm out, so any tips you have, tell the new sheriff instead of me. He or she will need all the help they can get." Then he turned to Schulman. "Who *has* the governor decided to make the new sheriff?"

She looked relieved. "Chester Biggle will be acting sheriff until the next election, and District Attorney Samantha Parr will be the governor's Special Prosecutor for this case."

Tip touched the brim of his hat in a salute. "For Sedalia's sake, I wish them success."

And with that, he strode off, but then turned in afterthought and said, "Ah. The Department SUV. Guess I don't have it any more." He tossed the SUV keys to Schulman. Who dropped them.

* * *

There was a temporary sense of lightness of heart, of freedom, of the lifting of a terrible burden as he walked home, no more than a mile out to the railroad house. The lilacs, redbuds, and dogwoods were in bloom. The dandelions had passed, and people had cleaned up mole hills and mowed a few times, so yards were perfect green carpets on the spring-moist soil. Retirees working in their yards waved and called "Hey Tip" when he walked by. Some wanted to schmooze, and all were curious about why he was walking.

"SUV break down, Tip?"

"Decide to walk off some of the winter, Tip?"

"Looking for clues, Tip?"

And in each case, rather than spend ten minutes explaining his situation, he just said, "You'll want to watch the local news tonight. All will become clear."

\* \* \*

Katy was outraged. "After all these years you've served the county?"

He shrugged. "Politics is a blood sport. Brandt knows this will piss off the voters in Howarth County, but voters in the rest of the state will see how decisive and effective he is, getting rid of a sheriff who lets three shootings happen in his bailiwick without catching anybody." He gave a mean grin. "Of course, now he and Samantha Parr and Chet have to catch the bastard. But even if they don't, Brandt will be clean. It'll be Chet's fault, and he'll drop him like a dog turd. Even drop Samantha if he has to. Even though she's his protégé."

But deep down, he was gratified that Katy cared. Home two days, and her whole attitude toward him had changed. Maybe it's the wisdom of age, he thought.

Or maybe it's just that he was the only one who cared enough to protect her against the faceless threats that had brought her back to Indiana.

\* \* \*

142

Which would eventually send him to Big Iva for help. He had little doubt she had friends and allies in low places who could help find what Margolis couldn't. Or didn't.

But first, he needed transport. Katy had to be ready to run at any time, given the threats, so no way he could use the F-150 and leave her home with nothing to drive. Which meant he needed another vehicle. Preferably something with serious power, like the SUV interceptor. Just because Brandt had decided to take his badge didn't mean he was going to stop working the cases.

First, he had Katy drive him to the bank. He had twenty-eight thousand four hundred and change in his account there, all the money he had in the world, forget retiring, and he took out five thousand in cash.

"Going on a trip, Tip?" asked Jim Brock, the bank president, looking at the pile of hundreds the teller counted out. "Awful lot of money. Sorry about your job. Brandt's certainly not going to get my vote when he runs for reelection."

"Just need some operating cash, Jim. Also got a house guest. Eats like a horse."

Brock looked through the plate glass at Katy leaning against the front of the pick-up. She was wearing jeans and a work shirt but still looked terrific. "Sure doesn't look like it's hurting her figure. Nice that she came to visit, though Tip. I know you missed her."

That was the damnedest thing about Sedalia. Everybody knew everything, your whole life history, and they could push your most sensitive button at any time. Without effort.

"Yeah I did. Happy she's back."

He stuffed the fifty hundred-dollar bills into his shirt pocket and had Katy drive him out to Luther McConnell's place. The mudholes in the lane had dried up, but the foliage was now on thick enough that you couldn't see the place until you were well back the lane.

"You sure you know what you're doing, Dad? This looks like a good place to get shot as a trespasser, then buried, and nobody would ever know where you went."

"Well, you're not far wrong. I put Luther away a few years ago for meth dealing, and he wouldn't shed any tears over me if I met with an accident. Even so, I still keep tabs on him. But we're here to see Toby, his son. Just drive up nice and slow, circle around the barn lot, and park facing the road so we can leave quickly if we need to."

"Right. Sounds really safe."

She did as asked, and he was happy to see that the '68 Chevy truck was there, though now in the paint shop and painted a uniform primer gray, which covered the Bondo and made it look pretty good.

He reached over and tooted the horn, then told her to stay close to the truck, and leave the keys in the ignition. He got out and slowly approached the barn-size workshop.

The screen door to the main house banged, and Toby came tearing across the parking area.

"What the hell, Tip? I thought I was done with you. You got some other crime you're looking to hang on a McConnell?"

Tip gave his best smile. "Nah. Thought we might do a little business."

"What kind of business?"

"That truck." Tip nodded toward it. "Got it running?"

Toby sensed the change and started to play coy. "Could be. Who's asking? And by the way, who's the babe?" His eyes moved up and down Katy's form, drinking it all in.

"The babe is my daughter. Katy. Katy, meet Toby McConnell. Toby, Katy. Stay away from her or die."

Katy nodded. McConnell flashed a smile. "OK, sorry. Nice to meet you. Katy." He turned his attention back to Tip. "So what about the truck?"

"For sale?"

"Might be."

"Running good?" Tip knew it was supposed to be "running well," but when you're talking about rebuilt cars, it's "running good." Otherwise, people think you're some kind of dick.

"Why? You wanna buy it?"

"Maybe, maybe not."

And so on.

Toby started it up for Tip. It sounded sweet.

"Magnaflow exhaust system, Edelbrock cam, new pistons," bragged Toby. "I'm gonna drive it myself." Standard ploy. He looked sidewise at Tip.

"Well, I was going to offer you a good price. But I guess I'll have to go somewhere else."

"How good?"

"What do you reckon a good price would be?"

And so on.

Eventually, Tip bought the truck for thirty-five hundred. Powerful engine, overhauled, redone body. Needed new tires was all. 3.73 rear-end ratio, so, not so great for pick-up, but decent for speed. And absolutely unnoticeable in Sedalia, where every other pick-up truck was covered with Bondo patches or gray primer, or both.

"Never realized you were a motorhead," said Katy after they both climbed out of their trucks in the driveway at the railroad house.

"Every boy who grows up in Sedalia is a motorhead to some extent." He looked at her sidewise and raised an eyebrow. "Could be other things you don't know about me, too."

"And vice-versa," she said, returning the glance.

# CHAPTER TWENTY

Tip went in to Big Iva's, took off the black baseball cap he wore now that he couldn't wear his Smokey hat, and stood quietly in the center of the dining area. He waited, hat in hand, for Big Iva to notice him.

Patsy Cline was singing "I Fall to Pieces" on the sound system. The smell of clean hot grease and frying onions lay on the air. A trucker sat on a breakfast-bar stool eating chicken-fried steak and gravy, his Cummins hat on the counter beside him. Another played the ancient pinball machine in the right-hand corner. Down at the left end of the dining room, Big Iva hulked in her chair looking at something on a clipboard. She wore an Elvis T shirt and her usual expansive denim pants. Al Stefano, the Porters man, waited beside her. She scrawled a signature and handed the clipboard back to him. Her oak love seat creaked as she shifted her mass to sit back.

Then she spied Tip.

"What in the HELL are you doing here?" she bellowed. Al winked at Tip and beat a hasty retreat. The customer at the breakfast counter put on his hat, slapped a bill on the counter, and took a final few bites. Then he, too, was out the door.

She leaned forward threateningly in her chair, pointed at Tip, and hooked a thumb toward the door. "OUT! You can't help me any more! I warned you they were after me, you piece of shit! Now the docs are saying Missy's arm will never be the same, and you let it happen! And now you're out so you can't DO a damn thing." She pointed at the door. "Out!" Her face was a swelling lava bed, threatening to burst forth.

He spoke in soothing tones. "I'm sorry as hell about Missy, Iva. We came close, but it wasn't good enough. And now I need your help."

"You want my *help*?" She wasn't done ranting. She leaned forward aggressively and her oak chair squeaked in protest. "You do know I've hired *armed guards* to sit outside her hospital room? 'Cause I don't think the bastards are done. And now you can't protect her." She raised a massive arm and jabbed her finger at him. "Goddamn jackleg excuse for a sheriff!"

Tip kept his voice calm. "Nope. Didn't know about the armed guards. But the Indy police should be doing that. And I'm still on the case. Just on my own."

Iva cocked an eye at him and blew a brassy curl off her forehead. She seemed to calm a bit and pushed her face forward. "You're still working the case?'

He nodded.

"Indy cops don't see it as a stalking case," she sneered. "To them, it was random violence that happened outside their jurisdiction. That way they don't have to guard her. And the State boys say they're undermanned. The usual crap. You need something from the government, they do a fast fade. They want something from you, they threaten you with prison."

"Not surprised. But good you're having her guarded, because I don't think they're done either."

"Goddamn right. Those Russian bastards won't give up. And your pissant deputy doesn't have a clue. Have you told him and this prissy little DA everything?"

"Nope."

"Why not?"

"Good question. So far, because I didn't want to get you into trouble for shooting Armando Dalek and his buddies last year."

"You got no proof of that."

"Damn it, Iva, get real. I know what happened. They tried to shake you down, you told them to go screw themselves, one took a shot at you, Cindy shot him from behind the counter, then the gunfight erupted, and you and Cindy shot them all. Then you had them hauled away in a reefer truck and dumped in Kentucky."

She heaved a sigh. "Not saying it happened that way, but sounds like something that could have happened."

"And I was too damn stupid to look back in the kitchen, where you must have had their bodies when I came in."

Big Iva said nothing.

"And if I shared my theory with Samantha, she would have used it against me to get me thrown out of office for incompetence or criminal collusion."

"Well?"

"Well, it *was* incompetence. But now it doesn't make any difference. To me. But how about you? You want me to tell them my version of that story? You ready to deal with that?"

Big Iva sat back. "Maybe not so much. Wouldn't accomplish anything."

"Didn't think so. But it might." He told her about Dalek's brother. She sat up straight.

"So you have made some progress." She sat back, calmer now.

"Yeah, but he's not the shooter, just the lookout. There's somebody else, and somebody local is feeding the bad guys information. Which is the other reason I haven't involved Chet. Thought maybe he was the source, even if he doesn't know it."

"Ah. I see the local angle. You mean because the murder victims were both going to die soon anyway, from cancer. And only somebody local would know that."

"Yup. How did you know that?"

"Got my sources."

"Damn it, Iva. Tell me. Could lead to the murderer."

"Mrs. Aubrey. Comes and sells me her cinnamon rolls. Drivers love them. She gives me updates on the smallest details of Sedalia life. She was on the prayer circle for George and the girl both."

"Ah, jeez. She neglected to tell me that. If she knew, anybody in town could know."

"Yup.

"All right. I'll tell Samantha everything. Except my . . . theory about Dalek. Which Chet knows, but keeps quiet for the same reason I do. But she and Chet and Temple won't get it by themselves. If I was in over my head, they're swimming in the ocean. Look, Iva. I'm still going to catch these guys. They've declared war on my town. And now, my family. And that's why I'm here. I need some help."

He told her about the threats to Katy, and how the timing coincidence was too much to believe. He needed some hacking work done to check out the threat calls to Katy, and now Temple was no longer available to him.

"Ah," nodded Iva. "Didn't know that was why Katy was home. There's naturally a lot of talk."

"I'm sure. But nobody else knows why. Don't want them too, either."

"Got it." She shook her head and sighed. "All right, I'll help."

She told him about her personal hacker, a guy who went by the screen name of Saruman, a guy who had been in Naval Intelligence, but who looked like a pure stoner. "Works in an internet service store on south Meridian in Indy. Gets pissy at times, but if he does, just say 'Barbry Ellen.' We have, let's say, a history. Don't wear your uniform. It'll cost you at least a thousand. Cash."

"Umph. OK."

"Running short? Could lend you some."

Tip knew about her interest rates. "Nah. I'll be all right. Just need some things, is all. Couple of good weapons, since they took my Glock. And Katy has my .38."

"See Ralph at Ralph's Sporting. I got an . . . account there."

"I imagine you do."

"Since you're now unofficial, you might want to take advantage of Ralph's special inventory: clean used guns with no record of ownership."

Tip didn't like that, not at all, but decided not to let on. He knew Ralph ran close to the edge on some things, but federal fire-arms violations were where he drew the line. Until now. He might consider it. Without a badge, he might end up having to shoot a bad guy anonymously.

* * *

Saruman had hair down to his ass and wore a Death Metal T Shirt. Tip hated him on sight. And he could tell the feeling was mutual. Even though he wore an old pair of cotton work pants from Sears, and a biker T shirt that said, "Kill 'em all and let God sort 'em out," he looked like a cop. Somehow it seeped into the DNA and came back out the pores. Once a cop, you always looked like a cop.

"I don't do business with cops," said Saruman. "There's the door."

"Not a cop," said Tip. "Not since yesterday morning. Sedalia."

"Ah," said Saruman. "You're that cop. Suck job, man. Jim Brandt is an asshole. So let me guess. It's like TV, and now you're working the case on your own."

"Something like that."

"Cool. You do know what I do is illegal. And you'll be breaking the law if you pay me to do it. And I'm not cheap."

"I do know all that."

"So first, how'd you get my name? As if I didn't know, you coming from Sedalia."

"Big Iva."

"That sow. Once she gets something on you, you're never free of her."

"I'm aware."

"And she told you to say a special phrase if I wouldn't cooperate."

"She did."

"So say it."

"Barbry Ellen."

"Damn that woman. All right. What do you need? And it's one thousand bucks, on the countertop, right now, before I do anything."

Tip plunked down ten Benjamins from his shirt pocket, plus the blocked phone numbers from Margolis. "Who are they, names and addresses, who have hey talked to in the last thirty days, and where were they when they talked?"

"Gotcha. You want recordings of any calls? Another two hundred per call. I gotta hack a secret government database.

Serious jail time to get caught, but I know how to cover my tracks."

Tip fished out the two hundred. "The last one from this list to this number." He provided Katy's number.

"OK. This could take awhile. Come back tomorrow, and I should be done."

* * *

Ralph Burke of Ralph's Sporting was about five nine, well-fed, with brown hair and blue eyes of unearthly clarity that always looked directly at yours. If you looked away, he would move back in front of you to maintain the lock. This gave an impression of over-voltage somewhere in the system as if somewhere inside was a person waiting to go bazingo. But he had been running a successful business for thirty years, and people had grown adjusted to his quirks, his opinion-page rants, and his preparations for the total breakdown of civil order. Sealed plastic buckets of survival food, $49.99, guaranteed to feed a person for one month, sat in a row before the counter.

"Never thought to see you in here, Tip. Except to arrest me for some bogus violation of the illegitimate laws of our dictatorial federal government. I know I'm not your favorite person. 'Specially after you sent me and the boys on wild goose chases the other night." He squinted a challenge.

Tip shook his head in denial. "Nah. I was wrong about the next target and the time, but not the need to protect those people." He ignored the favorite-person comment. "Look, I had to give up my Glock. Need a couple of good weapons, Ralph. Right away."

Ralph smiled. "I heard. So, you going rogue?" This was clearly an idea that appealed to him. "Don't blame you. Brandt playing politics like that. And us with a terrorist loose in town.

And Biggle in charge? Give me a break. What are you looking for?"

"Most accurate .45 you got, and the cheapest AR15. Plus ammo for each."

"Well, that'd be the Springfield GI M1911 for a thousand bucks, and an Adams Arms AR for $750."

"Holy shit, I'm not trying to buy a house."

"Iva said you might react like that."

"Iva called ahead?"

"Yeah. Said you don't have much money, but help you out anyway. Put it on her account if necessary. Tell you what. This is serious for Sedalia, so give me a hundred each and your promise to return them unscratched, and I'll loan them both to you. And give you fifty rounds for each. And some free jerky. Venison. Made it myself. That's all if you stop screwing with me if you get to be sheriff again."

"All right. I think you're safe in any case, 'cause long as we got Brandt, my sheriffing days are over. Also need a game camera."

Ralph perked up. "You got leads? A place to surveil?"

"I do. Can't say where."

"Like to sell you one, but mine are all top quality, and expensive. You're better off buying a cheap one at Huge Mart. It'll work well enough."

"Great. You got walkie talkies?"

"Sure."

"Your, uh, public safety committee boys got walkie talkies?"

Now Ralph was on full alert. "Sure. Tip, you need our help, we're ready. Just let us know."

Tip had been in exactly three gunfights in his life, if you counted the sniper's shot from the rise, and he dearly hoped he never experienced another. He was always amazed at people who seemed eager.

"Hope it doesn't come to that, 'cause it could mean a gunfight. But I'll keep that in mind."

"Want my cell number?"

"Got pretty much everybody in town. Comes in handy. I'll let you know."

## CHAPTER TWENTY-ONE

The '68 Chevy with the 348 Tri-Power was fun to drive because of its brute power. Three deuces—two-barrel carburetors—sat on the intake manifold dumping in gas like it was 1968. Hitting the accelerator got Tip's juices flowing like they did hadn't since he was a young man. On I-65 headed up to Indy he got a speeding ticket. It was Jasper, a state bull he knew.

"What the hell, Tip? You lose your badge, you revert to hickdom?" He nodded at the primered truck. "Start drag racing?"

Tip smiled. "Pretty much. Confess I used to be a motorhead, and couldn't resist this truck. Or passing that asshole in the Charger so he couldn't cut me off again. So, you got me."

"That asshole in the Charger is Crimmens. New guy in an unmarked. He gets a little . . . exuberant."

Tip sighed. "You dicks. All right. You got no choice but to give me a ticket. I was in fact, speeding." He smiled his best smile.

Jasper shrugged. "No remorse? All right. Your hundred eighty bucks."

"HUNDRED EIGHTY? Jesus! You do know I'm out of a job?"

"Too late. You confessed. And that's the rate for the speed you were going." He handed Tip the ticket. "Slow it down. . ., uh, Mr. Tungate."

* * *

Back home at the railroad house, he plugged Saruman's jump drive into the outdated desktop in his "office," an otherwise empty bedroom with a card table, folding chair, and the computer. Katy was rustling around in the living room, talking with Lucy Smith, the cleaning lady, answering her questions about what it was like to live in New York City. He figured it was safe to look at the data until Lucy left.

The phones naturally all turned out to be burners, except for Katy's. That was the bad news. The good news was that cell-tower triangulation had become a refined science, and locations where calls originated were identifiable by address. Nearly all came from a Polish/Russian restaurant in Cicero, Illinois, that had also been on Big Iva's list. Three went to Katy's number, two went to a phone that was in the Bronx when answered. And there was one from a New York number to Katy's number on the day she left. And here was the odd part. Three went *back and forth*— three each direction—between the Cicero location and:  a place near the VA in Indy.

Hammadi.

Of course, there was no smoking gun. Just a gigantic set of coincidences. And an overwhelming question:  what did George Sampson, Jennifer Clarkson, Missy, and Katy all have in common? And why target Tom Burton for patsy? It made no sense. But clearly, there was a common thread. And somehow, Hammadi was the key.

With Missy, the target was clearly Big Iva. Missy was dear to her, so the Russkis struck her favorite. And he could make the same kind of case for Katy: that they were trying to get at him through her. But why? What had he ever done to piss off the Russian mob? Other than not arrest Big Iva for their buddy's killing.

It had occurred to him a couple of times that more than one motive and more than one bad guy, or set of bad guys, might be involved. But he didn't believe in coincidences that big. And the note in his mailbox seemed to close off that avenue of thought.

He forced himself to listen to the recording of the last phone call to Katy, the one that drove her to end her ten-year estrangement with him. He turned the volume down so she wouldn't hear and come into the room. First, there was her bright voice saying hello, as if she was expecting a good friend. Then the heavy breathing, her saying who is this, and then finally the voice, with a New York thug accent: "Too bad you're gonna be dead in twenty-four hours, Baby. You're too good to waste. If it wasn't for DNA, I'd help myself first, then shoot you." Click.

Tip's vision clouded with rage, and his chest heaved. His mind filled with the violent things he would do with this son of a bitch. If only he knew how to find him.

"How did you get that, Dad?" came her voice from behind him. He hadn't heard her approach on the old high-profile carpet. He turned. She stood in the doorway.

"Never mind, Katy." He was barely able to speak. "Had to do something illegal you don't need to know about. Just know I'm gonna get the bastard." He forced himself to smile. "Look, I'm gonna have to go away for a day or so. I'll have my cell with me. Think you can take care of yourself here?"

She hesitated, looking worried, then forced a smile. "Sure, Dad. Just don't do anything to get yourself killed. I'm, uh, sorry. About, um, all the years. I was young."

His chest felt like it would explode. As if she wasn't still young. He fought back the emotion. "I'm glad you've come back, Sweetheart. At least temporarily. I know your life is in Manhattan, so I'm gonna make that safe again for you."

She came and kissed him on his bald spot. "Be careful, Dad." Then she left the room.

He heaved a sigh and took an extra blood pressure pill. Well, all right, he conceded to himself, he took the one he was supposed to have taken that morning, but he hated taking them, despite Doc Quick's warning that, even if he wasn't old, he could kill himself with bad diet and lack of fitness. He would start the cardio-pulmonary exercises—the running—just as soon as all this murder stuff was over. No kidding. No excuses.

The location for that last, threatening call had been Penn Station, the 7$^{th}$ Ave. exit. Totally worthless information. Except that online information suggested that exit as the best place to catch a Taxi going downtown. Where Katy lived, near Battery Park. Guy carrying a weapon would likely take a taxi instead of the subway, where his weapon might be detected. Sweat beaded up on Tip's forehead. Sweet Jesus, had the guy been on his way to kill her when he called? No way to know. Based on the time stamp, she had immediately called Sedalia, grabbed her go bag, and headed for LaGuardia. So this was one call she probably hadn't told Margolis about.

Didn't matter. What was clear was that a guy or group of guys who hung out in a Russian restaurant in Cicero, Illinois, had connections in New York, enough to get a hit man, or at least a guy to act like a hit man. And that same crew had some kind of connection to Dr. Hammadi at the VA. Or he to them. And they had connections to Andrei Dalek and Robert Miklaczewski, the

Chicago lawyer, both of whom looked suspicious as hell, particularly lookout man Dalek.

He ran the narrative through his head again to see if there was something he had missed. The mob guys are pissed off at Iva for shooting their guys last year, so maybe they reconnoiter and find out Iva keeps too close a watch for them to plant a bomb. So they send a hit man to shoot Missy. He misses, maybe accidentally, maybe on purpose. But what was the connection to George Sampson and Jennifer Clarkson? And why try to implicate Tom Burton? And why threaten Katy? How did they even know who she was?

He still just couldn't get it.

But it was clear he had to roust Hammadi. And he had to go to Cicero and meet the people in that restaurant. Maybe kick ass. Maybe it would be like in the movies. The head mobster either owns the restaurant, or hangs out there because the owner is too afraid to kick him out. The Big Guy sits at a back table holding court, eating while all his minions watch. Big, ugly guys in tight jackets with guns bulging under them stand around. There are few other patrons. Tip walks in. The big guy says, "Who the hell are you?" And Tip says, "I'm your worst nightmare." Then he cleans house. All the bad guys die or go to the hospital. Tip at most gets a busted knuckle.

But he knew it wouldn't be like that. Caution was called for, because in the crime novels he secretly read for entertainment, Russian mob guys were all former KGB agents who knew how to fight, and knew how to kill people with impunity. Worse, he would be outnumbered, and he might not even be able to recognize who was in charge. So he needed a plan.

* * *

Hammadi readily agreed to meet, apparently thinking he was still Sheriff and just wanted to ask more questions about Burton. Tip let him think both without saying either. So far, hacking and invasion of privacy were the only things on his potential rap sheet, so to avoid impersonating a law officer, he had carefully identified himself only as Tip Tungate when he called.

But by the time he got there, Hammadi had apparently googled him and found that he had been booted out.

"I not required, talk to you, Mr. Tungate," he said. There was extra emphasis on the "Mister."

"Of course you aren't," said Tip. "But even though I've been replaced, I still am curious about some things. Just trying to satisfy my own curiosity. About Tom Burton, that is."

"Patient records are private, require search warrant."

"You talked to me before."

"You were officer of law before. I was courteous, but I give no real confidential information."

"What connection do you have to the Russian mob?"

Hammadi's expression showed brief surprise, quickly covered up. "Please leave, Mr. Tungate. Or I call security."

"Pretty much what I expected. I'll be seeing you around, Hammadi. By the way, how long have you been in this country?"

"I am American citizen."

"Didn't say you weren't. Just curious. I met a lot of people named Hammadi in Kuwait and Iraq."

A sudden look of pure hatred crossed Hammadi's face. He tried but couldn't control it. His mouth opened and closed twice as he apparently stopped himself from speaking.

"It is common name," he finally said. "Much less common than before wars killed so many. But it will recover." Then his face darkened and his mouth screwed up, as if he was trying to keep something in that wanted to come out. He failed. "And it will be avenged, *insha'Allah*. Get out, Mr. Tungate."

He glared at Tip with an unsettling intensity. Tip looked into those dark eyes and said to himself, this guy is off his rocker, but he said nothing aloud. But oddly, at that moment, he had a flash of the recurring dream, which he quickly suppressed.

"Very unfortunate, those wars," said Tip. "Too bad they got started. Where you from in Iraq, Dr. Hammadi?"

"I didn't say I was from Iraq. I said, get out."

"I didn't say you did. But I'm betting you're originally from Iraq."

"Get out, Mr. Tungate." He picked up the receiver from the phone on his desk and punched a speed-dial button.

"Be seeing you around, Dr. Hammadi."

Tip passed the security people in the hall, two big men wearing uniforms but carrying no weapons, probably vets by the look of them: age, haircut, resigned, no-bullshit expressions. One turned around and looked at Tip quizzically.

"Just leaving, just leaving. You men have a nice day."

* * *

Something there, something there, but Hammadi wasn't the shooter. Provably in other locations when the shooting occurred. More, it was impossible to explain any connection to the shooter. What could a disaffected Iraqi-American have to do with the Russian mob?

He went back to Sedalia to think. Driving the streets the way he had done for more than a decade as sheriff helped him to clarify his mind. He had an idea and parked in the fisherman's pull-off by the Sedalia bridge over the Wapamoni.

He would give Agent Sanchez at the FBI's Asian Organized Crime Unit a try. Maybe he hadn't heard.

He had.

"I can't talk to you, Tungate. Not only are you no longer an officer of the law, if you ever actually were more so than in name only, you're a person of interest in an ongoing investigation into racketeering."

"Come on, Sanchez. You know damn well I'm not a racketeer. Look at my bank account."

"Didn't say you were a smart racketeer."

"So you're trying to get me to roll on Godiva Randall."

"Correct."

"Look, I'll tell you everything I know about Big Iva if you tell me what I want to know about the boys at the Golden Samovar in Cicero, and about a guy by the name of Halif Hammadi who works at the VA in Indianapolis."

There was a brief pause, then, "Maybe. Putting you on hold just a second."

To ask his superiors. For crying out loud. Did nobody make any decisions himself any more?

Sanchez came back. "OK. So you'll testify against her?"

"Didn't say that. Said I'd tell you everything I know. Not the same thing. What I know won't convict her of anything, but it still might be useful to you."

Another long pause, followed by a sigh.

"You're dirty as hell, Tungate. I know it, you know it, and we all know it. We'll get you in the end. All right. You first."

Tip told the story of the shootout at Big Iva's. The twin stolen Escalades. The absence of bodies. Big Iva's wound. The blood on the floor that Cindy washed away with bleach before he could get a sample. His suspicion, without proof, that Armando Dalek, Cicero Illinois, found in the Cumberland River a few days later, had been one of the drivers. His suspicion that the mobsters had tried to shake Big Iva down, thus precipitating a gunfight. His own shameful incompetence in failing to check the kitchen to see if there were any corpses in there. Big Iva's worry that the Russian mob was after her, thus precipitating his first call to Sanchez. And his collar of Andrei Dalek, almost certainly serving as lookout man for the local shooter. And the brother of Armando Dalek. He naturally left out the part about the calls to Katy.

"You're right. Some of that may be useful."

"Now your turn, Sanchez. What do you know about Halif Hammadi?"

"He's on a terrorist watch list."

"Why?"

"He regularly attends a mosque in Indianapolis with a radical-ized imam."

"That's it? So everybody who goes to that mosque is on the watch list?"

"Pretty much. How do you know about the Golden Samovar?"

Damn it. Forgot he'd found that out illegally. "Dalek is a Polish name. Looked up Polish restaurants in Cicero. Got a blip out of Andrei Dalek on it when I was questioning him."

"By 'questioning,' do you mean, beating the hell out of him?"

"Different people have different methods."

"It's a center of Russian mob organized crime in the Chicago area. Stay away from it. Otherwise, next time we talk, you'll likely be dead."

"Who is Mr. Big?"

"That would be Roman Dalek, the old man. Eighty if he's a day, but no one knows for sure."

Something occurred to Tip. "You're the organized crime unit. Why do you know about somebody on the terror watch list."

"Because there's a Chechen mobster we're watching who goes to the same mosque."

Tip knew about Chechnya. You couldn't spend a tour in the Middle East without continuing to follow up on the millennia-long struggle between Sunni and Shia, and Muslims and the west.

"Ah. The Chechen connection you mentioned before. Tell me more."

"Nope. That's all you get. Do not tell Godiva Randall what you told me about her."

"Gotcha."

* * *

He drove to Big Iva's to tell her about the conversation.

"It's all right, Tip. You didn't really give him anything. So, you gonna go after this Dalek guy in Chicago?"

"Cicero, but yeah. Just trying to figure out how to keep from getting myself killed."

# CHAPTER TWENTY-TWO

The game cameras were in place, one in the lilac bush in front of the house, and the other in a cedar tree out back, so that both the front and the back of the house were covered.

If anyone snuck around casing the place, day or night, he would get them on camera. Still, he didn't tell Katy about the cameras, the note in the mailbox, or his suspicions about connections between her New York harassers and the local bad actors. She didn't need worries she could do nothing about. But she was no fool. She knew there was a reason he had given her the old .38.

With these precautions in place, he got into the '68 Chevy and headed for Ralph's Sporting. On the way, he called. Ralph answered immediately.

"A favor, Ralph." He didn't bother to introduce himself. It still freaked him out a little bit, Luddite that he was, that everyone in the universe knew who you were when you called, even if they didn't recognize your voice.

"Might cost you, Tip."

"Figured. Probably worth the price. Going out of town for a day, maybe two, maybe three. Need somebody to watch over Katy without her knowing. Think your guys would be willing to do that?"

Ralph chuckled. "Based on the way I hear Katy looks these days, I expect I could get a lot of volunteers."

Tip pulled in to Ralph's parking lot and walked through the front door, still talking to Ralph on his cell phone. No one else was in the store. Both chuckled and put away their phones. Tip put both hands flat on Ralph's glass display case before he remembered: Ralph hated that because he constantly had to wipe people's fingerprints off. Tip smiled and used Ralph's ever-present cloth to clean the glass himself.

"Look, Ralph, I'm onto some seriously evil people. Major badass. People who stop at nothing. They're after Katy to get to me. Don't know exactly why yet. So I'm disappearing for a couple of days. To go . . . look them up . . . and find out. Think you can keep all that under your hat?"

There was a long silence. Ralph's clear-eyed, unblinking gaze bored into Tip.

"What are you into, Tip? You need some boys to go with you? I know some who will. Whatever it is you're doing."

Tip imagined the boys who would go with him: out-of-work guys who survived on deer meat, food stamps, beer, and popcorn. Guys laid off from the headlight factory in Elmira. He saw them as guys who liked running around at night with weapons, like boys playing capture the flag, but had no appetite for a real fight. When it came down to it, no sane person did.

"That's all right, Ralph. Appreciate the offer, but I don't want to get anybody else hurt." He handed Ralph a folded slip of paper.

The "else" reverberated for a moment in the silence.

"Gotcha. All right, Tip. You be careful. We'll make sure nothing happens to Katy. What's on the paper?"

"The address where I died if I don't come back."

Ralph didn't blink, but his eyebrows rose. Tip dug out his wallet and handed Ralph his credit card.

"Be great if you'd use this a couple of times a day till I get back. Fill your tank one day, fill your gas cans another day. At Altemeyer's. He's got no security cameras."

It took Ralph only a few seconds, then he nodded a conspiratorial smile.

"Ah. You bet, Tip."

\* \* \*

On his way north up I-65 to Chicago, Chet called.

"You neglected to make case notes on everything you know," accused Chet. "Temple and I are under pressure to come up with an arrest. We're looking hard at Burton."

"You got nothing."

"Yeah, but we're under a lot of pressure. The governor actually called and talked to me. I think you know a lot more than you've told us."

"I got a lot of supposition. But it's not worth much. Tell you what. Work on this awhile. Andrei Dalek was the lookout for the Missy shooting. Can't prove it, but no doubt in my mind. And here's the angle: somebody in Sedalia is the shooter, or somebody in Sedalia is feeding information to the shooter. The shooter knew George Sampson and Jennifer Clarkson both had fatal diseases. Left me a note in my mailbox."

Chet fell silent. "Left you a note? Why didn't you say anything? Jesus, Tip. That's evidence."

"Standard font, computer printer, simple wording. Nothing traceable. And no proof it was even left by the shooter. But it was. That's the only piece of hard, legal evidence I've not told you about. So I'm telling you now. It's in the SUV glove compartment. Figure out how he knew about their health conditions if he's from outside, or who from Sedalia had opportunity and motive, and you've got the shooter."

Chet sighed. Somehow, even his sigh communicated more sense of newfound responsibility than Tip had ever seen him display.

"Thanks a lot. What about motive?"

"Damned if I know. Good luck. Pray that your term as sheriff doesn't set new records for shortness."

"Thanks a hell of a lot, Tip. I know you're just waiting for me to fail."

"Actually, Chet, given what Sedalia is up against, for the first time in our relationship, I'm rooting for you."

\* \* \*

The Golden Samovar was surrounded 360 by nearly empty parking lot: two black Escalades in front, and a beater Toyota in back. The cook. No trees, bushes, nearby utility sheds, or perimeter fences offered cover to a running man. Not a coincidence, Tip was sure. The nearest cover was a tired strip mall four blocks away with enough cars in the lot to hide among. Tip parked there and unlimbered Dalek's binoculars. The department's nice Zeiss binoculars were no longer available to him.

His first plan, while driving north through the flatlands of northwest Indiana, was simple: go in and order a meal and scope out the situation. Identify Mr. Big if he was there, based on the people kowtowing to him, follow him home at night, and figure out the best time and place to kidnap him.

Of course it didn't work out that way. It was clear from looking at the situation on the ground—no patrons, though according to its posted hours it was open—that he would draw immediate attention if he walked into the place. His size alone had that effect on people. And then there was the cop look. He might as well have it stamped on his forehead. Even though he was no longer technically a cop.

He watched for hours, walking over twice to a nearby fast-food for coffee and a pit stop. Cars came to the Golden Samovar and went, usually after only ten or twenty minutes, always at least two guys, always dressed in flashy clothes of one kind or another: a few double-breasted suits, but mostly filmy, long-sleeve pull-overs open at the chest, often with gold chains, and a lump at the back or front pocket where the gun was concealed. Some were black, some were white, some were Hispanic. In one case, it was two cops in civilian clothes who parked their cruiser close to him in the strip-mall parking lot and walked down to the restaurant.

He assumed these were payoffs, because while some visitors carried small bags or packages in, all came out empty-handed. Except the cops. So the guy really was Mr. Big, holding court, taking tribute, and making payoffs.

At nearly eight in the evening, when Tip's ass felt as if he couldn't sit for another minute, after no visitors had arrived for more than ninety minutes, four men came out of the restaurant and got into the Escalades. Three were obvious muscle, based on their size versus the SUVs, but one looked to be about five three and eighty years old.

Mr. Big. Had to be. Roman Dalek.

Tip followed the cars at a great distance, because the '68 Chevy was distinctive and easily recognizable among Chicago-area's flashier vehicles. They drove three miles across town into an upscale housing development, nothing super fancy, no gates or guards, but expensive enough to keep the riff-raff out. He watched from five blocks away and around a bend as Dalek got out and walked with a slight limp to his front door. Only when he was safely inside did the cars drive away.

Tip waited for an hour, until it was nearly dark, and made his move. He left the truck outside the subdivision at a convenience store and walked in, feeling the whole time as if he was being watched. The worry was that Mr. Big would have security inside—another goon or two. Or he would have security cameras outside his house, too. Or that his wife would call 911 while Tip was strong-arming him. Or a butler who answered the door wouldn't let him in without a noisy ruckus.

So he decided on a little indirection.

The thing he was counting on turned out to be there. As a homeowner himself, he knew that men were particularly attuned to the sound of water running when it wasn't supposed to. Was it running all over the basement floor? Down through the living-room ceiling from the laundry closet upstairs? Into the garage, soaking the boxes sitting on the floor? The hiss of water running was also difficult to immediately locate, but eventually, the man of the house would check every possibility. And Tip was in luck. Two water spigots protruded from the front of the house, concealed by arborvitae. Tip turned one on, then hid behind a juniper bush beside the front door.

Sure enough, after three minutes, the front door opened, and the little man came out cursing. "Goddamn boys," he said to himself, then something in Polish or Russian.

He stepped down off the front step and headed for the open spigot across from Tip, whose stream was fanned out across the front walk.

Tip grabbed him from behind, one massive arm around his neck, the other hand on the side of his head ready to twist. "Who's in the house?" he demanded.

It took a moment for Dalek to recover some composure. "Four guys who are gonna waste your ass as soon as I scream."

"And then as soon as you scream, you'll be dead. Maybe they'll get me, maybe they won't." He twisted Dalek's neck as far as he dared. "Now, who's in the house?"

"Nobody, damn you. Go in and take what you want."

Tip hauled the man up and through the front door. He was light as a dried-up gourd.

The inside of the house was plain. No fancy furniture, no fancy decorations. Plain drywall. A forty-eight-inch TV was tuned to RT America, where a commentator was criticizing US policy in the Middle East. Still, holding Dalek, Tip found the remote and shut it off.

Then he pushed the small man onto a chair and said, "Who's your shooter in Sedalia?"

"Ah," smiled Dalek. "I thought you looked familiar. You're uglier than your picture."

Tip readied a back-hand slap, but at the last minute thought he heard the floor creak behind him. Then there was a sense of something massive coming into his peripheral vision on his left side.

* * *

He came to in serious pain. It wasn't waking; it was coming to. The left side of his face didn't work, and he couldn't see out of his left eye. His tongue felt swollen and he couldn't bite down. He concluded that his jaw was broken. He seemed to be propped up in a straight-back chair in a store room. Large cans of tomatoes and green beans crowded steel shelves beside him. Dalek sat in a leather office chair in front of him, smoking a cigarette. Ralph's brand-new .45 and a cop's telescopic baton lay in his lap. Under Tip's chair, a square of wrinkled plastic sheeting extended out a few feet in all directions.

"You didn't do your job last summer, Sheriff," said Dalek. "You let that fat sow get away with murdering my son and his associates. Didn't even bring her in for questioning. Now you will pay price. Not just to me, but, let us say, to client for one of our services. You and your stupid little town. You were very foolish to come here, but I heard you were not smart."

Tip spat, trying for Dalek's face, but falling far short, expelling a thick, sticky rope of blood that fell mostly on his own pants.

"You might think I, how you say, admire spirit, but I don't give shit about it. You see, we kill whoever we want, whenever we want, if they get in way. Now, before we, ah, send you to your reward, tell us how you find us. Because that part is problem."

Tip couldn't turn his head much because of the pain, and he had no peripheral vision out of his left eye. In fact, he was pretty sure it was looking in one direction while his right eye looked in another. But it felt like he and Dalek were alone in the room. He didn't sense any other presences. He wished he knew how many there were. And where they were in the house.

"I found you by your smell."

Dalek's hand moved like a snake, flicking out the baton to its full length and whipping it backhand across Tip's face. The good side. The pain was incandescent. He was pretty sure it laid his cheek open, because now his mouth didn't want to work right on that side either. But at least he could still see. And until he was dead, at least, he was on a mission. He wasn't going to cave.

"What was your son *doing* at Big Iva's?" he demanded. Why did she have to defend herself?" It all came out slurred and garbled, but clear enough.

"Not your business. But since you gonna die, fine. I tell you." This all came out in a heavy accent. "Big Iva is pimple on our ass. *We* control cash businesses, Milwaukee to Louisville. Not people like Big Iva. She won't play ball? No protection, no drugs, no laundry? She got to go. But only after we take everything from her, like she did my son. She going to suffer like I have. My first son? Her best girls."

"You started it, asshole, but OK. I understand that. But why is your shooter killing innocent people in Sedalia? An old farmer? A little girl?"

Dalek made a rattling sound in his chest. Tip realized he was laughing.

"Some boys that do this work, they like it too much. Makes them feel smart. Strong. They do for fun. You gotta be careful, even when they work for you." He laughed again. "Na, your guy? Just warming up." He rasped another chuckle. "See, Big Iva is one thing. We also got client. Pays good. So we get good mechanic."

"What client?"

"Somebody you piss off long time back. You and another asshole in your shitty little town. You gotta pay for that, too."

"Who's the shooter, damn it?"

"Think I'm stupid? I got people that make those connections."

"Who made the connection?"

"I tell you what, you big, stupid country boy. I tell you to, how you say, tantalize you, since you gonna die, anyway."

He clicked off the safety on the .45. Tip looked at the size of the bore. Damn, that was going to hurt.

"So who? Let me die at least knowing that."

"The Chechen made the connection."

Tip by now had determined that they were alone. His hearing was very good, and he had heard no other sounds in the house. But then the guy who hit him hadn't made much sound. Still, time to make his move or die. And he had that one piece of information. And Sanchez had mentioned a Chechen.

If he only had a move he could make, since he was duct-taped to the chair.

Except for his feet.

He extended his lower legs upward as far as he could, until they were straight out in front of him. Dalek laughed and pointed the weapon at his face. Tip slammed down his legs and heaved himself up and forward so that he fell across the small void between them and crashed onto Dalek, aiming with his head for the little man's head. The .45 poked hard against his chest, then turned flat between them.

And went off. Something ripped through Tip's chest, and the explosion in his ear sounded like the end of the world. The pain was enormous. He decided he was probably dead.

The two fell onto the floor, the little man's chair falling backward with Tip on top of him. The arm of the office chair poked into Tip's belly and hurt like a son of a bitch, and he decided, OK, I'm not dead.

But Dalek seemed to be. He was not moving. Of course, Tip knew anyone would have a hard time moving under his bulk, so he wasn't taking chances. He bashed his forehead into Dalek's forehead for good measure. There was no response. His forehead felt wet, and he smelled blood.

Suddenly, there was a knock at a door somewhere close.

"You need us to clean up in there boss?" asked a voice. "Take it away?" It sounded like somebody at the bottom of a well, given the ringing still in Tip's ears.

"Not yet," said Tip, trying his best to mimic Dalek's voice and accent. It didn't sound very convincing to him, but no one came in.

After three minutes of wriggling and straining, he managed to get his left arm loose. Whoever had duct-taped him had not taped his wrists together, only taped around his body and arms and the chair.

He found the end of the duct tape and untaped himself. Then he examined his chest. The bullet had plowed a bloody furrow half an inch deep through his left pectoral. He could hardly feel it in comparison to his other pains, and the numbness in his ears.

Dalek, on the other hand, had a neat entrance wound in the bottom of his chin, and part of his forehead was missing.

"Asshole," said Tip. He started to spit on him but decided not to leave any more DNA than necessary.

He found a gallon jug of bleach and a rag, and wiped up all of his own blood that he could find that was not on the Visqueen. Then he rolled up the plastic and stuffed it into a large waste basket.

He found his clasp knife and was digging the slug out of the wall when a knock came again at the door. "You sure you don't need me in there, Boss? Something don't sound right."

Tip jerked the door open with his left hand, the knife in his right. A monster two inches taller than him, with forty more pounds all muscle, faced him with a nine millimeter in his hand. He started to raise it but Tip stabbed him in the side with the still-open knife. The man said "Whoof," and collapsed onto the floor, making desperate grunting sounds. Tip stuffed Ralph's .45 into the back of his pants and took the man's weapon.

"Who's the Chechen?" he demanded. "Where do I find him?"

"Screw you, Jethro," gasped the man. "You're a dead man."

"The only reason you're not," said Tip, "is that I don't shoot people in cold blood. But I'd be happy to defend myself if you want to take a crack at me." He extended the man's Glock toward him.

"Later, asshole," said the man. "I'll get you later."

"Not unless you get the hell out of here."

He retrieved Dalek's cigarette lighter from the floor, lit the papers in the wastebasket containing the plastic with his blood on it, and pocketed the lighter. The flames came up nicely. Then he stepped over the man in the doorway, holding the man's own nine millimeter on him as he did so, and said, "Better move your ass."

* * *

Only when he made it out of the room did Tip realize he probably need not have bothered cleaning up DNA. Any cops who investigated here were probably paid off to not investigate. He was in the dining room of a closed restaurant, resplendent with brocaded gold wallpaper, gold-framed mirrors everywhere there wasn't a window. And on a side table stood a large brass samovar with a sign that said, "Help yourself to good Russian tea."

He was in the Golden Samovar, and he had a good three-mile walk ahead of him back to his truck. He looked at himself in one of the mirrors and realized his appearance would raise a lot of questions if he was stopped. So he cleaned off as much blood as possible with napkins and tea. Meanwhile, the flames grew higher, and he could smell smoke.

Security cameras? Did he need to find and destroy them? Nah, he decided. Place like this would never keep any kind of record of what went on here.

He went back to check on the brute he had stabbed. The guy was nearly unconscious. So Tip wiped the guy's Glock with a napkin, then, careful not to touch it himself, took the guy's hand, wrapped it around the Glock, and fired the weapon through the ceiling. Good. Powder residue on the guy's hand and his weapon.

And a corpse in the store room, whose entrance wound was about to get charred beyond measuring the difference between a nine millimeter and a .45. Let this asshole do the explaining. Then he dragged the thug out the front door and dropped him on the sidewalk with his nine millimeter on top of him. The flames were already invading the dining room.

Satisfied, exhausted, and in serious pain, he took off on foot down the dark, sidewalk-less road leading back to his truck.

He hated cities. He hated big towns. He planned to get the hell out of this city-town and back down to the sweet lands of Howarth County, Indiana, not far north of the Ohio River, and never come back. If he didn't pass out from shock and loss of blood.

Then he was going to find the Chechen.

## CHAPTER TWENTY-THREE

By the time Tip got back to his truck it was three AM and he was worse than exhausted. He just wanted to collapse and sleep. But he knew he needed help. He drove south in a stupor, biting his cheeks to stay awake.

His first stop in Sedalia was Doc Quick's office. It was only seven thirty in the morning, but he knew Doc started at seven. "Some people actually work for a living," Doc had explained. "They can't come to the doctor in the middle of the day, like the Medicare patients. And they sometimes actually pay me without any paperwork."

Tip pulled up in the parking lot behind the office and called Linda McConnell.

"Hey, Linda," he rasped. "Need some help." He knew she would recognize his voice and his number. "Unlock the back door."

"What's wrong, Tip?" She sounded worried. "People know you were gone all day yesterday but nobody knew where. They're worried about you. Thought you might be sulking somewhere. Did you even know somebody tried to kill Katy?"

The bottom dropped out of his stomach.

"*What?*" he croaked. "She OK? Nobody called!"

"She's OK, no thanks to you. People called, but your phone was turned off. Ralph Burke and a couple of other guys had your place staked out, nobody is sure why, and they saw this guy sneaking up in the night. There was a gunfight. Ralph got hit in the leg. The guy got away. What the hell do you mean leaving her alone like that?"

God, how stupid could he be? The New York threats had been a ruse! The whole point had been to drive her back to Sedalia, where the hired shooter could take care of her along with his other targets, whoever the hell they were.

"You're right. It is my fault. These guys have outsmarted me at every step of the way. But right now I really need some help. And I don't want anybody to see me in the front office. I'm, uh, not looking my best."

"*These* guys? There's more than one?"

"Sorry, misspoke. Look, I really do need some help. Privately."

"All right. Give me a minute."

\* \* \*

The steel door opened with a clank. Linda held it open against the tension of the closer. She looked down the two concrete steps at Tip in obvious shock.

"Holy crap, Tip. You look terrible." She looked both ways to make sure nobody saw them. "Come in, come in." She took his elbow and led him down the hall to an examination room, then pointed at the blood on his shirt. "Take off your shirt. I'll get Doc." Then she sniffed. "Whew! You smell bad, too."

"Thanks a lot. I feel better now."

She left to get Doc Quick. They were both back in less than a minute.

"Jesus H. Christ!" said Doc as soon as he saw Tip. "What the hell happened to you? Can you even see out of that eye?"

"Nope. Hurts, too."

"I expect so. Looks like somebody beat the hell out of you. With a stick."

"Yalp. Pretty much. But you oughta see the other guy."

"Well, both cheeks are going to need stitches. After we clean them out. It's gonna hurt." People swore Doc loved to say this, then make it true. "When those cheeks heal, you're going to look like some kind of primitive tribesman. And Tip, I'm not sure about that eye. For right now, I'd say the best thing is to make sure it doesn't get infected. Then wait until the swelling goes down and send you to an ophthalmologist. You could lose it."

"I know."

And what did this?" Quick poked on both sides of the gouge in his chest.

"A fast-moving object."

Quick looked him long in his good eye, then pursed his lips.

"I see. Working the case on your own? Well, I imagine you'll solve it before our hotshot DA and self-inflating governor. You do know, by the way, that Brandt plans to expand Medicare when he becomes President?" He shook his head in ain't-it-awful manner. It was awful. "I might've told you this before, but you know, I have to employ a person for the sole purpose—"

"Doc. I promise I'll vote against Brandt if he runs for President. Right now, I need you to patch me up as best you can and return me to action."

That stopped Quick.

"It's that bad?"

"It's not good. They're after Big Iva, they're after Katy, they're after my town, and they're after me. I'm going to stop it. If that's going rogue, I've gone rogue."

Doc nodded. "Good. Chet Biggle is a sorry excuse for a sheriff. You were gone yesterday, so you may not know. He's arrested Tom Burton and charged him with the murder of Jennifer Clarkson." He shook his head again. The world was going to hell in a handbasket. "But I happen to know Burton was up at the VA that morning."

Tip sighed. He wasn't surprised. Had even expected it. "Chet knows it, too. But it gives him and Samantha and Brandt an opportunity to preen front of the cameras."

"'Preen'?"

"My word of the day last Wednesday."

Doc irrigated the wounds with saline, followed by hydrogen peroxide that foamed and fizzed. Then he threaded a curved needle, clamped it in a hemostat, and looked at Tip.

"Don't have any local anesthetic on hand. Temporarily out. So this is gonna hurt." He smiled an evil smile. "Which do you want first? The cheeks or the chest?"

"Take your pick."

Doc started on his chest. It did hurt, but Tip was determined not to show it. "They'll have to let Burton go pretty much immediately. At most in three days. They got nothing."

"Well, the problem for Burton is, the psychologist he was seeing that morning, who could verify he was there, has disappeared. And Samantha is saying all the other physical proofs of his presence, sign-in sheets and so on, have also disappeared."

"And security videos?"

"Mysteriously missing."

"Ah."

Very neat.

The question was, what had Burton ever done to Hammadi?

\* \* \*

Katy wasn't home when he got there, but came in soon afterward carrying grocery bags. And carrying the .38 in a new shoulder holster. She took one look at him and her face screwed up in horror. She started to rush to him and give him a hug, then hesitated, then did it.

"Who did this to you?"

"The guy who ordered all this to happen. One of them, at least. He won't be giving any more orders. Problem is, things he set in motion are still in motion. And he wasn't the only driving force."

She backed away and looked at him. She clearly wanted to ask the question his use of past tense naturally raised. But she didn't. She crimped her lips and jutted her jaw like his father used to do when he was pissed off and determined. God, genes were mysterious things.

"OK," she said, drawing it out. "What now? And how can I help? Some guy, armed with a pistol, actually tried to sneak in here last night. Ralph Burke and two guys hiding outside saw him first, and they had a gun fight. I got off a couple of shots myself, but I don't think I hit the guy. Beefy guy, polo shirt, mask. It was dark, and I couldn't really see, but there was enough light I could see his arms. Looked dark. I just shot because I could see he was shooting at Ralph, who was clearly trying to protect the house. It would have been good of you to tell me you were putting a bunch of crazy militia types on me as bodyguards," she accused. "I might have shot some of them. Way it was, though, I think they saved my life."

Holy shit, Tip was thinking. Holy shit. It had been a spur-of-the-moment thing to ask Ralph to watch over her. But he couldn't let her see uncertainty.

"I didn't tell you because I didn't want to worry you. How did you know it was Ralph?"

"He yelled who he was and told me to stay in the house and get down. He was in the neighbors' yard in a clump of spirea behind some landscaping bricks. The bad guy apparently came down the tracks and was sneaking toward the back door. With a gun in his hand. They pinned him down behind that old cast iron cauldron sitting back there that somebody used to use as a flower pot. Obviously not you. Anyway, I think my shots drove him away, because he couldn't hide from Ralph and me both behind that cauldron." She pushed away. "Jesus, Dad. You stink."

"I was headed for the shower. He looked down at the .38. "You do know you can be arrested for carrying that in public without a permit."

"Somebody is trying to kill me, Dad. Chet Biggle tries to arrest me for carrying, I'll shoot *his* ass."

Tip couldn't help but smile. The apple and the tree, etc. "You should apply for one."

"Did already. And Ralph gave me this holster. Said carry the gun at all times. Same weird guy he's always been, but he took a bullet for me, so I'm doing what he says."

"Ralph is right. I'm working on it all, but I'm not there yet."

* * *

When he got out of the shower, he was just starting to look with his good eye through the game camera footage from the back yard when his phone rang. Sanchez from the FBI.

"Good morning, Mr. Tungate."

"Word travels fast."

"Indeed it does. Seems there was an unfortunate fire in a Russian restaurant in Cicero. Crispy critter inside. A Mr. Roman Dalek, by DNA analysis. Shot through the chin."

"Do tell. Very unfortunate. Nobody called the fire department?"

"Yes, an anonymous 911, from a burner phone, but too late. Caller sounded physically distressed. There were two kinds of blood on the front sidewalk. Quite a lot from an ex-con, ex-KGB agent named Surov. Local police are searching for him now. I imagine he'll be full of information. And a trail of small spots from somebody else we don't have a sample from. Got any idea who that other person might be?"

"Given Mr. Dalek's business, I imagine there are all sorts of possibilities."

"I'll take that as a 'no.' So, mind telling me where you were last night?"

"Drinking beer and fishing."

"Anybody see you?"

"Nope."

"Any proof you were not in Chicago?"

"Don't need any."

"Mind taking a DNA test?"

"Yup. You got nothing. No probable cause. Get a warrant."

"Thought so. You're dirty, Tungate. You know it. I know it. And you're going down sooner or later. On my watch."

"You're the South Asia crime unit. Why do you care about me?"

"Because my boss's boss and your Governor Brandt were roommates in college. He's going to be President some day. Word came down on you, Tungate. Brandt wants you nailed."

"Ah. Well, when your boss's boss talks to my buddy Jim next time, tell him for me to tell Brandt to go fuck himself. By the way, for the protection of all parties involved, this conversation has been recorded."

* * *

The pictures on the game camera were indistinct. Gun flashes whited out the picture every few seconds, but Tip got an image of a well-put-together guy, not too tall, but built strong in the upper body. He was wearing a black ski mask and a black polo or T-shirt, and you couldn't see his arms very well. Maybe that was why Katy thought he was dark complexioned. His hands did look dusky, but in the dark, in a game-camera picture, you couldn't expect to distinguish color tones.

The one thing Tip got out of the video was that the guy was very athletic, and ran pigeon-toed. If you were from Indiana, you noticed pigeon-toed. All the best basketball players were pigeon-toed. The condition kept you on your toes better than splay-footed.

So, he was looking for a guy, five-ten or so, good shoulders, athletic, and pigeon-toed. And who wore cologne.

* * *

He went to see Ralph, who was sitting in a deck chair behind the counter, eating a piece of jerky, explaining to a customer that his stiff leg and cane were the result of twisting his knee wrong while lifting a roof truss for the new pole barn he was building. Tip kept his face averted until the customer left.

"Looks like you may have found somebody you were looking for," Ralph said when he got a look at Tip's face. "You look pretty bad."

"Yeah. Wouldn't want to look better than I feel."

Ralph levered himself out of the chair, dug in his pocket, and handed Tip his credit card.

"Did just like you said. Bought gas at the bait house down at Hartman. No security cameras. Thanks for the gas, plus the crickets. Caught fifteen bluegills in three hours."

"Perfect. Thank you. And no thanks are enough for what you did for Katy. Really sorry about the leg."

"Katy told you?"

"Linda McConnell."

Ralph snorted and shook his head. "This town. Tried to keep it so nobody knew about the whole thing except Katy and the guys with me. That's why I didn't go to Doc for the leg. She told the neighbors she was shooting at a possum."

"Who patched you up?"

"Ray Haupt. Combat medic in 'Nam. I think it was a ricochet, 'cause it didn't go in deep. It's not bad. Lost some tissue, so it's gonna leave kind of a depression there, but not bad."

"Jesus, seems like those medic skills might go rusty after all these years."

"Says you never, ever forget stuff like that. He fished it out, no problem. Nine Millimeter, not deep. Hurt coming out, though. Used plenty of alcohol, but didn't have any antibiotic. Just hoping no infection."

"I really appreciate it, Ralph. You saved her."

"A promise is a promise."

"Hang onto that slug, case I'm ever back in good graces with law enforcement. I'll get ballistics. Might help. Look, Ralph, I didn't mean to get you hurt. I hope the leg heals fast."

"Gonna be fine. Just a scratch. Us survivalists are tough." He gave a fake smile, then became serious. "Tip, this thing is bigger than we been thinking. Nobody's safe. You need help, I'm with you. Whatever you need. Chet will never get there. And based on the way you look, I'd say you're making progress finding the bad guys. You might try to use something on them besides your face, though."

Tip smiled, then quit because it hurt. "Appreciate it, Ralph. May take you up on it."

\* \* \*

Tip went back home to think and catch some rack time. He hadn't felt this bad in awhile.

The question now was, how to find the Chechen? It looked like Hammadi was definitely the customer for the special custom services Dalek senior had mentioned. Question was, why? And where the hell was he? In any case, the Chechen was the key. He would know the shooter. Hammadi might not, even though he was probably the one paying.

He was surprised to learn on Google that there were half a dozen mosques in Indianapolis. He guessed that most attendees of those mosques were Middle-Easterners or blacks, but he knew there were some white Hoosier converts. He had seen a few interviewed on TV, pleading for common sense and religious tolerance, and asking the public to come visit and see for themselves. Still, he would likely stick out like a sore thumb if he simply visited them, one after another. He couldn't very well just show up and start asking for the Chechen.

There was only one thing to do. Talk to somebody in the Indy Police Department who knew which mosque the Feds had the watch on and get the skinny on the Chechen from them.

He knew just the person. The only question was, would she talk to him after the way he had treated her? No, actually, that wasn't the only question. The other question was, if she was happy to see him again, how complicated could that get? Especially now that Katy was home.

But before he did anything, he crashed in his bed and didn't wake up until nightfall. At which time he opened a beer and turned on the Western channel. A John Wayne was showing. *Rio Lobo.* The Duke was searching for a traitor. It would do. He settled in and was asleep again in twenty minutes.

# CHAPTER TWENTY-FOUR

**O**fficer Janelle Roberts sat across from Tip in the coffee shop near Monument Circle, looking if anything better than the last time he had seen her. Six two if an inch, her eyes nearly level with his, fit, trim, good-looking, she made the uniform look like a recruiting ad. She gave him an appraising look, her eyes traveling slowly up one side of his marred face, then the other.

"So I hear you're unemployed. Looks like it was a rough exit interview."

"I've had worse. I see you've been promoted. *Ser*geant Roberts."

She smiled. "De*tec*tive Sergeant Roberts to you, civilian."

He returned the smile. "You look great. Fantastic, actually. I'm trying to remember why I told you it was over."

"Because I'm black, you're white, and you live in a redneck southern Indiana town you won't leave. Where a sheriff with a black wife would be a constant source of talk."

"Oh yeah. Now I remember. Well, the sheriff part is no longer a problem."

"I heard. I'm sorry, Tip. I know it was your life."

"I'll figure something out. But first I've got to save my life. And the lives of the people in Sedalia. We've got a paid killer on the loose."

"We've all heard. And you're Jim Brandt's fall guy."

Tip ignored this. "The perp has killed two and tried for two more, one of them my daughter."

She raised eyebrows. "Your daughter is home? I remember that she never called you. You must be happy."

"Yes and no." Tip explained.

"Ah. So what is it, Tip? I'd say you broke my heart before, after we wrapped up the Danny Ortiz meth-cooking case together, but I'm smarter than you are. I could see down the road, and I knew it wasn't going to work long-term. So it hurt, but I didn't let it break my heart. And I know it made you feel bad, too, weaseling out so I wouldn't have to. So I know you're not here looking for a reprise. What is it?"

He told her most of it, leaving out inconvenient details. Including how he found out about the Chechen. He let her think it came from Sanchez.

"So you're not gonna tell me who beat hell out of you?"

"Fell over a chair."

She snorted. "You hardly have any chairs in your house. You're the only grown man I know who still has beanbags in his living room."

"It was someplace else. Look. I need to find this Chechen. He's the key to finding the shooter."

"The guy you're talking about is one dangerous hombre. We're sure he's killed several people himself, but we don't have the goods on him. Plus, the FBI won't let us touch him. They're watching him for his Islamic terrorism connection."

"So you know him. Know which mosque he goes to?"

"Sure. Al Ansar on the west side. But only on Fridays. Otherwise, he gets around a lot."

"Got a picture of him?"

She looked long and hard at him. "Giving you a picture of a suspect is a problem from all kinds of directions. It's not just that I could get in trouble for it. The main thing is, you could get yourself killed."

"How about a description?"

She shook her head in resignation. "You're not listening. I can do that, but for your sake, I shouldn't."

"Nobody else is going to solve this problem if I don't, Sergeant Roberts." He usually called her Janelle. "And if nobody solves this problem, my daughter will be dead, I will be dead, and at least one other person in Sedalia will be dead. Probably more."

She sighed. "You're a hard-headed man, Tip. Stubborn. What makes a good cop. And also a dead cop, if you're not careful." She shook her head. "All right."

She described a stocky blond man with a full beard and a buzz cut, with a badly-healed scar running from the corner of his left eye down into his beard toward his chin.

"So why is Indy Metro watching him? Just the killings?"

"That, and because he's the locus of mob activity on the west side. And according to the FBI, he feeds a lot of that money to a terrorist organization in Iraq."

"'Locus'?"

"Yes. We college-educated detectives speak precisely. He's the center of crime out there. The usual: drugs, guns, protection. And his empire is growing. Works with the Dalek family out of Chicago. Though we hear the old man just got burned up in a fire." Her head snapped up straight with a sudden thought, and she looked at him hard. "You don't know anything about that, do you?"

He scratched the back of his fringe. "I hadn't heard that."

"Well, you wouldn't if you did it."

"That's true. But don't worry. Sanchez at the FBI has already braced me on it. He's got nothing."

She held his gaze for a long time, then gave a slight nod. "Which is still not the same as saying you didn't do it."

"That's also true."

He stared back, poker-faced. She finally broke the stare-down.

"Be careful, Tip. I understand protecting your daughter. But if you get yourself killed, it won't help her. And I'll feel responsible, after giving you Kadyrov's description."

Ah. The Chechen's name. Progress.

"Would you feel bad as well as responsible?"

"Yes, because then I would feel duty-bound to fill out all the paperwork the FBI would want."

"Thanks, Janelle. It's good to be loved."

\* \* \*

He was back in Sedalia, freshly back home from filling the '68 Chevy with gas at Altemeyer's gas station. Katy was in an empty bedroom she had already set up as an office, talking to somebody in New York on Skype about the next show she was responsible for. He felt good that she was able to keep up her work, because he knew he would lose her back to New York eventually, and he didn't want her old life to go completely away. He didn't understand that life or what she did as a producer, but he was proud of her. His daughter had made it in the Big Apple.

He was looking into his thinning wallet, realizing he was going to have to take more money out of the bank. The 348 Tri-Power was an incredible gas hog, plus he had to eat.

A light tap sounded at the front door.

"Somebody outside, Katy," he called down the hall. "Get your weapon." He could hear her moving quickly.

"Got it, Dad! I'll cover the back!"

"All right."

He took a peak out the side of the picture window and at first didn't see anybody. It was times like this he was glad of the railroad house's construction: concrete blocks on a slab, with brick on the outside. Wouldn't stop a heavy round, but would stop almost anything else.

The tapping came again. He squatted down beside the door and yelled, "Identify yourself!"

"Open up, Tip. And don't shoot. It's Samantha."

"Why can't I see you?"

"Because I'm flat against the wall so if you shoot through the door you won't hit me. I know you must be jumpy out here."

So she had somehow found out about either the attack on Katy, or his visit to Doc Quick. Gun in hand, he opened the door. She stepped out of hiding, flinched when she saw his face, but said nothing. He faced her across the threshold. As always, she was dressed as if about to pose for an Indianapolis Today profile of young professionals, today in a dark pin-striped suit.

"So, you going to let me in?"

"Ah, sure." He turned and called over his shoulder. "It's OK, Katy!" Then he stepped aside and said, "Come on in."

After a moment, Katy appeared at the end of the hall with the .38 in both hands, firing grip, pointed at the ceiling, right forefinger straight alongside the trigger guard, just as he had taught her. She spied Samantha and Samantha spied her and stiffened. The two assessed each other. Then Samantha loosened, plastered on a smile, and said, "You must be Katy." She strode across the room in three long steps with her hand out. "Call me Sam. I'm the District Attorney of Howarth County."

Katy lowered her weapon and stuck it back in her shoulder holster. Then she took Samantha's hand and said, "Yeah, I've heard about you. Call me Kate. I'm the daughter."

"Who fought off an armed attack Tuesday night."

"Yes. In your county. After you got my father dismissed from office. Why am I not safe here, with you in charge? And how did you find out? I told the neighbors I was shooting at a possum."

Samantha gave a wolfish smile. She liked competition. "It's taking awhile to clean up the mess your father left us with, so you may not be safe for awhile. And I found out the usual way in Sedalia: gossip. Do you mind if I speak with your father alone?"

"Of course not. Though I can't imagine why he would want to speak with you after you just insulted him like that. But go for it."

Samantha watched as Katy turned back down the hall, flouncing a hip back at her as she went.

"She's beautiful, Tip. You must have some great recessive genes, or her mother was seriously good looking."

"Both. And her mother is still alive. What do you want, Samantha? There's a reason we're carrying guns around the house. You could be in danger just by being here."

"We're not getting anywhere, Tip. And I think you know that. And I think you know why. You haven't told us everything you know. You gave Chet some scraps, but there's more."

"You have no idea."

"That's why I'm here."

"Fine. Here it is in a nutshell, for all you can do with it. I don't expect much. The shooter is a hired gun contracted by a Chechen mobster who is also an Islamic terrorist. His two-fold mission is to terrorize Big Iva for the Russian mob in Chicago, plus get revenge for a private customer who has some kind of hard-on for Tom Burton and me. I believe the private customer is Dr. Hammadi at the VA. The Chechen, a guy named Kadyrov, is on the FBI's watch list, and they won't let the Indy police touch him. He attends Al Ansar mosque on the west side. There you have most of it. Take it away. I feel safer already with everything in your hands."

Her eyes were wide. "That's quite a data dump. How'd you find all that out?"

He smiled. "The usual way in Sedalia: gossip."

She smirked. "I don't think so. I think you may not be as unintelligent as I first thought."

"I like to be underestimated."

She flashed a smile. "I've noticed that. So what would you do next? If you were still working the case?"

He smiled. "It's not obvious? Find Kadyrov, beat hell out of him, and get him to talk. Who the hell is the shooter?"

"Besides being illegal, beating hell out of somebody is not something I can physically do. Or legally have done. What do you recommend?"

"Well, there's always your new sheriff. You could hint to him what needs to be done, while preserving your deniability."

She sniffed, then rolled her tongue around her mouth. "Look, I've been on the run all morning. Could I have a cup of tea or coffee? Whatever kind of caffeine you drink?"

"Sure. My manners. Sorry. Have a seat." He disappeared into the kitchen and came back with a cup of coffee. "It was fresh only a few hours ago."'

In his absence, she had sat down on one of the beanbags and crossed her legs. She had great legs, but he forced himself not to look. He was sure she knew exactly how her legs looked in the snug suit pants. She took the cup, drank, and grimaced.

"Look. I'll make you a deal. I'll reinstate you as a deputy, and you can continue to work the case."

"What makes you think I'm working the case?"

Katy came back in and sat down on a straight-backed chair at the dining table between the living room and the kitchen. She had her laptop with her, but made no pretense that she was not eavesdropping. Samantha noticed her but looked back at Tip.

"What makes me think you're still working the case? Well, there's the fact that your face looks like you've used it as a battering ram. And the fact that you mysteriously disappeared for a day or two. And the fact that your cell phone has gone dark several times in the last week, as if the battery had been removed."

"I can't believe you would be tracking my cell phone. Or that you think I would engage in suspicious activity."

"Of course you can. That's why you took the battery out. So let's get real. Look, I screwed you, with Governor Brandt's help. I admit it. But I also underestimated you. And overestimated what Chet and Temple could do by themselves. Bottom line is, we need you back on this case. I'll get Chet to deputize you, we put you back on your old salary, you help us with the case, and you say nothing bad in public about Governor Brandt or me. We solve the case together."

"And Chet remains as sheriff. And Brandt gets re-elected Governor. And you get elected Lieutenant Governor."

She crossed her legs the other way. "Yes."

"Tell you what. Give me a day or two to think about it. Then I'll give you a clear answer. I've got some private business to clear up."

She hoisted herself out of the beanbag as gracefully as he'd ever seen it done and came and stood in front of him, just fifteen or twenty inches away, looking up. Her breath smelled like chocolate mixed with coffee.

"Don't wait too long," she said. "The offer goes away if we catch Kadyrov and he talks."

"Understood. I'm terrified."

She left.

Katy snickered. "You do know, Dad, she thinks you're hot."

"What? The woman is an armored bitch on tank tracks."

"Yeah. But she thinks you're hot."

"What she thinks is, I'm going to find this Kadyrov and beat the story out of him, then she's going to show back up and try some threat or inducement to get the information out of me so she can close the case and prance for the cameras."

"Yeah. And the inducement might be something you really don't expect." She paused. "So, was Mom screwing around with Neal all along?"

This knocked Tip off center. Since she had been home, Katy had never mentioned Diane, even though he strongly suspected that, not only did she talk regularly with her mother on the phone, she probably had visited the two of them in Indy on more than one occasion. But he knew he had to talk honestly here. His daughter was a grown woman.

"I don't know. I suspected. The bottom line is, I just couldn't give your mother what she wanted because I wasn't the person she wanted. We were sweethearts in high school. She waited for me to get out of the Marines. Everything was good. Then her world grew. I guess mine didn't. She liked cities and sophistication, and money, and I'm just a Sedalia person, born and bred. I don't blame her. After all, we got you out of it."

Katy took two long strides toward him and gave him a hug. "I'm sorry, Dad. I've been mean to you. And it's because I didn't know you."

He patted her on the back. "I'm just happy to see you again. Sorry about the circumstances. But I'm going to fix things up for you. Don't worry."

## CHAPTER TWENTY-FIVE

**A**l Ansar's website said the mosque was open twenty-four hours a day. The muezzin's first call to prayer for Friday was at 5:24 AM. The five daily salah, or prayer, times were listed by date, along with the trigonometry used to calculate them based on latitude and longitude, the amount of horizon covered by pre-dawn light, the midday position of the sun, and time of sunset.

Tip remembered the haunting, beautiful sound of the muezzin's call to prayer, particularly Fajar, the pre-dawn call. By that time, most of the troops were stirring anyway, woken by those standing watch, so as to be prepared for dawn attacks, either receiving or launching them. But unfailingly, when the plaintive sound floated across the desert from the nearby towns, all the troops would stop to listen.

So he decided to stake out the mosque from first prayer at 5:24 AM to last prayer at 10:01 PM. Then he would follow Kadyrov to wherever he lived, even if he had to follow him all day. And there he would confront him and have a discussion with him.

He sat in his truck in a strip-mall parking lot much of the day in total boredom. He received two visits from Indy police, who wondered what he was doing there.

"Bird watching," he said, and raised Andrei Dalek's binoculars.

"Uh huh," said one officer, looking around. "Birds like to sit in trees and bushes. I don't see too many around here."

"I'm looking for the double-crested Russian titmouse," he said. "They like to sit on wires. I've heard there's one in this area."

"Uh huh," said the officer. "And you're also loitering. So move it along or get arrested."

So he moved to a convenience-store parking lot slightly farther away, but still with good line of sight. That lasted only an hour before he was again rousted.

"Second time you've been reported loitering on this street," said the new officer. "One more time and you're going to get charged."

So he finally just moved to the farthest corner of the mosque parking lot, and he actually spotted Kadyrov going in just in time for midday prayer. Based on the website, this prayer, or Dhuhr, would be followed by a sermon, so he assumed the Chechen would be in there for forty-five to sixty minutes. He settled back to wait. The problem was, one of the faithful spotted him sitting in the truck with the window open and came over to talk. He took a good look at Tip and diagnosed the situation.

"Come inside, brother. You are welcome. Everyone must have a first time. You are curious about Islam, and we welcome you. We want more people to be curious and to join us, to join the umma, the family of Muslims."

"Just waiting on somebody, thanks anyway."

"Please. I can tell you want to join us, but you are embarrassed, perhaps nervous and fearful. You think we are terrorists. But we are peaceful. I insist. You must join us. It will not hurt you."

Tip could see he was going to have to play along.

"You will make a big thing of my presence. You will introduce me to people, call attention to me. I don't want that."

"I understand. You wish to quietly visit, quietly learn about us, and quietly leave. I promise, that is the way it will be." He opened Tip's truck door and made welcoming gestures.

The problem, of course—besides that he would become obvious to the Chechen, who would almost certainly know what he looked like—was that he was packing the .45 in a holster in the small of his back. No way could he go in there. And no way could he remove it and the holster with this guy watching.

"Tell you what. You're nice and friendly, and I appreciate that, but I've changed my mind. I'm not ready to convert yet. I'll visit at another time."

And with that, he started up and drove out of the lot. He was reduced this time to parking in front of a second-hand store. He went in, bought a used recliner for fifteen dollars, and got the owner to help him load it in the back of the truck. Then he paid him another ten, telling him he needed to sit in the lot for an hour or two while waiting for a friend. He got the impression it was the first twenty-five the guy had taken in that day, and he seemed only too happy to oblige.

After an hour, the Chechen came out, and Tip followed him to a tea shop. There was Arabic writing all over the plate glass window, and it was a small place, so Tip figured it was best not to go in for at least two reasons. He would stand out, and it was probably full of the Chechen's friends. But he was able to walk by with his ball cap pulled low over sun glasses and get a glimpse of the Chechen and somebody else in a booth, arguing. He risked walking back past the place and was shocked and gratified to see that the other man was Hammadi. He took a picture with his cell phone hoping it would come out, but decided the picture was of limited usefulness. In his own mind, the connection was estab-lished. Hammadi was the customer. The only question was why.

Tip waited in another convenience store parking lot across the street, worrying because of the bars over its windows that the cops would come any time to roust him, but they did not. He then followed Kadyrov to an apartment block on the west side and watched him go in. Each apartment had its own external entry door, so there was no confusion that might be associated with a common entrance hall.

Then he waited. And waited. Fortunately, he had thought to prepare himself with what his father had called a doniker, with one-quart capacity.

When it was thoroughly dark he knocked on the door. He held a tire iron in his left hand, along his pant leg so no casual observer could see it. There was no answer. He knocked again. Still no answer. He quietly tried the knob. Locked. Taking a quick look over his shoulder and seeing no one, he raised the tire iron and started to pry on the door, but a sudden voice behind him stopped him.

"You must be really stupid."

The speaker had an accent Tip couldn't place, but he instantly knew who its owner was. And he instantly realized, he was indeed stupid. He turned slowly. The Chechen stood below him on the sidewalk with a silenced automatic pistol leveled at him. He wondered if the man had seen his .45 under his shirt.

"Looks that way, doesn't it?"

"I observed you following me. You have no skill at this. But it is a good thing. You have come to me. It will save time."

"I'm just a thief here to steal your stuff. I heard you're rich."

"Pathetic. You are Sheriff Earl Tungate of Howarth County. You will die tonight. But not by my hand. I will take you to the man who has been paid for this work. He will do the job. But only after you see your daughter die before your eyes."

Tip's vision dimmed with rage. "So that's what Hammadi paid for, is it?"

Kadyrov's eyes widened slightly, then his face went blank, but Tip saw it. Then he thought furiously. Would Katy be able to defend herself? Get help? With Ralph hurt, who would defend her? Would a 911 call bring Chet, and if so, what good would that do? Would she think the danger was past, that the would-be attacker was discouraged, now that he'd been driven off once? Did Kadyrov mean she was going to be kidnapped and taken to another location where Tip would be taken too, or was she going to be killed at home and video-taped?

There were a million questions, all of which meant he needed to get away from this guy, now that he'd lost the chance to get the drop on him. Maybe if he jumped sideways off the porch and drew at the same time, he'd be able to get a shot off at the same time as Kadyrov. It was his only chance.

He looked Kadyrov in the eye and prepared himself, and the Chechen calmly shot him in the left thigh. It felt like a blow from a baseball bat. The Kevlar pants he had taken to wearing when he became Sheriff did nothing to stop the bullet.

Tip stood stunned. It was one of those situations where you know the pain is going to hit, but it hasn't quite hit yet, kind of like when you accidentally touch a hot burner. But in the brief moment, he had a flash of clarity and made his decision.

Then the pain hit and he yelled, "YOU SON OF A BITCH!" and fell on his left hip. Simultaneously, he reached behind, drew his .45, and fired twice. Compared to the "phut!" sound of the silenced nine millimeter, it was ear shattering. As he fired, the Chechen fired again, grazing his right ear. Then the Chechen turned and ran, folded over as if he had been hit in the middle.

Must not have been too good a hit, thought Tip, or he would have gone down.

Oddly, the ear hurt worse than the leg, which was starting to go numb. He watched Kadyrov get into his car and leave. Tip realized he needed to do the same quickly, because the police would certainly be there at any moment. Surely someone who had heard his .45 go off twice would have called 911.

He levered himself up and looked at his leg. It was bleeding, but not pumping blood. That was good. He reached up and felt the ear. Not good. Pretty ragged, not all there. Plus it was ringing non-stop.

Twenty yards down the way, a front door opened and a man stepped out with a shotgun. He looked at Tip, still on his butt, and yelled, "Hey, you all right? Or are you the bad guy? Never seen you before." He leveled the shotgun.

Tip hid his weapon from the man and surreptitiously slid it back into its holster.

"No problem," he called back. "Just a minor misunderstanding."

He didn't raise his hands because that would make him look guilty. Slowly, he pulled himself upright using Kadyrov's front door knob. He was careful to use the side of his hand so as not to leave fingerprints, which the FBI would have because of his military service. Then he hobbled down the steps, trying to make it look normal.

"Thanks for asking," he said, and made for his truck.

"Hey, Buddy," called the man. "I called the police. You better stick around till they get here."

"I'll be all right," Tip called back, and went around behind the truck, unclipped the license plate, and threw it into the bed of the truck. Sirens sounded in the near distance.

"I'll shoot," called the man. "I think you done something wrong."

"Go ahead if you want to be charged with assault with a deadly weapon and attempted murder."

The man lowered the double-barrel and broke it open. "Yeah, you're probably right. But I got your description."

"It's the man in that apartment I was standing in front of you need to report to the police. Son of a bitch shot me. With a silenced pistol."

With that, he struggled to his truck and drove away.

\* \* \*

Using only back streets and county roads to get back to Sedalia took half again as long, and on the way, he worried himself sick. He could not get Katy or Ralph either one on the phone. In desperation, he called Chet. No answer. Finally, in total despair, he called Samantha. She answered on the first ring.

"It's nine thirty at night, Tip. What can it possibly be? I know you didn't call to give me more useless information. Certainly not to invite me out for a drink. What can it be?"

"They're after Katy. I can't get hold of her, and I think they're planning to kill her on video, like terrorists. I need Chet and maybe the State boys to find and protect her."

"What?" she demanded. "What's going on, Tip? And by the way, you don't sound so good. Are you all right?"

He ignored the concern for his well-being and did a thirty-second data dump, relating the info from the Chechen but leaving out the fact that he was shot. His main concern was Katy, and the fact that the Chechen got away. He implied he was still after the Chechen, and ended with, "I can't do it all myself, Samantha. I need help. Call Jarvis. He'll come if you call, but since I'm not sheriff any more, he might feel like he can't if I call. Please protect Katy."

"Holy shit, Tip. All right. All right. I'll get Chet, Jarvis, and Temple over to your house right away."

The relief was immediate. "OK, good, 'cause I'm not sure. . .." He was starting to feel woozy and faded out for a second.

"Tip, you sound hurt. I know you don't tell me everything. If you're hurt, go to the hospital in Elmira now."

He recovered slightly, and forced himself to sound more energetic.

"Hey, listen, have Chet call me back when he gets to the house. I want to know Katy is OK. I'm still too far away and . . . ah, busy pursuing a hot lead."

"Of course."

He immediately called Doc Quick. The phone rang five times before he answered. Tip forced himself to sound casual.

"You watching that naked survival show on TV again, Doc?"

"Yeah, for all that it's any of your business. What the hell you calling me for at this hour of the night?"

Tip explained. "Will just have to go without extra blood. Just need you to sew me up. And give me some pain killer. I've got my belt around my leg. Pretty sure the slug's still in there."

"Before you put the belt on, was the blood pumping or oozing?"

"Oozing."

"Then stop that stupid shit with the belt right now! Take off your T shirt and wad it up over the wound, then fasten it in place with your belt. Snugly, but not tight enough to cut off circulation. Tourniquets are only for arterial bleeding. Life or limb. I assume you'd like to keep the leg."

"It'd be nice. You can't tell anybody you've worked on me for a GSW."

"Figured that. You can't either. Then the government would get involved, and everything would go to shit. Do you realize, I employ a person full-time—"

"Doc, I'll be there in twenty minutes."

* * *

Samantha called just as he crossed into Howarth County and started down River Road to Sedalia.

"She's not there, Tip."

"Truck there?"

"Yes. We've looked all over town, and no one knows where she is. There's sign of forced entry at both the front and back doors, and blood on the kitchen floor. Couple of holes in the drywall. Looks like .38 caliber. But I'm sorry. She's just not there."

A five-pound lump of lead dropped into Tip's stomach.

"She's been kidnapped. Put out a BOLA."

"We've done that. But there's other bad news."

"What could be worse?"

"Somebody entered Missy Davis's hospital room in Elmira and strangled her earlier this evening. Video showed somebody in doctor's scrubs and surgical mask. Iva Randall's guard just outside the room didn't even discover it for two hours."

## CHAPTER TWENTY-SIX

**A** single light burned in Doc Quick's office. So he had beaten Tip there.

Exhausted, light-headed, Tip struggled up the back steps and tried the door. Still locked. As he raised his hand to beat on the door, his phone went off. An anonymous number. He answered with dread, thinking it could be the kidnappers. Instead it was Big Iva. She started right in.

"You miserable, no-count, worthless, lowlife scumbag son of a bitch! You let them kill her! I'm coming for you, Tip! You'll never know what hit you! But first, I'm going up and kill that Chicago son of a bitch with my own hands!"

Tip was aware the FBI could be listening, even though she was using a burner phone. He was not. So he had to be circumspect. "Somebody already took care of that a few days ago, Iva."

There was a long silence on the phone.

"Ah." More silence. Then a sniffle. Then an explosion of hacking and coughing, and Tip realized she was crying. "Who's doing this stuff?" she wailed. "Ahhh, my sweet Missy." She sobbed. He gave her a moment, then continued.

"I'm sorry, Iva. I really am. It's a prepaid hit man. Can't figure out who he is yet, but I know who paid him—which was

Roman Dalek, the Chicago asshole, and another guy I'm ninety percent sure of who is after me. And maybe Tom Burton, too. Just don't know why. Same killer, two different customers, two different motives, two different sets of targets. With a cut-out who contracted him." His throat constricted. "And now he's kidnapped Katy."

The sobbing subsided. "They kidnapped your daughter?"

"Yeah." Anger darkened his vision, and his breath came hard. "It's war."

There was a pause. "Did he die bad? Painfully?"

It took a moment. She was talking about Roman Dalek. A small lie was in order.

"Yes. Very bad. Burned up in his place of business."

"Good. Who the hell did that punk son of a bitch think he was, to try to shake me down? Launder his cash for him? For nothing! Without even a cut! Just started shooting the place up when I told them to fuck off. Look. I'm sorry I spoke sharply to you, Tip. And I can tell by the way you're grunting and breathing that you're hurt. I won't ask. I'll just say, whatever you need that I can give, it's yours."

* * *

Doc Quick was not as sympathetic.

"Get me off my couch and away from my beer at this hour of the evening? You think doctors like to do this shit?"

"No, but I was hoping your Hypocritical oath would get you in here."

"Hippocratic."

"Plus I figured you would want to keep me alive so I can pay my bill from last time."

Doc ignored this and looked at the ear. He whistled. "You always were an ugly son of a bitch, but that ear's going to put you in a whole new category. Best I'll be able to do is stop the bleeding and sew it up. Some of it's gone."

"Thanks for the kind words, Doc. How about the leg? I'm starting to get weak from loss of blood."

"But it never pumped, right?"

"Right."

"Hm. Lot of blood. Could have hit the femoral vein. The artery is right beside it, which means you are one lucky son of a bitch. Exit wound on the back?"

"No. I think it's still in there."

"Fantastic. You do know I'm not a trauma surgeon? You should have gone to Methodist in Indy. They get two or three of these a day."

"I'll remember that next time I'm shot."

"I don't even have the right kind of forceps. I'm going to have to probe with a long hemostat. It's gonna hurt."

"Already does."

"And I really need to get in there, find the bleeder, and suture it up if it's the femoral vein. That'll involve some cutting. "

"Do your best, Doc."

"Yeah, yeah. You're a tough guy. But I could end up killing you, or screwing up a nerve. I'm not a surgeon, Tip."

"Doc."

"All right. Damn it. I'm gonna need Linda for this. Somebody to sponge and vacuum out. I assume the reason you're here instead of a hospital is, like you mentioned on the phone, you don't want this reported to the police. Am I right on that?"

"Yup."

"What makes you think I won't report it?"

"'Cause you hate government in all its forms."

Doc sighed heavily. "All right. Sign a release, and we're good to go. I don't do general, so this is gonna have to be nothing but local anesthesia. Got some xylocaine this time, but it's still gonna hurt like a son of a bitch."

"I know. If I'm awake to feel it. But meantime, Doc, if you don't mind, I'm gonna lie back and go to sleep. It's hard to even keep sitting up."

"That's blood loss. All right. Go to sleep. If you die before you wake—"

"I pray the Lord my soul to take. Not the other guy. He's already trying to kill me."

\* \* \*

Tip woke up with his phone buzzing in his shirt pocket. He was on his back on the same exam table. His leg hurt like a son of a bitch. He struggled to exert consciousness, but wasn't fast enough to answer the phone before it stopped buzzing.

"Can't believe you stayed asleep during that," said Linda McConnell. She sat beside him on a straight-back chair.

"Where's Doc?"

"Cussing in the front office, drinking coffee. Says he might as well stay up all night and do paperwork."

Tip sat up painfully and looked down at his leg. His pants were gone. He was wearing nothing but his shorts. His leg was heavily bandaged, but no blood had seeped through.

"So, did he get it out?"

"No problem. Wasn't in that deep. And he was able to determine based on the depth of the hole that it didn't hit your main vein."

"My Kevlar pants."

"Yup. He stopped the bleeding with hemostats, then released them after twenty minutes, watched for bleeding for ten minutes, then sewed you up. You should be good if you don't overexert. He said you have to stay here all night."

"OK, thanks. Let me see who this is."

He brought up the missed call. It was a text that said, "See picture." The attached picture showed Katy, her face beaten up. She was on her knees, arms behind her back, presumably bound. Beside her stood a man with a black hood over his head. One hand gripped a bow saw of the kind used to saw off small tree limbs. The other hand had a handful of her hair.

It looked like they were inside an old barn. In fact, Tip was pretty sure it was the ramshackle Reinhart barn out on River Road. Abandoned for decades, partially falling down, the barn had once been the main barn on the Reinhart homestead. The house had been gone for sixty years, but the barn was made of sturdier stuff and served as a place of adventure for boys.

He sent the text and attached picture to Chet, Samantha, Temple, the State Police, and the Elmira city police with his own superseding text: "Need your help. Reinhart Barn, River Road, twenty minutes. I want that son of a bitch alive." Then he called 911 and told the Elmira operator to look up the email and keep calling its recipients until they answered.

Then he received another text and picture. This one showed Katy with a long, bleeding cut in her left cheek. The man in the hood held a straight razor in one hand, and was flipping the bird with the other.

"I'm out of here, Linda." He showed her the picture. "Tell Doc to send me a bill. And tell him, don't go home. We're gonna need some help for Katy."

"Want your pants?"

"Oh, yeah."

* * *

Tip idled the last two hundred yards of River Road before coming to the overgrown lane that led back to the barn. He didn't want to alert the man with engine noise by getting too close, so he parked beside the road near the end of the lane, leaving the lane open for Chet and Temple. With luck, he could sneak in and get the drop on the son of a bitch before they got there.

He quietly eased the gate open, and closed it so the cattle wouldn't get out. Then he crept back the two-hundred-yard lane toward the barn, gun at the ready. His leg hurt like hell, and his breath came with an effort. He was running strictly on adrenaline. The anesthetic had worn off, and walking was a challenge. He'd even had trouble managing the clutch in the truck.

A quarter moon illuminated spindly locust trees, hawthorns, pasture, even cow pies, but if someone had driven here, he had hidden his vehicle well. Tip took deep breaths to calm his pounding heart. The smells of blooming wild rose and cow manure lay heavy on the air.

When he got close, he could see light seeping through vertical cracks between the barn siding boards. This was definitely the place, unless it was a bunch of kids.

He crept in through the equipment door, safety off now, finger outside the trigger guard. He didn't care what the law might do to him. He was going to kill this son of a bitch.

But it didn't work out that way.

"You slimy bastard," said Katy down in the left end of the barn where the light was. "You're a coward. Come on. You want to kill me? Fight me. Or maybe you're too afraid. Of a girl. You're probably one of those guys Viagra doesn't work for, and this is how you make yourself feel like a man."

There was the sound of a slap. She grunted.

"You're even afraid to talk, for fear I'll somehow get out of this and identify you. What a piss-poor excuse for a man you are."

Another slap and grunt.

Tip was almost past the old wooden manure spreader that sat to the left, almost to the point where he could see what was going on. Then a stick snapped under his foot. Damn it.

He rushed ahead, gun at the ready, and looked left. A light and video camera were set up facing the barn wall. Katy was on her knees, hands behind her back. A loop of rope circled her throat. Tip knew the technique: it would be tied to her ankles to keep her on her knees. The hooded man stood looking in Tip's direction, holding a hand sickle, head cocked to one side as if listening, and Tip realized the man was blinded by the light. He could not see into the shadows where Tip crouched.

"Drop the sickle, get on your knees, hands behind your head. NOW!"

A shot came from a dark corner of the barn and whizzed past Tip's head.

He dropped to the dirt floor of the barn, rolled back up on his good knee, and fired off three rounds toward the source of the shot. Then he swung back toward the scene in front of the video camera to shoot the hooded man, but he was gone.

"Katy, get down!" he ordered. "Clear down. How many people are there?"

"Two at the house," she called back. "But I thought there was only the one inside the barn."

Suddenly there were flashing red and blue lights outside the barn. Tip had heard nothing. Chet called, "Hey Tip! You in there?"

"Yeah! Two bad guys! Can't see them. Bring a spotlight."

He fired another round in the direction of the shooter, then looked back toward the entrance. He saw Chet's dark profile, crawling in on hands and knees. Tip hissed softly to locate himself for Chet. Chet crawled up and handed Tip a department handheld spotlight. Tip sighed.

"I was hoping you would shine it while I shoot."

Chet missed the sarcasm. "They're gonna shoot at the spotlight, Tip! I don't want to get hit."

Tip snorted in disgust. "Jesus."

A rustling sound came from behind them near the door. Tip swung his aim around. Another form was crawling in.

"Who the hell is that?" hissed Tip.

"Samantha," said Chet. "She's got a gun."

"Jesus. Where the hell is Temple?"

"Needed her at the lab in Indy."

Samantha crawled up. "What do you need?" She asked.

"Shine the light in that corner," pointed Tip. "Keep it moving so he can't shoot you."

"Got it."

She took the light, pulled a pistol from inside her jacket, and stood halfway up. She raised the light as high above her shoulder as she could and clicked it on. Brilliant light bathed the corner of the barn.

Nobody there. Just barn beams still showing their adze marks and rotting vertical siding boards.

She swept it right. Nobody there. Just the old feed bunk and hayrack.

She swept it all around. Nobody was in the barn. There was a sound behind them, toward the very door they had entered, and she swept the light there. Two hooded figures were fleeing down the lane. She took aim and shot. They kept running. Tip took off after them, but he made it only fifty feet before he had to stop. The pain and exhaustion were too much. An engine started up in the woods along the right side of the lane, and a vehicle crashed out onto the lane, turned toward the road, and was gone. It crashed through the gate at the end. Tip swore and went back to the barn. Samantha was still standing there, extinguished light in one hand, and an automatic in the other.

"Damn," said Tip. "You're tougher than I thought. You could have killed one of them, you know. Lot of questions would have come up."

She stuffed the weapon into a shoulder holster. "Let's set your daughter free."

Katy was good. Tip was proud of her. She didn't whine, sniffle, or complain. She just stood up when they untied the rope and rubbed her wrists.

"How bad's my face?" she asked. "One of the cuts went clear through. I can feel it with my tongue."

Tip folded her in his arms. "It's not so bad. It was a razor, so it'll heal up nicely. I'll pay for a good plastic surgeon. Come on. Let's get you to the hospital in Elmira."

"It's something about you, Dad. Something you did maybe way back, maybe in the service. They didn't talk, but at the house when they grabbed me, one said, 'They will pay for what they did to my family.' Had an accent. Then they tied me up, gagged me, put a hood over my head, and tossed me in the back of some kind of SUV, maybe a Jeep. Rough ride. But I heard him say it. Otherwise, they didn't talk."

"You get a look at their faces?"

"They wore ski masks."

He turned to Samantha. Before he could speak, she said, "We'll do forensics on the scene, Tip. Could be prints on the camera, the light, the tripods. We are going to catch these guys."

For the first time since he had known her, Tip did not have to suppress dislike. In fact, he didn't want to admit to himself what he was feeling. But it was far from dislike. It was gratitude. And something else he didn't want to admit and immediately suppressed. He stuck out his hand. She hesitated, then took it, and they shook.

"Thanks, Sam."

She looked back at him in an appraising way, but even accounting for the low light of the quarter moon, it seemed like it was the first time she had looked at him without a hidden contempt.

He held her hand longer than absolutely necessary.

## CHAPTER TWENTY-SEVEN

The ER doctor at the hospital in Elmira used surgical glue to seal up the cuts on Katy's cheeks. "Minimizes scarring," he said. "But you still might need a cosmetic surgeon at some point."

Tip called Doc Quick to tell him she'd already been taken care of.

"Thanks, Tip. I'm pleased to have your permission to go home and go to bed. You'll be getting my bill. Pay it soon, will ya? Before you get yourself killed."

Then Tip checked them in to a couple of motel rooms in Elmira, making sure to hide the truck in an adjacent hotel lot. Both needed sleep, and neither was in condition to stand guard in the railroad house while the other slept.

When they woke, he checked Dalek's hotel, and incredibly, the jeep was there. And the front was banged up as if it had been driven through a gate. He called Samantha and laid out his case.

"Some of the paint from that jeep is gonna be on that tubular gate out at the old Reinhart place. By the way, did you and Chet wire up the gate so the cattle couldn't get out?"

"Didn't think of it. We don't have cattle penned up where I came from. Seems a little inhumane."

Tip spent a moment trying to imagine free-range cattle in Indianapolis. Samantha continued.

"The owner, a Larry Sievert, complained this morning that crime-scene people had let them out. I pointed out that he could be charged with maintaining a public nuisance, since he has not posted no-trespassing signs. But he got his cows back in this morning with no trouble."

What a gal. He could just imagine Sievert's reaction: a silent glare and a sidewise Skoal spit. "Yeah. Most people feed their cattle a little corn every few days to keep them coming to them."

"You mean, like chocolate to women?"

Tip hesitated. Diane had once told him his efforts at subtlety reminded her of bulldozers. He ignored the jab. "So you'll im-pound the jeep?"

"Can't. No firm link."

Tip bit back his first reaction. He would do better with this woman on his side. As much as that pissed him off. He leveled his voice. "After all I've told you?"

"Problem is, none of it's admissible. It's all hearsay. From you. There is no credible evidence to believe this Andrei Dalek has committed a crime. All you have is suspicion."

"I thought we had a moment there. Last night."

"*You* thought we had a moment. I thought I was helping save your daughter from kidnappers, which I would do for anybody."

"And does our new sheriff have a lead on those kidnappers? What does the FBI say? After all, kidnapping is a federal crime."

"We, ah, haven't reported it to the FBI."

"What? Why not?"

Silence.

Tip broke the silence. "You have to be kidding me. Brandt? It'd look like you guys don't have it under control after making a big deal of getting rid of me? Seriously? How far will you two go for ambition?"

"Easy, Tip."

This lit him up even more. "Tell you what. How about *I* report it to the FBI?"

"Easy down, Tip. Then I would have to tell them everything you told me. Everything."

"Which would also be hearsay. From me. Jesus. Whew! Look. You and Chet stay out of my way, and I'll get these bastards. Just don't be charging me with any crimes when I have to shoot somebody in, uh, self-defense."

"Don't break any laws, Tip, and I won't charge you with anything. But do keep us informed."

"So you can claim credit when I get this guy."

"Of course. That's politics."

\* \* \*

He needed a way to draw out the bastard. Ambush him. And the only way to do that was bait. But what kind, where? Roman Dalek was dead, and so was Missy, so it was reasonable to assume the shooter would feel his contract for the old man was taken care of. Of course, there was Andrei, who had lost both his old man and his brother, so he might have taken over the business and be lusting for even more revenge. If that was so, the question was, revenge against whom now, since by now the survivor of the fire would have identified Roman Dalek's killer to his son.

The burning question was who was driving the attempts against Katy, and the efforts to frame Tom Burton, and why. Just because Hammadi had disappeared and Katy said her would-be killer had an accent didn't mean they were one and the same, but there was that strange comment he had made at their last meeting. About the name Hammadi being avenged, God willing. But even that meant nothing in a court. Just that the guy maybe had family killed in Iraq. No connection to him or Burton.

Or was there? Maybe he hadn't looked closely enough at that possibility.

He decided to visit Burton again. Quibble had got him out on bail. Very low bail, as Judge Prechter expressed disgust with the quality of information Samantha had brought. "Ought to set him free altogether," he had said, "but I don't want the same thing to happen to me that happened to Tip. Hell of a thing our country is coming to. Rule of law is down the toilet."

It wasn't safe to leave Katy alone, so they went back to the railroad house, showered, or in Tip's case, partially showered to keep his leg and face wounds dry, and put on clean clothes. Then they climbed back in the '68 Chevy and headed out River Road.

"I never thought it'd come to this," Katy mused. "Jeans and a work shirt in a pick-up truck in Sedalia, Indiana, basically running for my life up a deserted gravel road along a river. It's so basic. My friends in Manhattan will never believe it."

"You don't have to tell them."

"The scars."

"Oh. Yeah."

* * *

It was another beautiful morning along the river. In fact, as far as Tip was concerned, all mornings along the river were beautiful, no matter the weather. On this morning, the fragrant strings of black locust blossoms were about done broadcasting scent, but the multiflora roses and honeysuckle were kicking in, and the effect was intoxicating. Tip wanted to just sit on the stone shelf along the bank and fish as he had done since he was boy, but grim urgency reasserted itself.

Burton was cold sober. He sat cross-legged on his front porch snelling hooks and laying them on a board across his lap. He looked up.

"Hey, Tip." Then he saw Katy in her jeans, chambray shirt, and shoulder holster. "Hey, whoah!" He clambered to his feet, dumping his snells onto the porch and stuck out his hand to Katy. "Pleased to meet you. You gotta be Katy. Whew!"

She smiled in spite of herself. "Likewise, Mr. Burton, isn't it?"

"Tom. Call me Tom." He turned to Tip. "So what is it this time, Tip? You can't be here to take me in, 'cause you're not sheriff any more."

"You silver-tongued devil. No, I'm here to try to figure out a guy by the name of Hammadi. You know him. He's conveniently disappeared, I understand, just in time to not back up your alibi in the Jennifer Clarkson case."

"Not only that. Before he disappeared, the son of a bitch turned in the paperwork to rescind my disability. I'm going to have to get a job."

"Damn, that's rough."

"Go ahead. Joke. You don't know how it is. Although I know you were there. But in your time, it was a short war. Hell, you guys were in and out in a few weeks. With us, it was just a long grind, living among people who hated us. Smile at you during the day; blow your ass up at night. Or bury a bomb on the road. Or smile at you then blow themselves and you up. Crazy people."

"So, I know you were a sniper."

"I was."

"Did the Iraqis know it?"

"They did. Called me Dr. Death. Sent assassins after me four times. Attacked my unit over and over to try to get me."

"So how many?"

Burton looked at Katy. "Not sure I want to talk about this."

Tip gave an appraising look at Katy. She gave a level look back. Tip nodded at her. "She can hear this."

Burton closed his eyes and crimped his lips. A facial tic caused a bony cheek to jerk. "Forty-six. Confirmed. Seventeen probables." He took a deep breath and opened his eyes.

"So do you know why Hammadi would have it in for you? Why he cut your disability off?"

"Well, sure. I mean, the guy's an Iraqi-American. At first I didn't even want to talk to him, because I thought he would be hostile, but he either wasn't or covered it up. Eventually, I came to trust him. Saw him probably fifteen or twenty times. Two years' worth. Gotta say, though, he surprised me with this disability thing."

"And what all did you tell him?"

"Everything."

"Did you know names?"

"I can still tell you most of them. Hard to forget the name of a man you killed."

"Any Hammadis?"

"Well, yeah. Common name. And I even thought about that, but he never let on. At all." Burton looked thoughtfully at Katy with her bandaged cheeks, then back at Tip. "You really think he's doing this? I mean, he's a nice guy. And to be honest, he's kind of a numbnuts." He turned to Katy again. "Sorry."

She waved a hand to show it was nothing. He turned back to Tip.

"Can't see him pulling it off."

"Don't know if it's him. For sure, that'd be pretty elaborate. Come to America and become a citizen just to get revenge. But it could be a crime of opportunity. He ends up by coincidence at the same VA as you and decides to do something."

"Maybe it's not a coincidence. He transferred in from DC about two years ago. Same time I started going to the VA. Maybe he looked up veteran records there and applied for a transfer." Burton cleared his throat uncomfortably.

"You ever take out any targets in southwestern Iraq?"

"Sure. Karbala. As Salman. Tallil."

"Funny. I was in First Marines, but a bunch of us were detached to serve with Army 24th division. Hell of a fight in Tallil. For the airport. And around the airport." Tip's memory of the house came flooding back.

"No shit?" Burton glanced at Katy. "Uh, sorry. No kidding?"

Katy shrugged.

"No kidding," Tip said. "Was there a Hammadi on your list in Tallil?"

Burton looked as if someone had punched him in the gut. "There was."

"I'm beginning to see a picture here. I had, a, uh, an incident in Tallil, too." He looked at Katy, who was now paying rapt attention. "Still gives me dreams. And I'm beginning to suspect a connection. Anyone who could read our alphabet could have read my uniform name tag. And remembered."

"You got one incident and it gives you dreams. I got sixty three. Think about them every day. They were all bad guys, but I still think about them. We got the intelligence from the Iraqis. Maybe some of them were just grudges."

Tip nodded.

Burton pursed his lips. "I just don't know." He sounded doubtful. "I mean, he did ask a lot of questions, but he seemed like a decent guy. Sympathetic. And him being Iraqi and all, it kind of made me feel better, if you know what I mean. "

"I do. And I don't think it's him doing it. I think he's paying somebody to do it. I think we got a professional on our hands. With at least one and maybe two cutouts between Hammadi and the killer."

"I think it was this Hammadi in the barn," said Katy firmly.

"Why?" Tip asked.

"Because, like I said, he had an accent. And he was going to film himself cutting my head off. Not something an American would normally do. Plus, this guy had delicate hands, like somebody who works in an office. And I'm sure I heard him say "Allahu akbar" over and over under his breath while they were driving me out to that barn."

"No shit?" said Burton. "Kidnapping? Attempted video decapitation? In Sedalia? Why haven't I heard about this?"

"No shit," said Katy. "Dad saved me at the last minute. But the cops are keeping it quiet, because they don't want people to think they're not doing their job." "But he had—" Her voice thickened and her face twisted up as if she were going to sob. Burton reached a tentative hand out to lay on her shoulder but then pulled back. She stifled the emotion and cleared her throat. "He had another bastard helping him. Ran his hands over me. Wore cologne. Smelled like cypress, or something."

Tip froze. He remembered that lingering smell in the clump of willows between the drain pipes under I-65.

Burton shook his head in sympathy and crimped his lips in determination. "You gotta catch this bastard, Tip. Or these bastards, if there's more than one. They killed the only guy who ever acted like a father toward me. Let me hunt. Showed me how to plant and raise a garden. Tried to get me to read the Bible, but I wouldn't do it, so he would tell me Bible stories. He was a good man, and some son of a bitch took him away. Same with Jennifer. Sweet kid from good people who treat me like a real person. But I'm seeing it now. George and Jennifer were the closest the sons of bitches could get to me, my folks being dead. Just killing me wasn't good enough. First, take everything away from me, then hang it on me. Make me suffer longer." He shook his head bitterly. "It all does have a Middle Eastern feel to it. But where does Missy Davis fit in? She was a damn fine looking, sweet gal, but nothing to you or to me."

"Two customers, same killer, I'm pretty sure," said Tip. "Big Iva pissed some Chicago bad guys off. You and I, if I read it right, have pissed somebody else off. Maybe Hammadi."

Burton looked thoughtful. Tip was glad he was sober. He was sure the man had good tactical judgment or he would not have survived two tours in Iraq.

"We need bait," Burton said. "We need to draw this son of a bitch out somehow. Might try for you, or Katy, or me. How do we draw him out without getting one of us killed?"

"Hmmm," said Katy.

Both Tip and Burton replied. "What?"

"Look, everybody in this town knows everything, right? I mean, I know it's true, because I never used to be able to get away with anything when I grew up here."

Burton smiled, perhaps imagining the things Katy tried to get away with. Tip nodded. "Lucy cleans the house. Only takes a few hours for anything I do or say with her there to get broadcast. Same with Chet at the jail, Mama Alma at Fishers' Groc, or Mrs. Aubrey at the church. Lucy was in the house once since you been home? Did the laundry? By now, half the town can tell you your waist size."

"OK," she said. "I have an idea."

# CHAPTER TWENTY-EIGHT

Tip, Big Iva, and Katy sat in Pastor Frank's study, facing the man across the corner of a massive old oaken desk. Pastor Frank was a tall man with good hands who looked like he could handle a basketball, but no one ever saw him do it. His salient feature was his kind face, always with a smile but a slight look of essential sadness. He looked like a big guy who could beat hell out of you but never would.

Tip sat in the straight-backed counseling chair right next to the desk, and Katy and Big Iva occupied pulled-up folding chairs of the ancient wooden variety found in old churches. Big Iva's chair creaked and groaned ominously.

"It's very unusual," said Pastor Frank. "The young woman was a prostitute if my information is correct. Some in our congregation will take offense. Why not have a discreet funeral in Hoffman's funeral home, with the in-house chaplain he hires down from Elmira?"

Tip could tell Big Iva wanted to jump Pastor Frank for this, but she held back.

"I want the best for Missy," she said in a controlled voice. "She was a good girl who struggled through life. She was in her first year of law school. She wasn't just some bimbo."

Tip noticed she didn't deny the prostitute part.

Pastor Frank looked at Tip. "Also, if what you're telling me is true, there could be gunfire. These evildoers could come after Iva. Or you. Or Katy. In the church! I can't put people at risk like that, independently of whether I should be conducting a funeral service for someone like Missy."

"'Her sins are forgiven, for she hath loved much,'" said Iva quietly.

"What did you say?" said Pastor Frank, surprised. "Luke? Jesus to the prostitute in the Pharisee's house?"

Iva said nothing, just looked at him. Pastor Frank looked at her for a long time, saw the tear in her eye, then finally nodded.

"Of course. I remember that passage well. I should be willing to take some heat." He sat back and sighed. "All right. I will need some details about her life, things I can talk about in the service." He turned to Tip. "But still, here's the question. You've all been targets of this person, and probably still are. Having you all in one place will possibly draw this guy. Look, I did a tour as chaplain in Afghanistan. I've seen what gunfire can do. I don't want that in my church. How will you prevent it?"

Tip waited until he was sure he still heard Mrs. Aubrey's weight shifting on the creaky hardwood in the hall outside, probably rearranging brochures on the hall table. Any old excuse to eavesdrop. Then he laid it out.

"I won't deny your concerns. Something could happen. We'll sit in a roped-off section by ourselves. Tom Burton will be with us, too. He wants to show solidarity with Iva, and respect for George and Jennifer Clarkson, whose funerals he couldn't attend because he was a suspect. But he says he's also a target, since the bad guys tried to frame him. So we'll all ride to the cemetery together in a limousine Iva has arranged. The funeral procession will have to go out around the mile square past Schniermann's, because the county's going to be working on a culvert on the usual route."

"So if some hidden gunman starts shooting, you'll be separated from everybody else."

"That's the plan," said Tip. "But Iva is adamant: she wants Missy to have a church funeral, since she never got to have a church wedding."

Pastor Frank raised an eyebrow at Tip, who realized he might have pushed it a bit far. While folks didn't talk to Pastor Frank about some things, he wasn't stupid, and he had probably figured out Big Iva's and Missy's relationship.

"Fine, I'll do it," said Frank, and looked at Big Iva with sympathy. "And I'm very sorry for your loss." He reached over and took her hand in his. It was as big as his. "Love knows no boundaries."

Big Iva choked and laid her other hand on top of Frank's. "Thank you."

\* \* \*

The church was two thirds full. All of Big Iva's people were there, an amazing assortment of barely acceptably dressed young women, and tattooed and ear-ringed young men in work clothes smelling of diesel fuel. A fair sample of the town's young men under forty made up the rest of the crowd. All had left their wives at home.

As promised, Tip, Tom Burton, Katy, and Big Iva sat by themselves in a roped-off area in the left front of the church. Big Iva had spared no expense on flowers and an organist. There was even a soloist who sang "Let it Be" *a capella*. And Pastor Frank did a graceful job, choosing as his text the very Luke story Big Iva had quoted. Big Iva sniffled, and so did the other young women in her

retinue, but the young townsmen remained stony-faced and digni-
fied.

There was one incident, in which the wife of one of the forty-
year-old men in the crowd came in, sat down beside him long
enough to whisper in his ear, then hauled him out by his elbow.
But otherwise, all went off without incident. The State boys concealed in the crowd got no play. So everyone moved on to phase
two of Katy's plan: the procession.

The limo was bullet-proof, according to Big Iva. The doors
closed like a safe, and all outside noise was cut off.

"Hope you're right," said Burton. "Cause we're sitting ducks in
here if it's not."

Tip put away his phone. "Chet says the woods out by
Schniermann's Cut are full of State boys. Everyone is in place
waiting for the shooter to show up."

"It's the most logical place for a sniper, I agree," said Burton.

"They've even put up their one test drone," Tip said. "If our
guy shows up to pick us off, they'll see him."

"But he hasn't shown up so far?" worried Katy. "Surely he
would be there an hour or two ahead of time."

"Yeah," said Tip. "There is that. They would have called me if
they had seen him. But in any case, even if he slipped in without
them noticing, we're in a bullet-proof limo. So if he shoots, he'll
give away his position, and they'll get him."

The surprise was, they drove through the cut, a perfect kill zone
between two fifteen-foot wooded cut banks, and there was no
shooting.

The other surprise was, Dr. Hammadi was at the graveyard. He
stood respectfully back at a distance during the burial service,
during Pastor Frank's recitation of that haunting line, "the sure and
certain hope of resurrection," that always brought a tightness in

Tip's chest. Then, once Missy's casket was safely in the ground, he came over and offered his hand to Tip.

"I'm sorry to have spoken harshly to you the last time we spoke, Mr. Tungate. I was having some personal difficulties. I had to go away for awhile. Please forgive me."

Out of Hammadi's sight, Katy cut her eyes and head toward him, signaling to Tip, "This is the guy."

"Of course," said Tip, nodding at Katy, but wanting to be decorous for Iva's sake. But he was thinking of the man's meeting in the tea shop with the Chechen—who had shot him in the ear and the leg. And of the scene at the barn. And of why he didn't just kill the son of a bitch on the spot. But he kept it under wraps. "I would like to talk to you after the burial, if you don't mind."

"Of course," said Hammadi. Then he took Burton's hand and said, "Tom, I have missed talking with you."

"Well, me too," said Burton. "You going to come back to the VA? Maybe reinstate my disability?"

"Of course," reassured Hammadi. "Forgive me. I was having bad time and, how you say, I take it out on you. You are actually favorite people."

And with that, he gave Burton the traditional Arab kiss on the left and right cheeks. Burton, having spent at least two years in Iraq, automatically responded in kind. Hammadi stepped back.

Suddenly, Burton's head exploded, then a shot rang out. Burton dropped to the ground like a deflated balloon.

"Get down everybody!" yelled Tip, and hauled out his .45.

Katy swatted at something as if a bee buzzed her ear. At the same time a blow to his shoulder knocked Tip down, and another shot rang out. He dropped and rolled. Big Iva stood tall, looking for the shooter. She pulled her Beretta Pico from her pants pocket, fired off three rounds across the river, then squatted behind a large tombstone.

Katy hit the ground beside Tip and rolled behind a grave stone. Then she pulled out her .38, leaned out at the side, and fired all six rounds across the river.

"I think he's gotta be in that clump of trees!" she shouted. Then she turned to Tip. "Dad, give me your .45! I'm out of ammo!" He didn't answer. "Dad! Dad! Can you hear me?"

He managed a look at her. And as he did so, he realized he could see out of his left eye again. She had a graze on the side of her forehead. "You're hit," he grunted.

"I'm OK. But you don't look so good. There's blood everywhere."

"Well, it hurts like a son of a bitch," he groaned. "Can you see where it came from or are you and Iva just wasting lead?"

"Across the river. Top of that rise. I'm sure."

"I think so, too," said Pastor Frank, still erect, shading his eyes to look across the river. He made no effort to seek cover.

"Yes," said Hammadi, squatting behind another tombstone, looking calm. "Delay between bullet and sound was half a second. So distance to shooter is maybe two hundred meters."

"That's right," said Frank. "Maybe five hundred, six hundred feet away." He pointed across the river at the wooded bluff upstream from the elevator. "Has to be there."

"Get down, you fool!" snapped Big Iva. "You think God is going to protect you?"

"Maybe," he said matter-of-factly, though he did step behind a tree. He took out his cell phone and reported the incident, saying the shot had come from across the river, from the bluff above the elevator. "Shooter could still be there," he said.

Then he squatted beside Burton, in the open, placed a hand on his chest, and bowed his head in a moment of prayer. That done, he stood in a businesslike way and said, "I also think, now that the shooter knows people here are armed, he's gone. During my chaplain tour in Afghanistan, I never heard of a suicide sniper."

Tip felt his shoulder. His right shoulder, damn it. His right arm was numb. The hole was above his collar bone. That was good. Actually more like a tear, though. Felt as if had severed his trapezius. He couldn't raise the arm. He rolled onto his back and looked up at the sky. Damn it, the corpses were piling up, and so were his injuries. Maybe this was all too much, and he should take Katy and leave the state. But then he gritted his teeth and rolled back onto his right knee. His good knee. He was beginning to feel like a car with two hundred thousand on it. Keep fixing, or tow it to the junkyard?

"Pastor Frank may be protected by God," grunted Tip, "but everybody else should stay down until help comes."

Within minutes, a siren sounded across the river, and two more came up the lane to the cemetery. It was Temple in a State car, and an Elmira ambulance.

"Chet's checking it out across the river," she reported. "I think you can all get up now." She looked at what was left of Burton. "Except for him. Tom Burton, right?"

"Yes," said Pastor Frank. "His struggle is over."

Tip struggled to get to his feet, a difficult task with his right shoulder and left thigh incapacitated. Pastor Frank and Katy finally helped him.

Temple took pictures from several angles of them all standing where they had been when the shots came. Then she recorded each of them telling what happened. Finally, she received a call from Chet, saying the bluff across the river was unoccupied, but that there was an obvious sniper's nest, no weapon, no shell casings.

"It is sad," said Hammadi, looking down at Burton. "But he had much to answer for."

This pissed Tip off and it was all he could do to keep from shooting the son of a bitch in front of witnesses. "And just what did he have to answer for?" he demanded. "He wasn't perfect, but he served his country well."

"Of course, I can't talk about that," said Hammadi. "Patient confidentiality."

"Why not talk about why you came to the burial of a person you didn't know?" insisted Tip. He was thinking of the two-cheek kiss. And Hammadi's meeting with the Chechen. "Maybe to identify the target to a sniper who wasn't sure what he looked like?"

"Tip," soothed Pastor Frank. "We are on hallowed ground here."

"Is not a problem," said Hammadi smoothly. "I came to apologize to favorite patient. He stopped going to VA, and I didn't know where he lived. I saw him get into limousine at your church. So I came to cemetery. That is all."

"And what were you doing in Sedalia?" snapped Tip. "Sightseeing?"

"I came to find Tom Burton," Hammadi said easily. "I feel, I treat him badly."

"You did," said Tip. "And eventually I will prove it."

"You are full of hatred, Mr. Tungate," said Hammadi. "You must let Allah cleanse you of it."

"I'll do the cleansing when the time is right," said Tip, getting into Hammadi's face. "*Insha'Allah*."

Hammadi gave a small smile. "Sooner or later, we all get fate we deserve. Good day, Mr. Tungate." And he walked back down the lane to his car.

Then Iva, who looked sad and forlorn and lost for the only time in the years Tip had known her, spoke in a small voice.

"Can we bury Missy now?"

And with that, she knelt by the grave and began raking in dirt with her bare hands.

## CHAPTER TWENTY-NINE

**D**oc Quick was his usual sympathetic self.

"How the hell am I going to get paid for all this?" he demanded, swabbing Katy's forehead with alcohol. He was talking to Tip, who sat in the chair beside the exam room desk, his shirt cut away and his shoulder heavily bandaged. Katy sat on the exam table. "You come in here and ask for these surgical procedures I have no idea how to bill for, and you run up a bill I can't imagine how you'll pay, now that you're out of work. And it looks to me like you're going to get killed before I get a penny. Nothing I can do for this, by the way," he said as an aside to Katy as he took a closer look. "An abrasion. Not bad. It'll heal on its own. How'd you get it?"

"Same bullet that hit Dad," she said matter-of-factly. "I actually heard it. Sounded like a bumble bee."

Doc shook his head and touched Katy's bandaged cheeks. Of course, everyone in town had now heard about the incident at Reinhart's barn. "You Tungates have more lives than a cat." He turned to Tip. "What the hell, Tip? Gonna get her killed, too?"

"I have medical insurance, by the way," said Katy. "It will pay for mine. Not sure about Dad's."

"I do too, actually," said Tip. "Still on my old insurance from the department. At least, for awhile. All you have to do is fill out the forms. I imagine they're quite detailed." He smiled at Doc, whose face darkened.

"You know damn well Carmen will fill them out, not me. And I don't appreciate you joking about the fact that I pay her to do NOTHING but fill out FORMS, mainly for the GOVERNMENT, but also—"

"I wish I knew what the hell, by the way," said Tip. "About Katy. And I'm doing my best to keep her breathing. But I could use some sympathy here. My shoulder hurts like hell, and my leg still hurts like hell. And my ear still hurts like hell. You suppose you could put some pain pills on my bill, too?"

Doc exhaled sharply, reached into a cabinet, and pulled out a sample bottle of pills. "Here. Don't ask me for any more of these. They're addictive. When they're done, they're done." He grabbed a pad from the desk and scrawled a prescription. "This makes them legal. Now get the hell out of my office, and don't come back with any more life-threatening injuries. Bring me the bastard who's *doing* this, and let me treat *his* life-threatening injuries."

* * *

It was clearly not safe to go back to the railroad house and stay there. It had come under attack once, and Katy had been kidnapped there. They needed a safe place to sleep, and Tip's finances were meager. Motels were out.

"Why don't we move in with Mom and Neal for a few days?" suggested Katy brightly. "Just until all this blows over."

Tip's rule had always been never to speak ill of Diane. It was unmanly and ungentlemanly. Besides being pointless. An insufferable bitch was an insufferable bitch. No amount of complaining to others would change it. And he certainly wouldn't do it in front of their daughter, who clearly had maintained a relationship with her mother.

"I'm pretty sure that would be an uncomfortable situation," he managed.

"How long since you've seen her?"

"Ten years."

"And you've never met Neal?"

"No."

"He's not so bad. Plus, he's loaded. Dentist. Drives a Mercedes. So does Mom."

"I'm so happy for them."

"Dad," chastised Katy. "We need their help. I'll arrange it. Whoever's after us would never think we would be there."

"Most people wouldn't."

"Plus, whoever's after us probably doesn't even know about them."

"There's that. But I don't want to put others at risk. They're after you, because of me, I'm sure. And they're after me. I don't want your Mom to get hurt."

"That's sweet, but don't expect her to act grateful if you say that. Also, I notice you left out Neal from that statement. Look, I'll set it up. All you have to do is be civil."

"I always get the hard assignments."

* * *

Carmel was a good seven gallons of gas from Sedalia in the '68 Chevy with the 348. But Tip insisted on driving it because it had speed and maneuverability over the old F-150.

The house turned out to be a gracious, two-story brick colonial on at least four lots on a cul-de-sac, with professional landscaping and a four-car garage.

Diane was standing on the front porch as they drove up. She still looked good: blonde, coiffed, thin, stylish. She pointed to the garage. One of the doors rose, so Tip drove on in. The floor was pristine, which caused him to hope Toby had done a good job seating the engine's front and rear main seals. But he quickly decided there was more to worry about than oil spots on the floor.

Diane met them at the mudroom door and was horrified by their appearance. "Katy, Katy, Katy, what's happened to you?" She enfolded her daughter in her arms, and Katy hugged her back. Then she glanced at Tip, still standing down in the garage. "Tip," she said with a curt nod. "You're not looking so good yourself. What have you gotten my daughter into?"

"Don't fully know yet, but it's dangerous. Somebody is trying to kill us both. They've kidnapped her once and shot me twice. And they've killed four other people in Sedalia. So if you don't want us here, I understand."

"Kidnapped?" She looked horrified. "We've been reading about the four. Lots on TV about what the governor is doing about it. But they haven't mentioned anybody being after Katy or you. They did show you being relieved of your position." It sounded like an accusation.

"The people now in charge like to keep the public informed."

Diane had not moved out of the doorway. She still looked as good as the day she left, perfectly groomed, dressed like a million bucks, still trim, tennis-court fit. Standing in this neat, clean garage, in this orderly subdivision, in front of this woman for whom things always went well, he was tiredly embarrassed that deadly, chaotic, down-and-dirty things had happened in Sedalia. His town. Why had he not prevented them? Why had he not at least caught the bad guy? Now he stood like a bum, in three-day-old pants with a blood spot where the bandage had seeped through, and a semi-clean but wrinkled shirt from the truck's go bag. He was a supplicant before his ex-wife. Only for Katy would he do this. He looked back at the truck, then back at Diane.

"Look, I'll just sleep out here in the back of the truck. I've got a sleeping bag. Just let me know where I can use the bathroom, and I'll leave you alone. Both of us need sleep and a little R&R, that's all. Then I'll be going back down to Sedalia. I've got one more thing I want to pursue."

Diane looked as if someone had bludgeoned her on the back of the head. "Oh, I'm sorry, Tip! My manners. Come in, come in. Katy told me what you need, and that you might be putting us in danger, but I said come ahead. We have a room ready for each of you, and I'm sure Neal can lend you some clothes. He's a big man, but they might be a little tight. He'll be home in a few hours, after his office hours. You'll like him, Tip. I know you will."

She led him through the house and upstairs to a room the size of his living room.

"One of our guest rooms," she said. "Has an en-suite bathroom, over there. Plenty of towels. Please. Make yourself comfortable. Dinner tonight at six."

"Sleep," he said, looking at the queen-size bed, and she left.

And he did. Like a rock, after a careful shower. All afternoon. And when he woke up, his clothes were gone, and a stack of clothes lay on the corner of the bed: a golf shirt, a pair of chinos, and a web leather belt. They fit fairly well, with the pants only a little short.

He went down, with the .45 in his waist holster under the back of the untucked golf shirt. A large man nearly as tall as him was coming down the downstairs hall.

"Earl!" he boomed. "You must be Earl! I'm Neal!" He stuck out his hand.

Tip took it and they shook. The guy had a grip like an iron-worker but his skin was soft.

"People call me Tip. I appreciate you and Diane taking us in for a short while under the circumstances. There could be danger."

"Nonsense!" He clapped Tip on the back, narrowly missing the latest wound. "Nothing's going to happen to you here! I know the chief of police! He's got two cars parked at the end of the street watching anybody who comes in or goes out! At my request! We're good! Come on down to the den and have a whiskey before dinner. We've got a lot of catching up to do." He winked.

"Much as I'd like a snort, I'll just have a Coke. Gotta stay sharp. People are trying to kill us, Neal. Katy and me."

"I'm sure it will all work out, Earl. If Jim Brandt doesn't have it taken care of in a couple of days, I'll give him a call."

\* \* \*

Dinner was in a formal dining room on a cherry table that must have cost a month of Tip's salary, with damask cover, cloth napkins, and place settings with three forks, two spoons, a water glass and a wine glass. Tip looked at the red wine in the glass and the blindingly white table cloth and was glad he had already told Neal he wasn't drinking. He'd make a spot for sure.

A Hispanic woman named Marta served, and Diane praised her cooking while she did so, and explained that her husband

Alvoro "takes care of the outside." She pronounced Alvoro with a Spanish accent. Marta only smiled.

Diane was doing all this fancy stuff to maximize his discomfort, Tip was sure, but he did his best, working the forks from the outside in and leaving the wine untouched. Katy, Diane, and Neal seemed perfectly at ease, and Tip suppressed a smile when he noted them holding their forks upside down in their left hands, and using their knives to push food onto them, European style. It was no wonder they were all so trim.

Nevertheless he was able to get through the meal without spilling anything, getting crumbs on the table, or getting anything on his shirt. And not acting like it was an unusual accomplishment. But Diane had to comment.

"Tip, your table manners have improved." She smiled.

He was instantly reminded, if he needed to be, why they had been incompatible. Grown up in Sedalia, she had increasingly taken on airs, until she finally found Neal, for whom they were normal manners, and he took her at face value.

"Thanks, Diane. It's good to see you haven't changed."

The ambiguity of this comment lay over the table for a moment before Neal took over with a good-natured harrumph. He seemed always to be full of bluff good cheer, a man for whom having a dark day would be bad form.

"So tell me, Earl—"

"People call me Tip."

"Tell me, Tip. What's it like being a lawman? It must be exciting."

"Mostly, it's boring. You hope. When it gets exciting, that's when you have to beg your ex-wife for a safe place to sleep." Dead silence fell around the table. "Sorry. That came out wrong. I am grateful you've given us a place to sleep. We're actually running for our lives, and you've taken on risk. That took courage. I'm grateful."

More dead silence. Such raw topics were clearly not discussed at the dinner table here. The Colts' prospects, golf, the weather if conversation flagged. Tip realized he had crossed a cultural line. He struggled to recover.

"So, Neal, you look as if you're in great physical condition." He turned to Diane. "Both of you. You folks golf, play tennis, go to the gym?"

The smile returned to Neal's face. "All of those, Tip. You golf? Happy to take you out to the Club some time. Gotta tell you, I'm not that great."

"He's hustling you," smiled Diane. "His official handicap is four, but he's really a scratch golfer. He takes money off of people all the time."

It appeared to be an old conversational ploy for both of them, and Tip played along, drawing them both out about their sports, their travel, even their financial situation. "He doesn't need to work," chastised Diane, looking sidewise at Neal. "But he says he enjoys it, so I let him. Instead of making him take me to France for a year, as he has promised."

Meanwhile, on the other side of the table, Katy's smile steadily became more frozen, and her gaze had settled on the middle distance. She paid no attention to either Diane or Neal. Tip knew what it was. She was thinking about Burton. She had never seen anyone killed before. And it had been her idea to make sure Mrs. Aubrey heard everything: that the four of them—the four targets—would go together to the funeral, through Schniermann's Cut together in the limo, and stand together in the graveyard.

During dessert, an irresistible pecan-covered cheesecake Tip was sure would require an extra belt hole all by itself, Diane went on at great length about her paintings. Neal smiled indulgently, and Tip nodded as best he could. He was considering how to reply to her invitation to her next showing, when Katy interrupted.

"I have another idea," she said, looking intensely at Tip, ignoring Diane and Neal.

Diane's mouth dropped open. She had almost had Tip corralled. "Katy, how rude."

Katy ignored her. "We need to talk about it. Alone. And we need everybody in Sedalia on our side."

# CHAPTER THIRTY

**D**iane's voice followed them out through the kitchen and mudroom and into the garage as Katy hauled her father along by his good arm. "Don't you *trust* us?" her mother called. "Your own mother and step father? You bring that man into my house and act like this?"

Katy ignored her. She was on a mission.

She closed the door on her mother's comments and turned to Tip. "OK. This guy is a sniper, right? Probably formally trained?"

"Sure looks like it. Except for that one case, where he strangled Missy Davis. Assuming it was the same guy."

"Snipers take great pride in their marksmanship, right?"

"They do. Whoa. I think I see where you're going with this. Not only will he come after us both again, he *has* to for the sake of his pride."

"That's what I think. The other thing is, he doesn't know how badly we're injured."

"Sure he does. By now, Hammadi, who for sure is the payer but I don't know why, knows the extent of our injuries. So does Pastor Frank. By now he's told Mrs. Aubrey, who's told everybody in town. The only thing everybody in town *doesn't* know is where you and I are right now."

"Sure. But I'm thinking you suffer a relapse, some sort of complication, and end up dead. Doc Quick tearfully announces it. You went in for a chest pain you thought was related to the shoulder wound, and you had a heart attack and died right there in his office. Sedalia will love it. It has drama. Pathos. So there's a big funeral. The killer *has* to come to the funeral because he doesn't believe it. So naturally, the dead person has to lie very still in the casket, no smiling or twitching, while people say how nice he looks, how life-like. Meanwhile, half the crowd is armed State Police in civilian clothes, waiting for something to happen. Neal arranges the police with the governor, to protect me."

Tip gave a wry smile. "I see you've given this some thought. So how does the dead person—who I notice *I* get to be—keep the shooter from leaning over the casket and stabbing him? Or shooting him with a silenced pistol? How do we recognize him?"

"Well, it won't be Hammadi, because he knows we already suspect him, and he'll know he's being watched."

"OK, so how?"

"The killer's going to test to confirm you're dead: poke you, pinch you, or stab you. So whoever does that is the killer."

"A brilliant plan. Except after he stabs me, I really *will* be dead."

Katy grinned. "Oh, all right. That's why you wear a Kevlar vest, one with sleeves, under your suit. As soon as you feel something, you pull out your gun and sit up."

Tip smirked appreciation and shook his head. "It's outrageous. But creative. I'll give it that. Both Hammadi and the shooter are going to want to make sure. But why me? You're the one with the head graze. Maybe it caused a concussion that killed you."

She shook her head. "Because you're the main target, Dad. They're only after me to get to you."

He sighed. "Yeah. You're probably right."

"Plus, everyone knows your injuries are worse than mine. So there's that." Then she smiled meanly. "And they'll believe the heart attack. Just the way you eat will make them believe that. Breaded tenderloins at Big Iva's. Grease burgers at Eileen's."

Tip's mouth watered. His stomach was already growling. The serving sizes on Diane's table were designed more to look great on her china than fill you up.

"Look. I'm not saying I'll go for this. But if I did, I still think *you* should die because I gotta be ready for the guy if he tries something."

"I can't die because I'm gonna sell this story to the network for a one-hour documentary. Plus, you'll make a much more imposing corpse than me. I'm too young. And skinny."

Tip snorted. "Learn that smartass stuff in New York, did you? All right, all right. So I'm the corpse. At least my part has no lines to screw up. But what, I just hold my breath for an hour so nobody sees my chest move? Take an allergy pill to keep from sneezing? After all, what could possibly go wrong with a plan like this?

"I've thought of all that. We leave the casket closed until after the service, "at the family's request," then let people file past."

"So I'll be dead from suffocation, and nobody will suspect a thing."

"You'll have an oxygen bottle in the casket with you, along with a tablet and earphone to watch and listen to the proceedings live. We'll set up a couple of very small video cameras. When Pastor Frank is done, Digger Hoffman will open the casket for the viewing. It'll work like a charm."

Tip heaved a sigh. Didn't like it, didn't like it, did not like it. But he had no better plan. And it just might work.

"All right. The worst that can happen, aside from complete disaster and death, is lifelong embarrassment in Sedalia. I'm willing to take that risk if we can catch these guys. You know, you're going to have to convince your mother to play along. No ex-wife misses her ex-husband's funeral. I believe the traditional response when a woman is informed of her ex's death is, 'Are you sure?'"

"Dad," she chastised. "Give yourself a break. Look, I'm really sorry I never called all those years. At first I thought I had a reason, then I was just embarrassed at what I said to you. I was pretty young. But I realized once I had lived in the city for awhile that you and Mom were just incompatible. She's just not a small-town person. You didn't drive her away. She left. But you're still both decent people."

Tip choked.

Then he hugged his daughter and she hugged back.

* * *

"What?" Diane shrieked. "You have to be kidding! It's a crazy idea! It sounds really dangerous!"

Tip nodded, astonished for once in his life to be in complete agreement with his ex-wife.

"Mom!" snapped Katy. "Of course it's dangerous. The part you're not thinking about is *why we are here*! They've *already* tried to kill us both. Twice! We have to get them before they get us."

Diane sniffed. "That sounds like such a Republican thing to say, dear."

Katy's eyes rolled back in her head. Neal reached across the table and took Diane's hand.

"I think it's a creative idea," he said. "You should be proud of your daughter. She's dealing with a tough reality. And she's asking for our help and giving us each an important role to play."

"Oh, all right," said Diane. "I suppose I'll need something to wear. I don't go to a lot of ex-husband funerals."

Neal smiled. "Yes, and you'll need to prepare your lines. People in Sedalia are going to have things to say to you. You must act your part."

"Which is what?"

Neal looked at Tip, than back at Diane. "'We grew apart, but he was a good man. I'm sure Sedalia will miss him.' Something like that."

Diane looked at Tip, really looked at him for the first time since he and Katy had come. "Yes, I think that's right. I can do that."

"And I will definitely play my part by calling Jim Brandt. After running Tip out of office, I'm sure he'll be magnanimous about sending some troopers down to his funeral. Of course, I can't tell Brandt exactly why we need them. The story will be, to protect Katy. The question is, who besides us has to know the truth? And how do you know that person isn't the killer?"

Tip looked at Neal with something akin to respect. Maybe the guy wasn't just a vacuous country clubber after all.

"That'll just be Doc Quick and Digger Hoffman, the undertaker. Doc has to tell the story, and Digger's got to be involved to put that terrible white make-up all over my face to make me look dead, and provide a casket and a hearse. And explain why the only viewing is just after the funeral. Family request, he'll explain, since it minimizes Katy's exposure. He's a big mouth, though, so I'll tell him Katy's life depends on keeping quiet. We'll just have to hope that does the trick."

\* \* \*

Tip decided to take one more run at Sanchez. Maybe he could find out something to make the funeral unnecessary. Did Sanchez know of any contract killers loose in the Hoosier state?

The FBI agent was not happy to hear from Tip, but not entirely unsympathetic.

"I have no reason to talk to you about law enforcement matters, Tungate. You're a private citizen. Who, unfortunately, seems to have somebody trying to kill him. We've heard about that."

"Bless your heart, as we say here in flyover country. And have you heard about my daughter's kidnapping?"

There was silence on the phone.

"What kidnapping? We've heard of no such kidnapping. All kidnappings are supposed to be reported to the FBI."

Tip explained why.

"That's actually illegal. They can't suppress information like that."

"But they did, and you're talking about the governor's fair-haired girl, even though her hair is actually dark as sin, so you'd be taking a career risk to pursue it. Look, I'm on my own here, I accept that. So what I want to know is, do you know of any professional snipers, military guys trained as snipers, who have gone rogue, gone private, who take money for contract killings? Who might be in Indiana."

"No. Not recently."

"What do you mean, 'recently'?"

"Well, we had a guy in witness protection out in Wyoming. You'd think that would be good enough for him. Nice big house, stipend so he didn't have to work. I mean, nobody goes there, and most people don't even know where it is. He was mob hit man who specialized in long-distance kills. He rolled on a capo in New York who had put out a hit on *him* to remove a potential witness. In the process, he created one. We put the long-distance shooter in witness protection, he stays there for like, six months, then disappears. We've been hunting him for five years."

"Description?"

"Can't tell you any more, Sheriff. Uh, Mr. Tungate. Already told you too much."

"All right. Thanks. Better than nothing."

So who had been in or around Indiana, or Howarth County, for around five years? Tip couldn't think of anybody. So much for that.

# CHAPTER THIRTY-ONE

Doc Quick pushed back when Tip called late at night and asked for a meeting at the I-65 rest stop north of Elmira.

"For Christ's sake, Tip.  I didn't take you for one of those."

"No, it's not that, Doc.  I have a much bigger favor to ask than that.  And only you can grant it.  It's going to take a lot of acting skill, won't cost you a dime, and more important, won't require any paperwork.  Just the opposite.  And it's going to save a couple of lives.  Including mine.  But you can't tell anyone anything. Nobody.  At all.  Except the story I'm going to give you."

"All right.  Count me intrigued."

Digger Hoffman was a little tougher.

"Why again, Tip?  This is a very odd request.  And I've got Mrs. Simms to prepare.  Her funeral is tomorrow you know."

"Actually, I didn't.  Been kind of busy."

"Yes, I've heard."

"And that's what this is about.  I need your help, Digger.  To keep from becoming one of your customers.  No offense intended."

"None taken.  Everybody says they like me, but nobody wants to be my customer.  I've even tried discounts."

Tip managed a weak chuckle.  Digger took it and continued.

"You mean this has to do with all these shootings. You know I can't give you information any more about the autopsies. Now that you're, uh—"

"Fired."

"Well, forced out, from what I heard. But I still like you, Tip. How can I help?"

"That's great, Digger. Meet Doc and me at the rest top. I'll explain everything. But tell no one. No one. No one."

"I've got it, Tip. Seems very odd, but I won't tell anyone."

\* \* \*

Both Doc and Digger understood the plan, both considered it crazy, and both agreed to go ahead with it. Tip warned them again that it hinged on absolute secrecy. The people of Sedalia, particularly its chief gossips—Chet and Mrs. Aubrey—had to believe he was dead. Not even Pastor Frank was to know. Tip provided Digger with an obituary to publish in the *Sedalia Democrat.* Digger glanced through it with a quick, professional eye.

"Kind of a puff piece, isn't it, Tip? Most obituaries are a third this long, and don't mention high school touchdowns, hotdog eating contests, or a single semester of college. Didn't know you had a bronze star, though."

"Hey, that's my life we're talking about here. Has to count for something."

Digger looked at Tip with a somber expression. "My business, we see that mostly they don't."

"Thanks, Digger. Wouldn't want to get above myself."

\* \* \*

The day of the funeral was a beautiful day, with summer-like temperatures even though it was still only late spring. The sun shone brightly in a cloudless sky as Neal drove them all down to Sedalia from Carmel. Tip's truck was far too recognizable.

They went in the back way to Digger Hoffman's establishment, where all dressed for their parts. Katy tested the hardware set-up, then went early to the church to set up the small cameras and microphones.

* * *

Sedalia Methodist Church's sanctuary was packed full. Tip could see pretty well on the tablet Katy had provided, and hear on the ear piece plugged into it. A miniature wide-angle camera on each side of the church provided a view of the whole sanctuary, including the rostrum, the pulpit, and his casket before the altar. He could even hear people on the back row, though not separate out words from the general hubbub, only recognize some voices.

It was a great set-up, just like Katy had promised. The only problem was, it was really, really hot in the casket. His shirt was already soaked. And he had to pee.

People fanned themselves furiously with the old-fashioned paper fans provided in the hymnal racks, and gossiped and buzzed and in general socialized in an excited but subdued way. Tip could just imagine what was going through their minds. And in some cases, he could hear their whispers.

This was a big deal. Tip Tungate, a fixture in their lives for decades, was dead. Effectively, killed by a serial killer he tried to stop, after being hustled out of office by the governor himself for not being fast enough. And now, his successors were looking worse than he had in the whole affair, except their PR spin was better. So they looked pretty good on Indy TV, but in Sedalia, people knew. Just let a couple of those reporters come down and talk to some regular people, by damn, and they would get a piece of Sedalia's mind.

There sat Chet Biggle, resplendent in a brand new dress uniform jacket Tip barely knew existed for sheriff's departments, with an honest-to-God loop of gold braid hanging from his shoulder. Beside him sat Temple in her Indiana State Police dress uniform. Despite himself, Tip couldn't keep from thinking about her ass. Jesus, he decided. He was hopeless. And he really had to pee. Damn prostate.

And on the front row sat Diane, Neal, and Katy, all looking suitably somber. Tip imagined the people in the crowd whispering back and forth. "Emmet, wasn't it? Diane Emmet? Treated Tip like shit, from what I heard. Daughter's a looker, though. Got her looks from her mother." Chuckle, chuckle.

Diane wore an expensive black dress and black hat with a veil, and Katy had gone out and bought herself a black dress, too, because she had brought only a few things in her flight from Manhattan. Both stared straight ahead with grim expressions, the way the bereaved do at funerals, trying not to cry, and the way they had discussed ahead of time. They had to be convincing. Tip wasn't sure, but he thought he might have even seen the glisten of a tear on Diane's face. Damn, but the woman was good. He remembered that she had been able to summon tears at the drop of a hat whenever she needed a trump card.

Hammadi was nowhere to be seen in the crowd, and Tip began to believe the whole charade was pointless. How would he explain it to the people of Sedalia if all went for naught? Wouldn't they be pissed off, being used as patsies? It was going to be embarrassing. But he would deal with that later.

He looked around hoping to see people crying, to give some validation to his life, but so far there had been no tears except Diane's. In fact, the saddest-looking people in the whole church were Samantha and Chet. They both knew the game was up, that they were going to get hung for this in the press and public opinion. No matter how good Jim Brandt was, no matter how effective his spinmeisters, there was no spinning this. This was total law-enforcement failure. Their careers were over.

He had to admit, though, that Samantha looked damn good in a black pant suit, snug in the thigh and the bust. Whew! Then he reminded himself again that he was a late middle-aged man with a prostate issue. Who really had to pee.

Finally, Pastor Frank took the rostrum and gave a fine sermon. He made no effort to pretend Tip had been a religious man, but he stressed that he had been a good man, working diligently to protect the people of his town, showing mercy where another sheriff might not, and in general behaving like a father toward the people of the town rather than a hard-bitten law-enforcement officer.

Now people began to sob, and Tip spied Jason Willetts, Toby McConnell's dope-smoking friend, and his mother, both clearly crying. Tip wondered if Jason had really given up smoking dope. But the one that really got him was Eileen, who had obviously shut down her restaurant this morning to come to his funeral. She always talked smartass with him, as if she didn't care, but she was sobbing so loudly he could hear her. He started to sniffle himself, but stifled it for fear people would hear.

Pastor Frank went on and detailed some things from Tip's life, including the big touchdown in his senior year, and the Legion hot-dog-eating contest. People smiled.

Finally, after recounting Tip's bravery in his military service, and Katy's and Big Iva's bravery at the graveyard during the latest shooting, Pastor Frank gave a benediction and asked if anyone would like to speak. The crowd had to wait for big Iva to stop coughing and hacking, which Tip by now knew was Big Iva crying. She sat on the back row next to the aisle, like anyone would who is accustomed to being shot at.

Chet got up to speak, unfolding papers out of his pocket. He praised Tip in such a way as to make himself look good, saying he and Tip had not always got along perfectly, but that he was sure Tip was a good man, and he had let Tip lean on him on various occasions because his heart was good, even if he wasn't a professional lawman, being elected and all. He then told of their involvement in the shootout at Big Iva's last year, again referring clumsily to his own heroism. A couple of sharp comments went up. One or two boos sounded. Tip made retching noises inside the coffin but again stifled himself. Chet realized he had overstepped, but took another minute to assure the town that he and the prosecuting attorney and her special investigator had this all under control. Arrests would follow soon.

"Sit down!" someone called, and Chet sat.

At this time, Tip noticed Hammadi come in the double doors at the back of the sanctuary, and sit down by Al Stefano, the Porters driver. It was nice that Al came to his funeral, Tip thought, even though he didn't live in Sedalia. He was in the township all the time, it being a big part of his area, delivering his frozen shrimp, boxed dinners, meatballs, egg rolls, and cheesecakes. Tip had never resolved the difference in the way the guy looked—compact, hairy, brutish—with the way the guy acted: everybody's friend. Everybody liked him, no exceptions.

Eileen got up and sang "Precious Memories," and Tip nearly burst out crying inside the coffin, but he didn't, because he knew the pressure on his abdomen would make him pee. He had now given up on the whole catch-the-bad-guy-at-the-funeral idea, and was just overwhelmed by the show of affection by the whole town.

He was really going to have to figure out a way to apologize to them all. Maybe a big party at Big Iva's.

But then Digger Hoffman got up and said the coffin would be open for a short time if people wanted to pay their respects. Tip was on.

He quickly put on his Raybans. *("You'll always look cool if you wear these.")* People were accustomed to seeing him in them so he thought he could get away with wearing them dead. But mainly, they would hide any eyelid twitches. Then he stuffed the tablet, the ear plug, and the oxygen cannula down into the coffin and composed himself. He really hoped this would be over soon so he could pee. He took a couple of deep breaths and closed his eyes. The lid creaked open and light streamed through his eyelids.

The first couple of people to file past went, "Whew!" and one said, "Man, Digger must have been sweating hard when he worked on Tip. You can still smell it. But doesn't Tip look like himself? Very lifelike. And those ridiculous sunglasses. He must have thought they made him look cool."

"It's really too bad," whispered Dave Schulz, whose voice Tip easily recognized. "He was slow to act and not real smart, but once he got started, you could always depend on Tip to go the distance."

Tip immediately began to wonder just how good an idea this was. Was he going to hear everybody in town's real opinion of him after all these years? He wasn't at all sure he wanted to.

Then a sobbing Eileen stood at the side of the casket and whispered, "I loved you Tip. I always loved you. Even back in high school. And Diane stole you away."

Tip nearly sat up and hugged her, but he restrained himself. Maybe this gig wasn't so bad after all. Except for the fly walking all over his face.

Someone shooed the fly off of his face, and he heard Temple's voice. "He was always such a horndog. Always looked at my ass whenever I turned my back."

"Mine too," said Samantha. She sounded almost wistful.

"You young ladies," scolded Mrs. Aubrey quietly. "The day will come when no man will look at your bottom. Enjoy the attention while you can."

Tip held his breath and bit the inside of his lip to keep from laughing. Mrs. Aubrey. Of course Mrs. Aubrey had been young once. But enjoying men looking at her bottom?

Then someone loomed up and he heard Hammadi's voice, speaking quietly. "I think is trick," he said quietly to a second presence that loomed up. Tip was surprised at how he could feel the presences, even with his eyes closed. Then he recognized the same cypress-smelling cologne he had noticed in the wind-becalmed willow clump in the drainage ditch. He went on instant alert.

"We'll find out now," said Al Stefano, the Porters man.

Of course! The Porters man! Could go anywhere at any time without arousing suspicion! Had brazenly stopped on River Road and asked Tip if he could help, shortly after—if he was the guy—shooting Missy!

Tip felt a hand against his right arm, blocking any movement, then a strong pressure on his rib-cage. Finally, something slipped through the Kevlar, and a sharp pain shot up his side.

"You dirty son of a bitch," snarled Tip. "I've got you now." He opened his eyes, swung his left arm up out of the casket and grabbed Stefano.

"What the hell?" shouted Stefano. The crowd said a collective "What?"

Tip wanted to pull his weapon but he couldn't because his right arm was blocked. All he could do was grab Stefano by the back of the neck with his left hand and pull him down. But the pain in his side was intense, and he had to get whatever was stabbed into his side out. Finally he yelled. "Katy! It's him! He's stabbing me!"

By this time, the crowd was on its feet. The tumult was tremendous. Suddenly something hit Stefano on the back of the head, once, twice, three times. "Get away from him, whatever you're doing!" demanded Mrs. Aubrey. Tip realized she was beating Stefano with her purse. "I thought there was something odd about those sunglasses."

Tip heard the sound of a revolver being cocked.

"On your knees, you scumbag," snapped Katy. "Both of you. It was you two getting ready to cut my head off at the barn. I'm sure of it."

"I am just onlooker," bleated Hammadi.

"Doc!" roared Tip. "Come help! Something is stabbed into my side!"

Doc Quick appeared, reached down a hand, pulled, and the pain subsided, but did not go away. He held up a syringe with a long, heavy-gauge needle. It contained a clear liquid.

"There are four CCs here," snapped Doc at Stefano. "How many were in it to start with?"

"Eh, I don't know," said Stefano casually. "Enough."

"What is it?"

By this time, Tip had sat up. Temple was handcuffing Stefano. The crowd stared at Tip in stunned silence.

"I got nothing to say," said Stefano. He still sounded his old, genial self. "Call the FBI. Send my picture. You can't touch me."

Chet had come up behind him. "What the Hell, Al?" he said. "I thought you were my friend! And you try to kill somebody? At his own funeral?"

Stefano shrugged. "Eh, what can I say? We had some times. You do what you're good at."

By now, Doc had Tip out of his shirt and vest and was examining the wound. "He sure as hell got you, got some of it in there, but without knowing what it is—"

"Hey Doc," said Tip. He was having trouble breathing, and his heart was racing. "You know what?"

Then the world went black.

# CHAPTER THIRTY-TWO

"**E**pinephrine, I'm pretty sure," Tip heard Doc say. "First thing I can think of that would make his heart race like that."

"I concur," said a voice Tip recognized but couldn't quite place. Then he realized it was Neal. Who, that's right, as a dentist would have gone to med school.

His heart was still pounding, but not as fast as before. And now he was starting to feel sleepy. His arms and legs felt like rubber.

"Damn good thing I had the amyl nitrate in my bag," said Doc. "Just a guess, but we'll have to wait and see."

Somewhere close by, Diane was weeping. He would never forget that sound. She had used it on him so many times it was burned into his brain. "Such a foolish thing to do, Katy," she sobbed. "I mean, we are divorced, but I still care for him. And this was *your* idea."

"He caught the guy," said Katy. Her voice was tough, unemotional. "Red-handed. The son of a bitch. And the only reason Hammadi would have been with him was that he was paying. What a weasel."

"We have them both in custody," said Samantha. "We'll get the truth out of them."

"What the hell?" said Tip. He sucked air greedily. It didn't seem to be doing that much good. Still, he opened his eyes and tried to sit up. He discovered that he was on the carpeted floor of the sanctuary in front of the casket. The crowd was being shooed out by State police and Chet's part-time deputies.

"Easy there, big fella," said Neal. "We still don't know what he hit you up with." He put a finger on Tip's carotid and went silent for a few seconds. "Still running about one-twenty. Much better than the one-eighty, though. Gotta get you calmed down, there, Earl. If he'd gotten that whole five CCs in you, you wouldn't have stood a chance."

"I'm fine," protested Tip. He struggled to get to his feet, leaning on Katy's shoulder as he did so. The room was off-level, but he felt sure he could walk and the worst was over. He looked at Samantha, who for once didn't look totally sure of herself. "Where's Stefano?"

"Chet took him to jail."

"You know those two are good buds, right?"

"I do, but Chet saw what happened. He may be a weak reed in a strong wind, but he'll do his job here. He was seriously bummed."

"What about Hammadi?"

"Who's Hammadi?"

"The guy with him, for Christ's sake. The guy who's paying Stefano. I'm ninety-nine percent sure Stefano's the mob hit man the FBI told me about. Disappeared from Witness Protection in Wyoming five years ago. About the same time Stefano showed up as the Porters man. Charge Hammadi. Do it now."

"We'll question him just because he was standing beside Stefano, but charge him with what? You have probable cause?"

"No, damn it. But I know he's behind George Sampson, Jennifer Clarkson, and Tom Burton. Check him out. Get with the State Department. I'm betting he's from a town in southern Iraq called Tallil." Tip paused, forced himself to go on. "There may be shared history there between Burton and Hammadi."

"Ah," said Katy quietly. "And you?"

He turned to look at his daughter, fully grown up now, as much as any child can ever appear fully grown up to a parent. She had a firm set to her jaw that ran in his family, not in Diane's, and a look of calculated reassessment in her eye.

"And me," he admitted. He held her gaze.

There was general silence in the group as everyone took this in.

"We'll hold him on suspicion and question him about that," said Samantha. "But even if he is from there, it won't prove anything or provide probable cause."

"It will for me," said Tip. "But I already know what the answer is."

Doc Quick broke the mood.

"Tip, you're going to the hospital in Elmira. No argument, no ifs, ands, or buts. I'll have Samantha put you under arrest if necessary. You need toxicology tests and observation for at least twenty-four hours."

Tip had backed up against the casket to maintain his balance. Otherwise, he would have ended up back on the floor.

"You make a persuasive case, Doc. But there's gonna be paperwork."

* * *

Katy stayed with him in the hospital. The drip flowing into his arm was laced with a sedative, the nurses told him, and he would sleep for twenty-four hours. The last thing he remembered was Katy sitting asleep on a fiberglass chair in his room, despite his telling her he would be fine and that she should go and stay with her mom.

When he woke, the sun was again shining brightly. It was a new day, and Katy told him that during the night, two masked gunmen had broken Stefano and Hammadi out of the Howarth County jail. Chet was down the hall, wounded and pissed off. Tip pulled the needle from his arm, wrapped the ridiculous hospital gown around to hide his ass, and went down to see Chet.

"Deputize me," he demanded.

For once in his life Chet didn't argue. "It's only because you can walk and I can't," he insisted.

"Whatever you say, Chet. Just write it out on a piece of paper I can show to Samantha and Temple so they know I'm legal. I know she's OK with it, because she offered before, but I didn't take her up on it."

Chet's face twisted up. "Damn it, Tip, I trusted the guy. I thought he was my friend. It's not like I have a lot."

Tip had never thought he'd feel sympathy for Chet, or the need to buck him up, but he did now.

"You been a faithful lawman, Chet. Not worth a damn some-times, but faithful. I never worried about you breaking the law. Maybe bending it a little. But the law comes before friends. And you showed that at the church. When the time comes, if I can, I'll set it up so you can arrest him."

* * *

The question was, where would these guys go after escaping? The good thing was, Hammadi was now legally arrestable, having escaped from jail, which ironically enough was illegal, even if you had committed no other crimes. But they wouldn't stay in the area.

Tip put his old uniform back on, found a deputy's badge, and slipped back into the jail as if he had never left. It was like putting on an old pair of shoes.

He sent the digital mug shots and fingerprints of Stefano and Hammadi to the FBI, then called Sanchez.

"You know I can't talk to you."

"Just emailed you a scan of the, uh, acting sheriff's deputization order now. Take a look. Should be on your phone now."

There was a pause.

"Anybody could have written that."

"But they didn't. And you know I wouldn't fake something like this. Because it would be impersonating a law officer."

"All right, *Deputy*. What is it?"

Tip told the story of the funeral, and before he finished, he heard an uncharacteristic sound out of Sanchez. He realized the FBI man was laughing.

"I've heard of some cockamamie plans before, but that one tops them all. So this Stefano tried to kill the corpse, which was you, with a poison injection."

"Basically. And I'm asking for your help with this Stefano. He's been around here for about five years, everybody likes him, and he's never given any reason to suspect him of anything. Until now. He's our shooter. And it's pretty clear he's working for this Hammadi guy. Maybe arranged by this Chechen guy who shot me in the leg."

There was silence on the other end of the call. Tip pressed.

"So what about it?"

"He may be our guy from Wyoming."

"Come on. You have his mug shot and prints. 'May be?'"

"The guy from Wyoming's name is not Stefano."

"What is it?"

"Can't tell you. What can you tell me about where he is?"

"Ah. So he *is* your guy from Wyoming."

"Maybe, maybe not. If he is, it might be characteristic that he couldn't resist going back into the business. Still not saying it's the same guy. But he might be somebody we would want to talk to."

"You're a hell of a lot of help, Sanchez. So you know the guy's name is not Stefano, you won't tell me what his name is, he might or might not be your guy from Wyoming, but you'd like to talk to him if we catch him."

"That's pretty much it."

"That's so helpful I can't believe it. Anything else you can tell me?"

"Yeah. Don't relax. If your guy *is* our guy from Wyoming, not saying he is, he won't give up. The law means nothing to him, and he's not afraid of you. The guy is a diagnosed psychopath. He's charming, intelligent, and plans carefully, but has no regard for others beyond his personal goals. And most of all, he feels no guilt. He's more concerned with the fact that you've made him look bad for not succeeding at every hit. His reputation is that he never gives up. He'll still come after you. But as he's getting ready to shoot you, he'll likely smile and tell you it's nothing per-sonal."

A chill settled over Tip.

"OK, thanks for the warning. What about this guy, Hammadi?"

"Don't know much. Immigrated from Iraq in '04. Degrees from Iraqi universities. Licensed shrink. Your prosecutor already asked this question."

"Where in Iraq?"

"Tallil."

\* \* \*

"Stop looking at my ass, Tip. It's so unprofessional." Temple moved from in front of the jail window and sat down at Chet's desk.

Tip sighed. "Temple, I am not looking at your ass. I am actually looking out the window. Besides, the day will come, according to Mrs. Aubrey, when you'll be sad if no man looks at your ass."

For the first time in their acquaintance, Temple smiled. It was a little like ice breaking.

"Heard that, did you?"

"Yeah." He grinned. "It's gonna be hard for me to talk to Mrs. Aubrey from now on without thinking about that."

"How are we going to find Stefano and Hammadi?"

"Good question. One way would be to just forget about them and wait for Stefano to come and kill Katy or me. But I'm not into that idea so much. I'd rather bring it to a conclusion on my own terms."

"You told me about that mosque, and the Chechen cutout. Maybe stake out the mosque?

"Tried that and stuck out like a sore thumb. I'd say, the usual way. Start with Porters. Find out where Stefano lived in Elmira. Hammadi in Indy. Stake out their places. Get their credit cards, accounts, phones, all the standard stuff. Follow their electronic trail."

"You don't think they're too smart for that stuff?"

"I do. But we can't make it easy for them. The other thing is, we find and squeeze Andrei Dalek and the Chechen. One of them knows how to get hold of Stefano."

# CHAPTER THIRTY-THREE

For a couple of days, Tip could hardly get anything done in the Sheriff's office because he had become a media star. The tabloids couldn't get enough. Repeatedly, the office phone would ring, and it would be a reporter from the *Enquirer*, the *Sun*, or the *Star* asking for exclusive information about the "Tom Sawyer Funeral."

"The what?" he would say, though he knew very well. But he played along and portrayed himself as a simple country sheriff fighting for his town, and for those two days, he rode high. The peak was when an Indy TV interview in front of his house went national: "Sedalia's Crafty Hero." Within thirty minutes he took a call from Jim Brandt.

"Maybe I was rash," said Brandt.

"No, you just behaved true to form. Once an asshole, always an asshole."

"Hey, I sent troopers to your funeral."

"That's because you thought I was really dead."

"Well, what can I do to help? And get some good PR out of it?"

"Seriously?"

"Yes, seriously."

"Help me find the guys trying to kill Katy and me. Who kidnapped Katy and were going to cut her head off on video. Put all the State boys on it. Call the FBI and get them to help. It's kind of hard for a deposed small-town sheriff to motivate the forces of truth, justice, and the American Way all by himself."

"Will do. And, maybe when this is over, you give Samantha and me credit, I'll get the court to put you back in the Sheriff's chair. She's an up-and-comer, Tip. You want to stay on her good side."

"Right." Tip spent a moment thinking about her front and back sides. And about how far up the governor's ass the court must be for him to promise such a thing. He suppressed his disgust. Help was help. "I'll send what we have on these guys. Mainly pictures, names, and prints."

"OK. To my personal email address. I'll make sure the stuff gets into the right hands." Brandt paused. "So we have a deal?"

Tip paused. "Deal."

* * *

In the end, it wasn't the governor who provided the lead. It was Mrs. Aubrey. She glided into the sheriff's office in a filmy lavender dress, smelling of lavender as she always did, moving as gracefully as a dirigible. She hadn't lost a pound since Tip was a boy. He suppressed a smile as he recalled her comment at the funeral. Temple, at Chet's desk running facial recognition on Stefano's mug shot, also appeared to suppress a smile. You had to have very sensitive instruments to detect the signs, but she had loosened a bit since she had been working with them at the jail.

"Good morning, Mrs. Aubrey," said Tip. "To what do I owe the honor? By the way, I appreciate your coming to my funeral. Everybody worries that no one will come to their funeral, and it was nice to see who all came."

She gave a rueful smile, pointing a forefinger at him and stroking it with her other forefinger in a "shame-on-you" gesture. "You were a very bad boy, Earl, fooling us all like that. We're all glad you're all right, but you gave us a terrible fright."

"Sorry, but it was the only way we could think of to flush out the guy trying to kill us. Only problem is, he's now escaped."

"Yes, I heard. So sad. Al Stefano. Such a nice man, all of us thought. Always cheerful. But it must have all been an act. Which is why I'm here. I think I know where he might be. Certainly not at his home in Elmira, after what he did to you."

Tip's ears perked up. "Do tell. How do you know?"

"Well, I talked with Al a number of times to try to get him to sell my cinnamon rolls from his truck. And he did a few times. Such a nice man. And he opened up a little with me. Not that I pried or anything. But I suppose you know that I . . . sort of collect information. It's kind of my hobby. I try to find out as much as I can about everybody. It helps me know who they are. "

"Never really noticed," lied Tip. "So what do you know about Al Stefano? Or whatever his real name is?"

"He has a daughter who lives in Shelbyville. You can tell from his accent that he's from somewhere out east, which he never talks about. But his daughter is why he moved here. And his grandson."

Tip sucked in a breath. "Know his daughter's name?"

"Cecilia. He said it once, though I don't think he meant to. It was the first time I thought there might be something Al wanted to hide. But I gather she and her father had had a falling out."

"Anything else I can use to find her? Husband? Employer? Last name?"

"He said something odd. He couldn't even get his own son in law to write his will."

"A lawyer?"

"That's what I think. I hope this helps, Earl. No one wants anything more to happen to you or your daughter."

"Thanks, Mrs. Aubrey."

And as she walked out, he looked at her dumpy ass. Temple saw him do it.

"You're terrible."

"Just paying my respects, even though she won't know it."

\* \* \*

Shelbyville boasted some eighteen law firms, a surprising number for a town its size, but it didn't take Temple long on the various social media sites to figure out which one had a lawyer whose wife's name was Cecilia: James Teal of Teal and Teal. And it didn't take long to find a home address.

Tip knew he should notify the local sheriff and city police that he was serving an arrest warrant in their town, but he feared the local connection would produce a warning and an escape. To hell with them. He could apologize later.

This time, instead of reprising his Lone Ranger act, he took Temple, Jarvis, and three other State Police along. Chet was still laid up, and didn't want to face Stefano in any case, so he declined the chance to go.

They waited until dark so as not to unduly embarrass Teal with his neighbors, then surrounded the house in the leafy neighborhood of well-kept houses from the Twenties and Thirties. An earnest, perhaps self-important young man of thirty or so opened the door and did a double-take at Tip's uniform.

"Mr. Teal?"

"Yes."

"I have an arrest warrant for Al Stefano," said Tip. "Is he in your house?"

"What's he done?"

"That's between him and the judge. Is Al Stefano in your house?"

"I assure you, Sheriff, no one born with that name is in this house. We're pretty Anglo here. And I must tell you, I'm an attorney. An officer of the court."

"No shit. Is your father in law in your house? Whatever his real name is?"

A voice from inside the house floated out. Al Stefano's voice.

"Don't get yourself in trouble, Jim. I know who it is. I'll go with him. His arrest warrant don't mean nothing anyway."

A beautiful, dark-haired young woman appeared and looked back into the house. Then she confronted Tip. "What's this about? I demand to see the arrest warrant."

Tip unfolded it from his shirt pocket and handed it to her. She read through it.

"Murder and attempted murder?" she shrieked. "No way!" She turned to Stefano. "You said it wasn't true! And I finally believed you!"

"Yeah, well that makes one of us," mumbled Teal under his breath.

Teal stepped between Tip and his wife and took the warrant from her hand. "Let me see that." He looked at Tip officiously, then read through the warrant. "Hm," he said. "Appears to be in order. But Sheriff—"

"It's actually Deputy—"

"Deputy, we had no knowledge of these alleged crimes. Only that Mr. ah—"

"Stefano," supplied Al, coming into view in the living room, hands up.

"Only that Mr. Stefano is in witness protection."

"I never did hits like they say I did," offered Al.

"You tried to kill me," said Tip without emotion. "And you escaped jail at gunpoint. And one of your confederates wounded the . . . sheriff." He twirled his finger for Al to turn around. "Hands behind your back."

Stefano complied with a shrug. "Your warrant don't mean nothing. The FBI will show up once they know you have me, and they'll take me somewhere else."

"We're peaceful, law-abiding citizens," said Teal. "We have no involvement in anything Mr. Stefano has done, and we are reluctant hosts for his visit."

Tip decided he didn't like Teal. "Relax, kid. I'm not after you. But it is your house. You can throw out anybody you don't like."

"I take it you've never been married," said Teal under his breath.

"I heard that," said Cecilia.

* * *

Back at the jail, Stefano immediately asked to call the FBI. He sat cuffed and ankle-manacled in a straight-backed chair next to Chet's desk, smiling pleasantly. Tip ignored him and asked Temple to take a walk.

"So you can do what?" she challenged.

"Beat hell out me," answered Stefano cheerfully. "What else?"

"Damn right," snapped Tip. "Until you tell me what I want to know. Who helped you escape? How much is Hammadi paying you? And where is Hammadi?"

"You think I'd be an accomplice in that?" demanded Temple.

"Well, I was hoping."

"I have a better idea."

She placed a call on her cell, said "Need you at the jail right away. Got him, but Tip's about to go Neanderthal to get the info he wants. And the guy says the FBI will spring him."

"Samantha?" asked Tip.

"She's smart. She'll figure out something legal. If not, then you can beat hell out of the son of a bitch. And I'll help."

"Maybe run a weedeater on his dick?"

Temple struggled to keep from smiling.

"Might work. I was thinking more, a taser on his balls."

Tip was getting aroused by this conversation, even though he knew Temple was only playing along. She never talked like this. Stefano was listening and trying to act like he wasn't scared.

\* \* \*

Samantha arrived in another black ensemble, this one more casual since she had been at home, but still stylish and form fitting: creased black Capri pants and a runner's pullover zipped down to show more décolletage than Tip thought she possessed.

"OK, Madame Prosecutor," said Tip. "He's all yours. Here's what we gotta find out." He handed her a list of questions. "Work your magic. Says he's going to call the FBI and get sprung as soon as we give him his phone call."

"I see." She sidled up and looked Stefano over. "Well, Mr. Stefano, it won't do you any good. Because you see, I've already called them. And they tell me you're on your own. Here. If you don't believe me, call your contact." She handed him her phone.

He smiled at her. "You're the best looking DA I've ever seen, but I know you're bluffing."

"Call them."

He did, and as he spoke to his contact, his face fell. He punched the End button and looked at Samantha, dismayed.

"They been looking for me for five years so I can testify. He said they don't need me any more. The guy died. The guy they wanted me to testify against died last month. I never even heard about it."

"So now you have to deal with me. I am prepared to offer you partial immunity—you would do five years—for your attempted murder of Deputy Tungate, and any other crimes you've committed in Howarth County."

"In return for what?"

"All information regarding the murders of George Sampson Jennifer Clarkson, Missy Davis, and Tom Burton. What involvement you had, who paid you, who helped you escape, where we can find that person, and where we can find Dr. Hammadi."

Stefano took on a sly expression. "You'd let me off with a nickel if I tell you all that?"

"Wait a damn minute!" exploded Tip. "This son of a bitch tried to kill my daughter and me, and he damn sure killed all those other people! And you're going to let him off with five years?"

"All we have him for is your attempted murder, Tip. The rest is your supposition. This way, we clear the other crimes, we get whoever paid him, and that person or persons goes down for murder one."

In a flash, Tip grabbed Stefano by the throat. Stefano was strong, but Tip was stronger. He squeezed for all he was worth, until Stefano's struggles began to slow.

"Tip!" yelled Samantha, then he felt something poke into his back and thousands of volts coursed through his body. He let go of Stefano and fell to the floor.

It took several seconds to recover and get back to his feet. Temple stood with the taser in her hand. She looked sheepish.

"You were going to kill him, Tip. You didn't really want that. End up as a criminal?"

He looked long and hard at her. For the first time since he had known her, she looked filled with doubt. As if he might do something else violent. Finally he took a deep breath.

"You're right. I don't want that. I want that weasely, sneaky son of a bitch to go down, but I don't want to have to go down to take him down." He turned to Samantha. "He's all yours."

"Fine."

She took out her cell phone again, set it to record mode, and started asking questions, starting with the ID question: "Are you currently operating under an alias?"

"Yes."

"And is that alias Al Stefano?"

"Yes."

And so on. Until it came to confession time.

"Put it in writing," he said to Samantha. "The deal. I tell you nothing without the deal in writing. On a signed copy I have in my pocket."

"Fine."

She sat down and wrote out the deal. Then she signed it, made a copy, and handed it to Stefano. He read through it carefully, then looked cagily at Samantha.

"I don't talk and I don't accept this deal without my lawyer. Call Miklaczewski. He's in my cell phone."

"You call your lawyer, the deal goes away. Completely. Without the deal, we're looking at life, and possibly the death penalty if we can prove you did any of the murders. Word is, the hospital security video of you strangling Missy Davis shows enough of your ears for identification. Turns out ears are unique, like faces. The video's a little fuzzy, but you might be identifiable."

"Keeping my lawyer out of it is not fair!"

"You're right. It's not. Talk."

* * *

He got so he missed the old game. He had been really, really good at the old game, so much so that he could charge fifty K a pop. And he never, ever, disappointed a customer. Then the sons of bitches in the Bronx rolled on him, so he rolled right back. He had names, amounts, everything. And he was willing to testify. So they put him in Wyoming until the trial, which kept getting de-layed, delayed, delayed.

And he hated Wyoming. There was just nothing there. Then Cecilia had her baby. His only grandchild. She was ashamed of him and moved to her husband's home town in Indiana of all places to get away from him. And her husband hated him, but he thought if he moved close, he could reconnect. At least there was action in Indy if he wanted it, so he set himself up close to both.

But Indiana was a snooze, man. He missed the old action. Then the Chechen found him and offered him a job, and he couldn't resist. He didn't know who was paying, but the money was good. They didn't pay as well here in this Podunk state as they did in New York, but ninety K to shoot Burton and Tip, and forty K to shoot the gal at the truck stop was a welcome windfall.

The Burton and Tip hit turned out to be a real charity job, though, since he was first supposed to take from them the people they valued most. Those were the words the customer sent along with the target names. And it was kind of a long list. The Chechen set him up with a hacker who gave him all the local ad-dress data he needed. He could have got most of it from Chet, the man absolutely had information diarrhea, but it might have raised suspicions. An old pal from the City helped scare Tip's daughter back to Indiana where he could get at her. So he was set.

And the plus of the long list of targets was, the old farmer and the girl would muddy the waters on motive. The yokels—"No offense, Tip"— would think they just had a nut-job mercy killer on their hands. It was just a great coincidence that the first two were sick. He did feel a little bad about the girl, after all he had his own daughter, but it was better for her since she was going to die anyway. This way she didn't suffer. Same with the old guy. He really did him a favor. And it was really enjoyable using the old guy's .22 to shoot him, and Burton's .22 to shoot the girl. He had laughed his ass off thinking about Tip trying to figure those out.

Plus, doing those distance shots really got the old blood flowing again. The best was when he shot Missy in the shoulder, a phenomenal three-hundred-yard shot. The shoulder shot was intentional so she would suffer. The Chechen was clear about the customer's desire for that. She was to suffer awhile so Big Iva would suffer, then he was to kill her.

But best of all, what really got him going again, was watching from the willows as Tip went through the drain pipes after him. He had almost given himself away by laughing.

But there had been problems from the start. That dipshit Dalek had to reveal himself and get involved. A very, very unprofessional situation. So, fine, he used him as a weapon delivery man and lookout. But the guy left evidence everywhere. Then that fuckup Hammadi revealed *him*self, that he's the customer for the soldier and the sheriff and his daughter. This is the first Stefano knows there are two customers. Which is the whole reason for the Chechen cutout in the first place, for crying out loud. Holy shit, these people don't know business.

So things started to go wrong from the start. Hammadi decided he wanted all of a sudden to get *personal* revenge on Tip while Stefano stood guard. The deal at the barn. What a clusterfuck. So after they escaped he told Hammadi to stay the hell away while he did his job. But *then* the asswipe showed up at the graveyard like the amateur he is to establish an alibi, or maybe just watch his targets die, who knows with people who want to cut heads off, but he screwed up the lines of fire. So Stefano got Burton with a clean snot but missed Katy's head badly and hit Tip. He began to see he was too old for this shit. It wasn't as much fun as it used to be. But he'd been paid, and he had his principles. His code. You been paid, you finish the job. No matter how messy.

So then when he heard the sheriff was dead, he didn't believe it, because, let's face it, this guy was smart, had come closer to catching him than anybody, ever. So he went to the funeral to prove it to himself: the big bastard was really dead.

"And you know the rest." He smiled at Samantha.

Tip inserted himself into the process. "What about the note in my mailbox?"

"What note?"

Ah. So, Hammadi.

"So where are Hammadi, Dalek, and the Chechen?" demanded Tip. "They're all guilty of conspiracy and murder, just the same as you."

"How should I know? The Chechen somehow knew how to find me—I think the New York Russian boys must know and told the Chicago Russian boys, which is scary, they got all these old KGB connections, but they hate the Italian boys I ratted on, so maybe they're OK with me staying alive—but I don't even *want* to know how to find him. He's a scary bastard."

Tip meditated on the irony of this statement for a moment before going on.

"Yeah, I've met him. So what about Dalek and Hammadi?"

"I don't know shit about Dalek, either, except that the hit was revenge for Big Iva killing his brother. That's all I know. Hammadi? What a numbnuts. He's probably holed up with his mother, pissing his pants. He's kind of a wuss."

"His mother?"

"Yeah. Lives in Indy on the west side in a Muslim neighborhood. The guy just pukes information. I'm surprised he ever made it out of Iraq."

"You wouldn't happen to have the address?"

Stefano looked at Tip and snorted.

"You want me to go and arrest him for you? No, I don't have her address. For God's sake, Tip."

The use of his name jolted. Al had been a friendly acquaintance.

"So what was the deal with the damned cologne? Smelled like cypress, or cedar, or something. I smelled it in your sniper's nest after you shot Missy. Katy smelled it on you at the barn. And I smelled it on you at my funeral. But I've never smelled it on you otherwise. I've known you for years, and you never struck me as a cologne kind of guy. What gives?"

Al smiled. "I always take a bath and put it on before I do somebody. It's just what I do."

The hairs on the back of Tip's neck stood up. He realized he was looking at a monster.

"How could you do it, Al? We all liked you. You been here five years or so. Everybody thought you were one of us."

"You know, I like all you guys here in Sedalia, too. Ridiculous Podunk little town, and people are so nice it makes you want to puke, but after awhile it grows on you. But I just couldn't resist, Tip. It's what I used to do. I was really, really good at it." He smiled again. "It wasn't nothing personal."

Tip hit him with a left to the jaw that knocked him out of his chair. He groaned and rolled onto his side and pulled his knees up into fetal position. Blood dripped onto the floor from a split in his lip.

"Neither was that, Al. It wasn't personal. It's just what I do."

Samantha turned off her phone recording function.

"I could charge you with assault for that," she said. She didn't sound convincing. "And we don't want him too marked up when the FBI arrives."

Stefano stifled his pain and half sat up.

"The FBI? They told me I was screwed!"

"They did," said Samantha. "Because I arranged it with them. It was the least they could do in return for taking you back and not allowing us to convict you for murder and send you to the gurney."

"You mean, all that shit about the partial immunity deal was bogus?"

"One hundred percent. If they weren't taking you away from me to put you back into witness protection, I would prosecute you to the full extent of the law. And go for the death penalty."

"But I got a copy of it in my pocket."

"If you'll take a second look, you'll notice that I signed a bogus name."

Stefano smiled. "Young lady, you're good." He turned to Tip. "You too, Tip. For a dumbass country sheriff, you're smarter than you look. Remind me never to come back to Howarth County."

# CHAPTER THIRTY-FOUR

**"S**o here's your guy," said Tip to Sanchez over the phone. "The guy you want to put back into witness protection somewhere and let roam free in the general public."

He played the recording of Stefano's confession.

Sanchez conferred in mumbles with someone else in the room. "All right, all right. You've made your point. Collateral damage has reached threshold levels."

Tip spent a full twenty seconds biting back enraged comments. Finally, he simply said evenly, "Your 'collateral damage' is my friends and neighbors, my daughter, and me."

"We're going to take him back," continued Sanchez, "but we may owe you one. It *is* kind of embarrassing. Sometimes the greater good gets a little expensive. What do you want from us?"

Tip again came to a boil. The idea of some federal asshole considering what had happened as "embarrassing" and "expensive" was almost more than he could take. He wanted to strangle Sanchez. But he finally succeeded in stuffing back his anger enough to control his voice.

"Help us find Hammadi's mother's address."

"That's it?"

"That's it. That, and make this Stefano, whoever he actually is, pay somehow. After all, here is a guy you essentially turned loose on the public, who cheerfully confessed to all manner of horrible crimes. The guy's a monster."

"Like I said, a psychopath according to our shrinks. But yes, there's the, um, possibility that even though he has immunity from us, he will end up paying. The longer such people try to live anonymously, especially after they testify, the greater the chances the ratted-out guy's friends find them. Despite our, um, best efforts."

"Ah," said Tip.

The address arrived on his phone within the hour.

* * *

Tip enlisted the aid of Indy Metro Police through the good offices of Detective Sergeant Janelle Roberts, who when she met Samantha did the finest exhibition of female squaring off and circling Tip had seen in awhile. The mystery was why. But the two were able to overcome what appeared to be instant mutual hatred and put together a legal raid plan.

So when they went in for Hammadi, they had Chet— still limping from a bullet hole in *his* left leg, pissed off and looking for revenge, any kind of revenge—Sergeant Roberts, an Indy Swat team, and Tip. But Tip took one look at the burr-cut, black-clad, heavily-armed SWAT team and insisted he be the first to go in. He wanted Hammadi and his mother alive.

He had a dark, dark suspicion and needed Hammadi alive to purge him of it.

The SWAT team surrounded the house. Chet uncharacteristically volunteered to take the back door, and Tip claimed the front. Both had serious risk because this was a daytime raid. But Tip had insisted, just to make sure that if bullets started flying, he and Temple and Chet would be able to see who was shooting whom.

"Alive, Chet," he warned. "This guy did nothing to you."

"Except get me shot when his buddies came for him." One of the buddies being the Chechen, Tip had already confirmed from the description of the blond beard sticking out from under the ski mask.

No one answered when Tip beat on the front door, so he took several deep breaths and readied himself. Then he kicked the door open with his good leg and crouched into a nightmare.

On the couch across the room sat the woman from Tallil from twenty-five years ago, only much older. Same position relative to the door, same layout as twenty-five years ago. Recognition passed between them.

"You," said Tip.

"You," she said simultaneously.

To her left, Tip's right, as before, looking like the very boy who had screamed at Tip, sat a boy of about thirteen or fourteen years. And on Tip's left as he swept the room with Ralph's M1911 .45, stood Hammadi, holding an AK47 with banana clip, pointed at Tip.

Many things flashed through Tip's mind, the first being that he ought to shoot. The second was that he should do so soon, because even his Kevlar vest would not stop an AK47 round at this range, only slow it down. The third thing was that there was a terrible, beautiful symmetry to the scene, which, knowing they were outside, Hammadi had obviously staged. The fourth was that maybe he deserved to get shot like this, after not understanding that the young soldier in Iraq was trying to give up. All this in less than a second.

He did not shoot.

"Put the weapon down, Hammadi. I'm wearing a vest." Hammadi might not know the vest would not protect him. "You're probably not good enough to get my head. And the odds are I'll get you before you get me. But I get your point. Was it your father?"

"My uncle."

"And the boy?"

"It was I."

"This boy?"

"My son. My wife is dead. Killed in Iraq. By Shia militia. Your intelligence people told them she was spy for Sunni militia."

"Was she?"

"She was not. We are Shia. Later, they admit mistake. Let me come to States."

"And this is your mother?" Tip nodded at the woman, who pulled her hijab closer around her face.

The woman spoke in a chilling voice full of hatred. "Yes, I am his mother. And sister of boy you kill in 1991. And mother to boy Burrtawn kill in 2003. They say he was Sunni terrorist." She gave a ghastly smile. "You people know nothing." She shook her head. "Nothing, nothing. Ignorant. We are *Shia*. Now Burrtawn has paid, and you will pay, too."

She started a screaming ululation and came out from under her robe with her own AK. Tip started for the floor as she started firing on full auto. She was awkward with the weapon and didn't get it aimed directly at him. He felt rounds pass and he hit the floor firing his .45. She took three rounds, center mass, and slumped back onto the couch. Her finger jammed the trigger down, and the weapon continued blowing chunks out of the wall and ceiling. Tip rolled away from the hammering death just as its magazine emptied. He looked for Hammadi, but he wasn't there. Neither was the boy.

Suddenly from the back of the house two short bursts of automatic fire broke the sudden, eerie silence, followed by a single boom—Chet's .44 magnum—and Chet's shout. "Got the son of a bitch but I'm hit, Tip! I'm hit!"

At the same time, there was an anguished shout from the boy. "Dad!"

In the kitchen, Hammadi lay across a wooden table beside a bowl of grapes and a stack of flat bread, a neat hole in the center of his forehead and the back of his head missing. Chet sat on the floor across the room with his back to a closet door, bleeding from his nose, his chest covered with blood. His face was ashen, and he was panting hard. The boy was violently ransacking a cabinet drawer. He finally came out with a butcher knife and headed for Chet.

"No!" said Tip.

He lunged and grabbed the boy's wrist. They struggled. The kid possessed a wiry strength, and turned and kicked and fought hard. And Tip did not want to hurt him. His heart was full to bursting with sympathy as he looked into the enraged, twisted, bereft face of a son who had just seen his father killed. Finally, he got the knife, but not before taking a slash to the chest which his Kevlar vest stopped.

"Do I have to cuff you, or will you go with the police and answer questions? Nobody is going to charge you with anything."

The kid glared at Tip, then at Chet. His body language was pure American. "No cuffs," he said. "But the same as my grandmother swore revenge, I swear I will kill you." He looked at Chet. "Both of you. Painfully. If it takes my whole life."

Tip sighed. "You'll never understand, and you'll never forgive us. But try to remember this. Revenge will steal your life away and end up killing you. Like it did your father and grandmother."

Tip took him to the kitchen door and called out to the SWAT team. "Need you to take this kid, question him, and put him with Child Protective Services. He's just lost his whole family. And we need an ambulance. Officer down in here."

A burly cop took the kid away. Tip turned back to the scene in the kitchen. Chet's head was lolling from side to side.

"I don't think I'm gonna make it, Tip. Tell Mom and Dad I love them, and tell Andy McCall I'm really sorry about that dope I planted in his back lot last year."

Andy was Chet's illegitimate half-brother, whom he had tried to run out of town to keep his father's indiscretion from being exposed.

"I will, Chet. But first, let's get you to the hospital." He called for the SWAT team medic.

Soon an ambulance was on the way, and the house was full of SWAT team, Temple, Samantha, and Sergeant Janelle Roberts.

"I thought you went in instead of the SWAT guys to try to keep the Hammadis alive," Sergeant Roberts accused. "Now two are dead, and your favorite deputy is not looking too good."

Janelle's tone bothered him. It was the rebuke of one professional to another, and that was not how he liked to think of her. After all, he would have married her if he thought he could get away with it. But that time had passed, and this was her turf.

"Look, I knew, this being the big town, this might get political. Which is why I wore this thing," and here he fingered the body cam Temple had provided. "Chet has one, too. The woman opened up on me, and Hammadi opened up on Chet. Neither of us had a choice."

"That's good," said Samantha, with a dismissive glance at Janelle. She wanted to be the one throwing *her* weight around. "I'll review the video closely and provide it to the Metro police.

But to me, it looks like Sheriff Tungate, rather, deputy Tungate, is right."

"We'll see," said Janelle evenly. "It'll have to pass our review board."

"I'm sure it will," said Samantha. She did not have to say that the governor would ensure it.

* * *

Outside on the front lawn, Samantha turned to Tip.

"So, this is how it ends?"

"Well, the shooter is in the hands of the FBI, and Hammadi is certainly not going to be paying him any more, so maybe yes. But we do still have this Chechen running loose. Who shot his way in and out of our jail. And Andrei Dalek still blames Big Iva for his brother, and might think I was involved in his father's death."

Samantha looked at him sharply. Tip ignored the look.

"So we gotta catch those two guys to feel completely safe. But that'll be Chet's job. If he survives."

"Hey, I heard that," said Chet, who was being carried out on a stretcher. He struggled to sit up. An ERT team member tried to hold him down.

"Easy there, Biggle," said Tip. He was not accustomed to showing concern for Chet, but this was different. The man was possibly mortally wounded. And he had behaved bravely. "You'll make yourself bleed to death."

"Actually, I don't feel all that bad now. Now that I've caught my breath." He felt around on his chest for the hole. "Not sure where he got me." He turned to the guy pushing the gurney. "Hold up a minute. I want to see something."

He sat up and removed his bloody shirt, followed by his bullet-proof vest. His T shirt underneath was white. No blood.

"So where's all that blood from?" asked Temple, averting her eyes from Chet's pudgy form.

"I'm sure I felt a hit to my chest, but maybe it's just from my nose. When I tried to open the screen door the first time, it was stuck. Then I pulled really hard and it opened and hit my nose."

"So you're not hurt at all?" Temple demanded.

"Well, my nose hurts. And so does my chest."

Tip caught Temple's eye and gave a small head shake. The guy had risked his life. "You got him, Chet. That's what matters. Good job."

Chet reacted like a petted dog, ducking his head and raising it again. Then to avoid saying anything, he picked up his bloody shirt, looked at the front, and pulled a pocket-sized, inch-and-a-half-thick book out of his left breast pocket. It was his much-thumbed turf directory, giving statistics on horses and tracks. His face turned white as he looked at it.

"Jesus," he said. "I knew I felt a hit. This is what saved me." He held it up. The book had two 7.62 mm sized holes, one at the bottom and one at the top. "Slowed them down enough the vest did the rest." He pulled up his T shirt to expose a small belly roll, milky white skin, and a purple bruise on his chest the size of a fist. "Holy shit." He started gasping for breath.

"Easy, Chet," Tip said. "You'll hyperventilate and we'll have to put a bag over your head. Looks like you're going to live. Do you still want me to tell Andy McCall you're sorry about the dope?"

# CHAPTER THIRTY-FIVE

Tip had Brandt on the phone. It was pay-up time. The governor chuckled.

"First I want to see the news conference. She's going to be on the ticket with me next year, and that publicity is key. It's golden. For both of us."

"So I gotta trust you first?" snorted Tip. "You do know if you welch, I'll come after you. I recorded that call where you told me you'd make me sheriff again if I gave you credit."

Brandt chuckled again. "Stay out of big-time politics, Tip. You can't lie worth a damn. You don't have a recording. You're too straight-up for that. But I won't welch."

And he didn't. The order of appointment came through the morning after Tip's news conference.

Tip held the "presser," as the newsies called it, on the steps of the jail, despite threatening rain clouds and the news people's request to have it inside. He knew well, as they did, that if it was inside, he could not escape by simply walking in and closing the door.

Indy and Louisville news crews were there, along with two na-tional-network stringers, to hear him announce in a simple sentence that the murders were solved. Samantha had given him a script, but he did not use it.

Then, suppressing his nausea, he went on to stress that help from Samantha Parr, the district attorney, and direct personal involvement by the governor himself were critical factors in catching the bad guys. Without them, the killers would still be at large. He declined to go into detail. It might prejudice future judicial action, which he also could not talk about. Even Temple appeared to gag on some of this, so Tip dialed it back a bit and finished strong by introducing Samantha to the cameras. He had not warned her ahead of time, but she handled it like a champ.

"The Howarth County Sheriff's department did the heavy lifting," she said humbly, but looking directly into first one camera, then the other. "They are the ones who took terrible risks and sustained serious wounds protecting their citizens and finally catching the bad guys. I'm sure I speak for the governor when I say that he and I are just happy to have played small, supportive roles in helping this town, one like many others across Indiana, indeed, across America, to rid itself of evil," blah, blah, blah.

Then rain began to fall, at first a few large spattering drops, then faster and faster, until it turned into a downpour. The news people fled for their vans. The news conference and the spring drought were over.

* * *

It turned out Chet actually didn't mind his demotion.

"I didn't like being sheriff by appointment," he said. "I want to beat you fair and square in the next election, and be sheriff in my own right."

"Fine," said Tip, feeling unaccustomed respect for Chet. "We'll go back to the way it was before."

But both knew it was now different. First, there was Chet's shame at being duped and used by Stefano. Not only duped, but disappointed. They had been friends. Had gone to horse races together, gone fishing together. While Stefano pumped him for information. And Chet didn't have that many friends.

Plus, there was the fact that Chet had shot and killed Hammadi, at great risk to himself. This was the first time Chet had stepped up to the plate and done seriously dangerous lawman work, and done it creditably. So Tip could no longer say he was the next thing to worthless. And as Tip well knew, killing a man is a life-changing event. Chet had changed, quieted, become less obnoxious. More thoughtful.

There was the also the fact that Chet had formed a good working relationship with both Samantha and Temple, which Tip had never quite been able to do. He had to give credit where credit was due.

But the kicker was the fact that blabbermouth Chet kept quiet about seeing Samantha at Tip's house the day after the raid in Indy. .

Katy had been gone. Tip thought she was in Elmira. And Samantha had stopped by to mend fences. She had been a bitch at times, she conceded. And she had treated him with less respect than he deserved. And so on.

He offered her a glass of tea. When she took it their fingers touched, and her other hand reached out and rested on his arm. "You are the least modern male I've come across lately, Tip, but you're brave," she said quietly. "The genuine article." Her hand ran up his arm and rested gently on his wounded shoulder.

The hand set off a pleasant glow. He put a hand on top of hers. A look passed between them, and a spark. Then the spark ignited a fire, and that was it. Despite their mutual loathing, they ended up in each other's arms, kissing, groping, pulling clothes, then plunging down the hall to the bedroom where in the time-honored, excitingly illicit way they released the tensions built up over the previous weeks.

Immediately afterward they were disgusted with themselves and each other, and Samantha looked at Tip with obvious disgust and actually said, "Oh, Jesus, what was I thinking?" And Tip said, "I don't usually do this with women I started out not being able to stand." Samantha's shoulders shook as if she were shivering away the taste of bitter medicine, and she said, "This never happened." She rushed down the hall to make her escape, still tucking in her expensive silk blouse.

Only to run into Katy, who had come home from Elmira earlier than Tip had expected. Who said, "Oh, Jesus." Then Samantha fled out the front door still tucking in her blouse, only to be met by Chet, and the icing was on the cake.

"Jesus, Dad, she's only a little older than me," Katy yelled down the hall. "And a bitch on wheels." But he could hear the smile in her voice. So anyway, he was grateful that no one—not Katy, not Chet, certainly not Samantha—spoke of the incident again. He knew this because nobody at Fishers' Groc or Eileen's Café gave him the fish eye. They only talked about the coming party.

* * *

Normally, it would have been Big Iva who would suggest a gigantic party for the whole town, like she did with Andy McCall and Sherry Fisher's wedding. But even though it was rumored she had a new favorite, the memory of Missy was too raw for her to feel that social. Still, when Eileen started telling people they had to have a big party to celebrate the end of the murders, a street party in front of her restaurant, between it and the court house, Big

Iva agreed, and agreed to provide a couple of flatbeds to serve as stages for musicians. After all, what was a street party without a country dance band?

It turned out to be an even bigger deal than the carry-in supper every month at the Methodist Church. Those were necessarily dry occasions, because, though it was whispered that Pastor Frank enjoyed a nip, and half the congregation—the men—were closet beer drinkers, the church could not be seen to condone, certainly not promote drinking. Taking alcoholic beverages to those occasions would have been like pissing in public.

This was different. Taking a page from the book of the current presidential administration, Samantha declared that, for this occasion, she and the sheriff's department would not enforce the local laws against closing off streets and drinking in public. A few, notably including Ralph Burke, no teetotaler, nevertheless loudly raised the issue of government overreach in a letter to the *Democrat*, the point being a single person was arrogantly deciding which laws to enforce and which not. But while most agreed Samantha had no such authority, everyone liked the idea of a party in the middle of the street, at the cusp of summer. Food was to be brought by everyone, Elaine would sell some, and Jimmy Ray Cheatham was to set up a drinks tent.

Tip was seated at a table for dignitaries, with Katy beside him. Judge Prechter, Samantha, and the whole town council were there. People came by to shake Tip's hand.

"I'm glad you caught the guy who killed Dad," said Ella Sampson, looking fantastic as usual, holding a longneck between thumb and forefinger, towering above nearly everyone in the crowd. "Even if the FBI took him away and nothing's going to happen to him for it." She looked at Katy. "And I gotta say, Tip, your daughter got her looks from her mother."

Tip smiled at this traditional insult. "She did. Good thing, too. But don't worry about Stefano. Odds are, once he testifies, he ends up dead. I have it on good authority that the FBI will somehow slip up and leak his location and identity. His enemies will find him. Besides, he was just the shooter. The people who paid him are dead. Dr. Hammadi and his mother. And you know, they had your dad killed strictly because he was important to Burton. You knew that, right? He was one of the only people in the community that Burton loved, because your dad acted like a father figure toward him when he was a kid, when his own dad had left. Plus, your dad had the inoperable colon cancer."

"Yeah. I was gone by the time he kind of took Tom Burton under his wing, but I knew about it." She sighed. "If you look at it in a certain way, though, it was kind of a mercy to Dad. Probably better than dying in the hospital in pain from the cancer. I doubt he ever knew what hit him."

"I guarantee it. It was a professional shot." He paused a moment. "So. Back to California?"

She snorted. "Much as I love all you people, and as much excitement as we've had, this place is a snooze. I'm out of here. Lulu Phillips has the farm listed."

He gave her an appraising look. "Sad to see you go."

She smiled. "In another life, Tip," she said, and trailed off.

"Yeah," he said, and watched her go.

* * *

Luther McConnell found Tip. He too had a beer in hand. "Heard you got shot." He nodded at Tip's leg, which he had extended beside the table.

"'Fraid so. Couple of times. Hurt like a son of a bitch. Still does."

Luther gave a mean smile. "Good. You deserve it. But I come over to thank you for not just taking the easy road and arresting Toby or me, or Tom Burton. You done good, Tip."

* * *

Eileen came and set a plate with hamburger and fries on the table in front of Tip. He looked up and smiled. She was dressed in civilian clothes, not her normal diner-waitress's dress. She looked damn good, Tip thought. She was gray at the temples, but in decent shape despite the business she was in. She filled her slacks and blouse very nicely.

"Thanks, Eileen, though I gotta say, you're an enabler. Doc Quick is trying to get me to quit eating fried foods."

"Well, you may die early, but you'll die happy." Then she got serious and looked at Katy, then back at Tip. "Came over 'cause I got something to say, Tip." She looked again at Katy.

Katy roused herself. "Hey, Dad, look, I see somebody over there I haven't seen in years. Excuse me for a minute." She got up and went over to the drinks tent and sat down at Jimmy Ray's makeshift bar.

"She's a great kid," said Eileen.

"She is. I couldn't be prouder of her. She and I were on the outs for ten years there, but I think we're good now. That's a good thing about all this trouble. It drove her home and we got re-acquainted. She's made of good stuff, Eileen."

"Got it from you, Tip. Look, there's, mmm, something I'm curious about."

He knew what it was, but he played along. "Which is?"

"How well could you hear while you were in that casket?"

He smiled. "I heard everything."

She looked shocked. "Everything?"

"Everything. And I think you and I have some talking to do. Maybe do some things together. See, I've always admired you, too, Eileen. I just didn't think you'd ever go for an ugly old bastard like me, with a paunch and a fringe. So, you still want to go fishing?"

She smiled, came around the table, removed his Smokey hat, and kissed him on his bald spot. "Tip, you're the stupidest man about women I have ever seen. Just my kind of guy." She kissed him again.

* * *

Katy came back when Eileen left.

"Get all that straightened out? I mean, you're the last person in town to find out she's in love with you. It's a wonder I ever got born at all, given how you are with women."

"Show some respect for your elders. So, you gonna stay, or go back to New York? I'd do everything I could to make it easy for you to stay. I understand you might not want to live in a place like Sedalia, but you could maybe live in Indy or Bloomington. You might find them more sophisticated."

"I'm glad I came home, Dad. We needed to do this. But New York is my home now. That's where my career is, where my friends are. But you could come and see me. I have a spare bedroom I use as my office, and it has a futon you could sleep on. I could show you New York. I expect given your size and the way you look, you'd draw some stares, 'cause you're clearly not the kind of male they've come to expect in Manhattan. But you would enjoy seeing some stuff, eating in a fancy restaurant for once in your life, and maybe going to a Broadway show. It would be a case of country boy goes to the big city."

Tip leaned over and gave her a hug. "I will definitely take you up on that, if for no other reason than to just come and see you."

\* \* \*

Ralph Burke came by and vociferated awhile about government overreach, and in a pause, Tip removed Ralph's M1911 .45 from his holster, removed the clip—he never kept a round in the chamber—and handed the weapon to Ralph.

"I really appreciate it, Ralph. But now that I'm employed again, I get a Glock from the department. What do I owe you?"

"Like I said, no scratches, and you don't owe me a thing. Plus, this thing has some history on it now that I could use to get a premium price. But I'd rather you kept it, Tip. My gift to you."

"Why?"

"'Cause I think it brought you luck. And 'cause, you will need it. The world is falling apart, Tip. Our country is falling apart. Going to Hell in a handbasket. With cheerleading by our leaders, who are chopping away at every stable thing we've ever had. Chaos is on the way, and we'll all need to be prepared."

This was nothing new from Ralph, so Tip chose not to respond to the doom and gloom.

"Thanks, Ralph. I'm sure it saved my life, so I really appreciate it."

\* \* \*

Big Iva trudged up and put a massive hand on his neck.

"How you holding up, Tip?"

He looked up into her huge face, round as the moon, with its two wicked-smart pig eyes close together in the middle. He was not normally this close to her, and he couldn't remember her ever touching him. She smelled of Dial soap and onions.

"That's my question for you, Iva. I'm really, really sorry about Missy. I just didn't think fast enough."

"Well, life moves on. Missy was sweet, sweet, sweet," and here her voice broke, "and she died bad, but she was good. Never hurt anybody. If what goes around comes around, she's in a good place. You think it's all over?"

"Well, Dalek and the Chechen are still on the loose, but I think they'll lie low for awhile. Hopefully they'll forget about us. But I'm not sure Sedalia will ever be the same. You told me once we were the town that time forgot, and not equipped to deal with the rough world you live in out on the interstate. I think you were right. But it looks like time woke up and remembered us. Now I'm afraid it won't be able to forget us."

# ABOUT THE AUTHOR

William Crow Johnson and his wife live on their farm in southern Indiana, where they grow pecans and enjoy visits from children and grandchildren. It is not far from Sedalia.